Dear Reader,

This month we are trying something a little different: *Renton's Royal* is set in 1969 and is more of a saga than anything we've published so far. Do you enjoy this type of romance? Would you like to see more sagas on the ***Scarlet*** list? Or historical romances? ***I'm*** a great fan of Regency novels, but perhaps you prefer other historical settings?

Wild Justice is the first part of 'The Beaumont Brides' trilogy, telling the stories of three, very different, sisters. We do hope you'll enjoy the chance to be involved with the same characters over the course of three books. *A Dark Legacy* combines romance with a dash of mystery, while *No Darker Heaven* is the story of a woman who's torn between two men – a father and son!

Do write to us with your views on ***Scarlet***, won't you, as it's only by hearing *your* opinion that we can continue to make sure that the books we are offering are pleasing you.

Best wishes,

Sally Cooper

SALLY COOPER,
Editor-in-Chief – ***Scarlet***

PS Have you filled in a questionnaire yet? If you haven't, please complete the fom at the back of this book and we'll be happy to send you a free gift as a thank you.

About the Author

Stella Whitelaw is a former professional actress whose stage roles included Eliza Doolittle, Kate and Miss Prism. She began her working life as a cub reporter on a newspaper and became the youngest female chief reporter in London. Stella has had 27 novels and 208 short stories published and has won various national prizes for her short stories. In 1995, she was short-listed for the highly prestigious Catherine Cookson Fiction Award.

In her (very limited) leisure time, Stella enjoys walking around Britain's coastal and scenic routes and caring for her six beautiful cats.

STELLA WHITELAW

NO DARKER HEAVEN

Enquiries to:
Robinson Publishing Ltd
7 Kensington Church Court
London W8 4SP

First published in the UK by Scarlet, 1996

A copy of the British Library Cataloguing in Publication data is available from the British Library

ISBN 1-85487-488-8

Printed and bound in the EC

10 9 8 7 6 5 4 3 2 1

CHAPTER 1

It was a case of throwing herself out of the plane or never making the jump at all. Lyssa sat with her back against the vibrating fuselage, frozen with fright, ashen-faced, staring. The plane smelled of fear. She had been mistaken about her reservoir of courage. There was very little left after the last few years, and this jump was going to pull at the corners.

As the plane began to roll forward across the tarmac, Lyssa pinned her thoughts firmly on Bethany and that morning's unexpected invitation. She would have to go for Bethany's sake. The child's sunny face came into mind, her dark hair flying as she ran across the playground to meet Lyssa. This will-o'-the-wisp, unfettered, sweet-smelling child of her body for whom she was going to change her whole life. Her pearl of pleasure.

'Bethany, I'm doing this for you,' she breathed.

Lyssa knew it had to happen. She could not

carry the burden of Bethany alone any longer. Matthew was kind and loving, the sort of man any woman would be glad to marry. And he loved her, which was surprising considering the kind of mad life she led, the rushing about to find locations, the stress of keeping her financial head above water, the protective blanket that Bethany needed constantly. Pity she didn't love him.

The plane turned at the end of the runway for take-off and Lyssa felt her stomach heave. What if she said she felt sick? Changed her mind? Had to get off at any cost?

At any cost . . . that was a joke. Several thousand pounds were riding on her back at this very moment.

The training had been a challenge. She had enjoyed every moment, felt very brave, and everyone had said she had done well. The practice landings had gone smoothly and the procedure for leaving the aircraft was drilled into her head.

Sponsorship money had rolled in. Her colleagues at the television company were especially generous. She had been amazed as people pledged ten, twenty pounds.

'It's all for a good cause,' they'd said. 'And you've got guts, girl. I wouldn't do it for an Emmy award.'

Matthew was less enthusiastic. He had listened

to her excited plans with caution. He had taken her hand across the restaurant table and squeezed it gently.

'You don't have to do this,' he said. 'There are other ways of raising money for RAS research.'

'I haven't time,' she'd said, firmly. 'I have to do it fast. Bethany hasn't the time to wait, either. I'm doing it for her and you can't stop me. She always comes first.'

'What about me? I shall be worried sick,' he'd replied carefully, his handsome face shadowed. 'You might get hurt.'

Lyssa removed her hand from his clasp and touched his dark hair. He wore it a little on the long side, brushing his collar, long dark lashes framing deep brown eyes. He was good-looking, his face unmarked by any stress. He worked as an accountant in his father's firm and the steps of promotion were marked out for him in concrete. He didn't have to worry about the future.

'Don't be daft, Matthew. It's safer than crossing a road. I know what to do. I've been practising for weeks.'

He sighed deeply. 'If you have to. I suppose nothing I say will stop you? I don't want my bride on crutches.'

'I'm not your bride yet,' said Lyssa, shaking her long strawberry-blonde hair. She had been in too much of a hurry that evening to do more than brush the reddish gold strands into a sleek tail tied back with a chiffon scarf. 'Nothing will happen.'

'Then I'll look after Bethany on Saturday, if that'll help. We'll go somewhere. The zoo.'

'That would be wonderful. Thank you, darling. I know I can always rely on you.'

Saturday saw her dressed in orange overalls, her kit inspected and passed. She joked with the others, gazed at the clear windswept expanse of wispy blue above her, and not felt connected to it. It was some other sky, some other person.

But now, as the plane rumbled over the runway, gathering speed, all Lyssa's courage fled. She had left it somewhere on the ground, in her locker with all the clutter that belonged to Lyssa Pasten, single parent, high-flying film locations manager for a television company, mother of five-year-old Bethany who had RAS, fiancée of Matthew Arnold.

The aircraft lifted off into the air and all sensation stopped. The smoothness of the climb did nothing to settle her nerves. Nor did the noise. Everywhere inside the fuselage shook with the powerful thrust of the engines. Her stomach pitched.

'Can I change my mind?' she asked as if it was a joke, but the jumpmaster pretended not to hear her.

The doorway was open and Lyssa could see the patchwork of earth disappearing like child's toys being cleared away. They went through a thin layer of swirling mist and cloud, then suddenly came out into the brilliant sunshine that had been there all the time. She went a shade of white and gasped.

One of the other jumpers gave her the thumbs-up sign. She grinned back, nodded, nervously checking straps that had already been checked and rechecked.

She saw the jumpmaster coming towards her, swaying. Surely not that old-fashioned 'ladies first'? She could have done without it at this height.

He bent low and spoke against her ear. 'Keep your head up and back arched. A clean exit. You'll be fine. See you in the clubhouse. First in the bar buys the drinks.'

Lyssa tried to answer but her voice had deserted her. It was cowering somewhere in her boots. She couldn't remember a single thing she was supposed to do. What was her name?

He signalled to her to move to the open doorway. She stumbled forward, her boots leaden with weights. Outside, the roaring gale deafened her; her overalls were flattened against her body, the wings creaked like a ship at sea. Her goggles misted over, then cleared. There was nothing outside. Absolutely nothing. It was space as vast as in a *Star Wars* film. He was saying something, but she couldn't hear.

'Go. Go! *Go*!'

Someone thumped her hard on the back and she was out. A thin scream came from her mouth like a thread of pain. She fell, plummeting like a stone towards the shaped brown earth that looked alien and hard. This is the end, she thought, all that fine talk had just been talk. Bethany, what will you do?

A voice came into her head, sweet, plaintive.

'Mummy, I've missed you all day. Do I have to go to school tomorrow? Please, Mummy, can I stay at home with you?'

Lyssa's training took over, robotic. 'One thousand . . . two thousand . . . three thousand. Pull. Check canopy.'

She felt her shoulders jerk back with the nylon risers and the steering toggles shot from their pockets with a reassuring snap. Her legs subsided down into their rightful place and her hands caught at the toggles.

For a few moments she did not dare believe that she was actually floating in the air. Even with her helmet on she could hear flapping . . . or was that her heart pounding? Then she saw the huge, round orange canopy billowing above her and she could have wept with relief.

And what a brilliant location! If only she could book this broad landscape of tiny fields and smudges of forest and thin pencilled rivers charting old courses, oast-houses like Lego. How the television bosses would applaud her ingenuity, her originality, give her a bonus . . . give her a day off?

It was so peaceful. She saw other orange blobs in the sky and waved, but the distance was too great. How nice it would be to just stay up here. No worries, no problems, no difficult decisions to make, no rat-race to run. Just to float forever, knowing that Matthew was looking after Bethany. She was his responsibility now. Lyssa could be herself for once, alone with her thoughts and feelings. This was a pocket of time off.

She steered herself away from the direction of buildings, tried to relocate herself towards the airfield and the tall packing shed. It was all coming towards her at a rate of knots and there were people now in sight, looking upwards, arms pointing. What was she doing wrong? What could she do that was right? Tall shapes loomed ahead . . . they were trees!

Where was the drop zone? She had absolutely no idea. Her wits had deserted her. But it was too late to do anything except try to avoid the trees and remember her landing-roll. The earth flashed forward at a tremendous speed.

She rolled over the instant she hit the ground. It was the perfect reflex action, although the impact winded her for a moment. She expected to be struggling with yards of canopy but the 'chute was caught in the lower branches of the trees and she felt the tug of the ropes. She unfastened her straps and stepped out of the harness, wondering if she would have to pay for the damaged 'chute. There was a big, flapping rip in the material.

The jumpmaster was not particularly pleased. 'Didn't you see the drop zone? It was clearly marked.'

'Sorry, I didn't see it at all,' said Lyssa, too elated to worry too much about him. 'The view was so marvellous.'

She showered quickly in the ladies' changing room and put on slim grey trousers and a bright red T-shirt, unplaited her hair and left it loose and frizzed round her shoulders. The summer was almost over and a chill was touching the air. It would be a winter wedding. That made her shiver. Taking a new marriage into a cold winter did not seem a good omen.

But she shook off her apprehension and went into the bar. Everyone was congratulating everyone else. The jumpers had all landed safely, no broken bones.

'When are you going to jump again?' they asked Lyssa.

'Not for a while. I'm on hold,' she said, smiling over her St Clement's. 'I want to be safely married.'

It was not until she was driving home in her old, reliable navy BMW that she realized that had been a strange phrase to use. Safely married. People did not marry to be safe. They married because they were head over heels in love.

She did not love Matthew. She was fond of him, oh, yes, very fond of him, and she hoped that love would follow if they were married. She knew what love was like, and she was not mistaking this different feeling she had for Matthew.

Love was the passion she had felt for André, Bethany's father. A French law student she had met on holiday in Minorca. She had only been able to afford Minorca, but the whole package had been transformed when they'd met that musky evening near the harbour wall at Mahon. The attraction had been instant, electric, mutual, and they spent every day of their holiday together, walking, sightseeing, dancing far into the night in the Caves of Xoroi. Their love had consumed all caution.

It was not till Lyssa returned to London that she discovered she was pregnant. She'd been dismayed at first, wandering round in a bewildered daze. But then she realized that she loved André more every day, and wanted his child. She knew he would marry her even if the wedding was a little late. There were problems to solve . . . where they would live and work . . . but with the optimism of youth Lyssa felt sure there were solutions.

André was overjoyed about the baby. He wanted to marry her. The date was set for a month's time. Lyssa bought a low-waisted cream dress to wear at the registry office and a room was booked at a hotel for a party afterwards. Lyssa was very happy.

But some youths, high on drugs and drink, stole a car. It was a fast Ferrari and they had no idea how to handle it. The police were in pursuit and the chase went through deserted streets of London in the early hours of the morning. André had arrived on the overnight ferry, was walking through the streets to surprise Lyssa with his unexpected arrival.

The Ferrari went up on the pavement, tore through street furniture and the man walking. André was flung across the windscreen as the car went through a shop window. It shattered and shards of glass pierced his face, his chest, his throat.

Even now, nearly six years later, Lyssa could not think of his death without shrivelling inside. She gripped the steering wheel of her car to steady herself, swallowing the bitter taste, and glared at other drivers as if they were also driving stolen cars and high on drugs. André, her darling love . . . It had been so cruel and so unfair, so like some drama on television. She could have located it for some show.

Bethany had arrived in due time, all rosy and sweet-faced with an angelic smile and the same sunny nature. Lyssa had not minded being a single parent. She earned enough to keep them both, worked like a Trojan, juggled sitters and baby-minders so that she could work her absurd hours, somehow survived the responsibility and the exhaustion. There was neither the time nor the energy for a social life. Lyssa could not remember when she had last been out on a date. Life revolved round Bethany and work. The television industry supported them.

It began to get heavy when the doctors finally diagnosed what was wrong with Bethany.

'RAS is very rare,' the consultant said gravely. 'We get about ten cases a year. There's no known cause and, as yet, no known cure. I'm very sorry.'

Lyssa thought that was really reassuring but

held back her distress. 'So what can be done?' she asked crisply.

'Nothing, I'm afraid. We know very little about this condition. Just try to give Bethany as normal a life as possible. Don't wrap her in cotton wool.'

'That's not enough. You've got to do something!'

But they couldn't. Bethany had become very clinging over the years. It was not surprising, because Lyssa kept a close, watchful eye on her and there had been many scares, many panic drives to the hospital. A young doctor in Casualty had said to Lyssa after a midnight drive to hospital, when Bethany had fallen out of bed and bumped her head on a table leg, 'You need a husband. This is too much for one person to cope with.'

The words had sunk in. Lyssa had begun to look for a husband. Not consciously at first, but then she'd realized that she was looking at available men in case they were husband material. Her colleagues in the television company were wrong. They lived the same kind of frantic, fast-paced life as she did, and with a social life that rated practically nil, she had little chance of meeting anyone else. She soon decided that all the best men were already spoken for and she was not a poacher.

When she'd met Matthew Arnold at a lunchtime media function, with flowing red wine and noisy talk, she could not believe her luck. He was like a calm island in the middle of all the frenetic activity. True he was younger than she by several years, but that didn't seem to matter. He was pleasant and easy-going and unmarried. He almost had wings. She did not push him; she did not hurry him, but the one thing she did was to make sure they kept in touch. He was a prize almost within reach.

They went to the cinema, concerts, took Bethany for walks in the park. He liked Bethany and the little girl adored him. He did not even mind an evening watching television if Lyssa failed to get a baby-sitter.

'This is so nice,' he often said, stretching out his long legs in front of the fake log fire. 'Just you and me. The world shut outside.' Lyssa was almost happy. But nothing was settled. Something was holding her back.

Matthew wanted to settle down. He wanted a town house in some quiet square and Lyssa sharing it. He also liked the idea of a ready-made daughter, well past the baby stage.

'No sleepless nights,' he'd said, tweaking Bethany's small ear. 'That's a bonus.'

'Can I be your bridesmaid?' Bethany had asked him, hopping about. 'And wear a long dress with frills and silver slippers?'

Lyssa imagined her tripping over stone steps, flying head over heels, and her heart constricted with fear. 'A short dress would be much prettier,' she'd said quickly.

She phoned Matthew as soon as she got back to her flat from the airfield. It was in a high-rise building overlooking a muddy flowing Thames. Her flat was on the seventeenth floor and it was murder when the lifts were out of order. 'I made it,' she said, rubbing her bruises. 'I told you it would be all right.'

Matthew groaned into the phone. 'Don't you ever put me through that again! I've been glued to the television in case there was a newsflash. Only your daughter has any confidence in your ability. Of course my mummy can jump out of an aeroplane, Bethany kept telling me; she can do anything.'

'I've had a summons,' Lyssa said uneasily. 'From Sussex. From your Aunt Sarah. She says it's time we all met.'

'She thinks I'm hiding you, keeping some dark secret.'

'I suppose it must seem like that. I'm a bit scared of meeting your people. They might not like a ready-made family.'

'My father will be back from the States next weekend.' Matthew hesitated. 'Why don't we go down for lunch then?'

'Aunt Sarah's letter was very pleasant. And yet . . . there was something odd about it. She didn't mention Bethany.'

'We could take Bethany with us,' said Matthew eagerly.

Lyssa drew a deep breath. 'No, I don't think so, not the first time. It'll be difficult enough. Bethany has a ballet class and my friend Maggie will keep her till I get back.'

Lyssa sat beside Matthew in his sleek and powerful four-litre Jaguar XJ6. It was the right kind of car for an up-and-coming accountant in big business. She was not sure what Arnold Consolidated Industries controlled, but knew it included transport, newspapers, media and heavy metals. Some mixture, she thought, hoping she'd worn the right sort of clothes.

The thought of meeting Matthew's father was almost as scary as jumping. Yet she always got on well with older people, enjoyed listening to them, found their reminiscences fascinating.

'You look lovely,' said Matthew, touching her bare knee. Not completely bare, but almost, with the sheerest of nearly black stockings covering her legs. She had decided she ought to look feminine and rushed out to buy a suit. She worked in trousers, never knowing whether she would spend the day halfway up a chimney or halfway down a mine shaft. So there were not many girl-type clothes in her wardrobe.

It was a deep apricot suit that went perfectly with her amber hair, with a short, curvy jacket and skimpy skirt. Lyssa knew her legs were good even if her body was on the skinny side. Her make-up was discreet but flawless. She'd been on enough film sets to see how the experts did it. Her hair was caught into a smooth chignon at the nape of her neck.

'I wasn't sure if you had legs,' he said, keeping a straight face and his eyes on the road. 'You've never let me find out. And you always wear trousers.'

'I borrowed this pair from props,' she said, smoothing the skirt down. It was a bit on the short side but there hadn't been time to shop around. She hoped his father wouldn't disapprove. Matthew had told her that his father was a stern workaholic, an absentee parent most of his adolescent years, and that he had been brought up by his father's elder sister, Aunt Sarah.

'Don't return them,' said Matthew fondly. 'They look good on you. I like legs. Particularly yours.'

They were leaving London behind, driving through the suburbs towards the twisting leafy lanes of Sussex. A watery sun peered through the overhead canopy of browning leaves and rustling branches. Horses cropped peacefully in the fields. A flock of sheep concentrated on decimating the grass. This was the kind of place Bethany ought to live in, Lyssa thought, not hemmed in by fume-belching traffic and concrete buildings.

'You're very quiet,' said Matthew, sensing her concern. 'Are you nervous?'

'Of course,' said Lyssa forcing a cheerful note into her voice. 'It's not often one meets an industrial tycoon. He might take an instant dislike to me; decide I'm after your money.'

'He's going to love you,' said Matthew, his eyes warm with affection as they met in the driving mirror. 'As I do, my sweet. I can't wait till we're married. Not long now.'

'Nothing is settled,' said Lyssa.

He took her hand and kissed her fingers gently. Lyssa warmed to the gesture. Matthew was such a dear. She was sure she would grow to love him if they were married.

They drove through a picturesque tree-lined Sussex village that had clearly become a museum piece. Each cottage had been reconstructed true to its period, even if modernised inside. Ducks waddled to the pond, diving into the verdant water.

Matthew turned the car off the road, taking a concealed driveway that Lyssa almost missed. She saw a notice saying 'Private Road. Trespassers will be prosecuted. Guard Dogs Patrolling. Surveillance cameras.' She shuddered.

'Are there really guard dogs?' she asked apprehensively. She was afraid of big dogs.

'Just two, Bill and Ben. They won't hurt you. They look ferocious but they're really a pair of softies.'

The driveway took a turn and the trees cleared. In the hollow was a rambling low-roofed, mellow-bricked house that looked as if it had been there forever. Lattice windows glinted in the sunlight, Virginia creeper crept up the walls in a profusion of red leaves and suckers, and chimney-pots of all different designs and heights lifted the slated, gabled roof to the sky. A house charged with dreams, lost behind the trees.

'Welcome to Hollow House,' said Matthew, and there was no mistaking the pride in his voice. 'It's been here hundreds of years, part farmhouse, then small country manor house, odd cottages added on. Now my father has turned it all into one big house. It's easy to get lost inside, there are so many odd staircases and floors that don't seem to belong.'

'It's beautiful,' said Lyssa, drinking in the

mellow beauty, her passion for old, strange places in her voice. 'No wonder you hate living in London.'

'I don't hate it now that you're there.'

She heard the possessiveness in his voice and hesitated before making a cool retort. She was still independent enough not to want to belong to anyone. But the moment passed as Matthew opened the car door for her and she swung out her long legs, showing a lot of thigh. She looked up sharply at the windows. She had a strange feeling that she was being watched, but there was no one there.

'Come in,' said Matthew, taking her arm. 'I want to show you everything. There are lots of gardens and a tennis court, and Father put in a heated pool last year. Then the heath stretching as far as the sea. That's the Channel.'

'It's a bit cold for swimming.'

'The pool is heated and in the old stables. You won't find it cold at all.' He opened an oak door inches thick.

The galleried hall was part of the old manor house. It was full of light from a stained-glass window that filled one wall and went up to the next floor. The window was early Victorian, with a half-clothed damsel being rescued from a fierce fire-breathing dragon by a knight in armour. But the colours glowed with life and threw patterns on to the tiled floor. There was a profusion of cut flowers, obviously Aunt Sarah's work.

Matthew led her into the sitting room, which ran the length of the front of the house to the left of the main doorway. It was oak-beamed, low-ceilinged, a big fire burning in the recessed stone fireplace, and Lyssa counted six deep sofas grouped about the room. Shelves and tables were cluttered with books and magazines. Lamps were everywhere, casting a pleasant glow. It was a restful, family room where one could relax and read. When had she last had the time to read? Her nervousness began to evaporate.

'I'll go and find Aunt Sarah and tell her we're here. Make yourself at home. Tea or coffee?'

'Coffee, please,' she smiled.

She stifled a yawn. It had been hectic getting ready to come away that morning and she had worked late the previous day on finding an ordinary suburban house for the series. They were the hardest and most time consuming locations to find. People were worried about being exploited and the loss of privacy, and usually didn't want to know. In the end she went to a local estate agent's and asked about renting an empty house. It was often the best way. Ordinary households didn't really want an invasion of media people stamping through their property.

She sat on a long chintz-covered sofa and without thinking kicked off her shoes. The heat from the spitting log fire was making her drowsy and she half closed her eyes, hoping the ballet teacher was taking special care of Bethany. Maggie was a good friend. They had met when Lyssa had needed a practice dance room for a ballet set; Maggie had been only too happy to let out her dance school for a couple of days.

'It beats working,' she'd said with a laugh, pocketing the cheque. 'And I'll give you special rates for Bethany.'

Lyssa heard the door open and thought it was Matthew arriving with the coffee.

'Just put it down anywhere,' she said sleepily.

'Anywhere special?' a voice asked.

'Just so I can reach it,' she said. 'I'm too tired to move.'

She was aware of someone, then realized that the person was standing in front of the fire, blocking the heat from her. She half opened her eyes and became aware of a tall man standing with his hands clasped behind his back, staring at her.

'Any more orders?' he said coolly.

She struggled upright, pulling down her skirt. He was staring at her with deep-set, granite-grey eyes, vivid with intelligence, a hard jaw set into unrelenting disapproval. She felt she could hardly breathe under his scrutiny, as if he were peeling away, not layers of clothes, but all the layers of her character, and finding her wanting. She was nothing, an irritation.

Yet she did not feel the same about him. He was like a rock, like a man who carried a gun, like a man who could deal with any situation. He was authority; he gave commands, he didn't take them. It was his powerful presence she felt most, before taking in his undeniably good looks.

She looked away from the width of his shoulders, the long legs astride the rug, and her heart faltered. He was looking at her with direct and cool appraisal, as if she were a specimen under a microscope. Matthew should have warned her. She had not known that there would be someone else at Hollow House, that there would be other visitors.

'They weren't orders,' she said with a hint of spirit. She had to keep calm. 'Only thoughtless remarks made when I was half-asleep. I had a busy day at work yesterday and the fire made me drowsy.'

'A lot of people work hard. They don't make a song and dance about it. You aren't the only one on an eighteen-hour day.' The room seemed to be growing smaller and hotter.

'I didn't say –'

'Sorry, I must have misheard. I thought you said you had a busy day.'

His voice was like gravel, ground up and spat out. The vowels did not have the mellow modulation of a trained actor; the tone was roughened by some dialect, some accent she could not place. It thrashed over her like a rough sea, pricking her nerves with alarm.

'I see you've made yourself at home,' he went on. Her toes curled up with embarrassment. 'Do you always put your feet up on other people's sofas?'

'I took my shoes off, as you may well have noticed since you're staring at me,' she retorted. 'You crept in on me and caught me by surprise. Don't you ever knock or cough or something when coming into a room?'

'Knock?' He raised a dark eyebrow. 'Is that what I should have done?'

Lyssa had a feeling he was mocking her now. She was too tired for a slanging match. She stood up swiftly, pulling down the short skirt which would not stretch another inch, and slipped her feet back into her shoes. She felt trapped by his presence, wanted to get away. A log split with a spark of running fire.

It was an unconscious gesture that made her pull out the pins fastening her careful chignon and shake out her hair. The long strands fell round her shoulders in a smooth curtain of silk, giving her the freedom she wanted from the tightness. This man was beginning to annoy her.

'I don't know who you are or what you are doing here,' said Lyssa, 'but I would much appreciate it if you would kindly leave me alone. If you're waiting to see Mr Arnold, perhaps you could wait in a different room.' The visitor was wearing a dark city suit, striped club tie, gold cufflinks. He was obviously a colleague, a director in some other industrial empire. Lyssa was used to dealing with irate television executives. 'I'm sure a house this size has plenty of other rooms, a study or office. This is, I believe, the family's private sitting room.'

She emphasized the word family, hoping the man would take the hint. But he showed no sign of moving.

She felt a frisson of awareness run through her body. It was a long time since she had known an actual stirring of her sexual needs. André's death had killed off physical sensations as if she too had died in that accident. But suddenly her traitorous body was responding to this man, unlocking her hunger. There was no mistaking the sudden weakening of her limbs, a tightening of her stomach. She caught back her breath, appalled how easily she was being trapped by the man's unnerving assessment of her. The room was very still, breathing on its own.

Lyssa had to break the spell. She said the first thing that came into her head. 'I'm dying for that coffee.'

'No doubt Sarah has dropped the tray. She's all butter-fingers today,' he said with an undertone of dry amusement. 'I can't think why.'

Lyssa heard warning bells but their message was fused, unclear. As if to save her further futile thought, the door opened and a middle-aged woman hurried in, brindled hair awry, flustered and breathless, fixing small pendant ear-rings.

'Matthew's bringing the coffee,' she said, unnecessarily because he was standing right behind her. She came straight over to Lyssa and took both her hands. 'My dear, this is so exciting. We are all so happy to meet you at last. Of course, now we know why Matthew is bowled over. You are very lovely.'

Lyssa wished she could stop the colour sweeping her cheeks. She hated it when people commented on her looks. She didn't agree with them. Her hair was too straight, skin too pale, her eyes too big and she was scrawny and thin.

Matthew put the tray of coffee down on a low table, pushing aside some books. Lyssa saw that there were four gilt-rimmed bone china cups and saucers, a big silver coffee pot, and a jug of cream. The aroma of good coffee brought a superficial layer of civilization to the group.

'Lyssa is lovely,' he said. 'But she doesn't believe it. She brushes aside all compliments as if she's never seen herself in a mirror. Ah, that's good, I see you two have already met. Then I don't have to make any introductions.'

'Met . . .?' Lyssa echoed weakly. She looked at Matthew for help. Surely he didn't mean . . .? What had she said and done? Had she given herself away in that one silvery moment of awareness?

'My father. This is Jeth Arnold, my father. Dad, this is Lyssa Pasten, my fiancée.'

Lyssa felt the room spinning but it was only in her head. In reality the room was as substantial as the man before her. Somehow she dredged up her manners and held out her hand formally.

'How do you do, Mr Arnold,' she murmured.

He nodded briefly, ramrod-straight. 'Mrs Pasten,' he acknowledged.

CHAPTER 2

It was the most uncomfortable lunch Lyssa had ever sat through, and yet on the surface it was eminently civilized. Aunt Sarah was an excellent cook despite giving the impression of being totally at sea in her kitchen. The meal was served by a fresh-faced young girl from the village called Emily, in the dining room which was to the right of the main hall. It was a long, cool room decorated in pale blue with a polished walnut dining table that could have seated twelve without any trouble.

The windows were draped with pale blue velvet curtains and cabinets along the interior wall held good china and crystal glassware. Another cabinet housed a collection of Georgian silver that would have delighted a burglar's eyes.

The four of them were placed together at one end of the table, and Lyssa wondered if Jeth Arnold had deliberately chosen this imposing room in order to intimidate her. But Aunt Sarah had put bowls of flowers and fruit and a cheese-board on the unoccupied half of the table and the space was soon forgotten. Matthew was very attentive, happiness written all over his handsome face.

'What a lovely room,' Lyssa murmured, trying to be the perfect guest. 'And you do all the flowers?'

'Oh, yes,' said Aunt Sarah. 'We have such a lot in the garden. You must take some home.'

Jeth Arnold was playing the charming host but there was an edge to his voice that only Lyssa seemed to detect. She caught him looking at her several times. What had she said? What had she done? Taken her shoes off in a stranger's home and put her feet on the sofa? Was that so much a sin? Or had he, too, felt that pull of sexual attraction and was shocked by it?

Lyssa went cold at the thought. Perhaps he thought that she reacted that way to every new man she met, that she used her sexuality. In which case, he would certainly not approve of her as being a suitable member of the family, as his son's future bride.

She turned to Matthew, tried talking to him exclusively so that Jeth would slide to the fringe of her mind.

'This is such a change,' she said. 'All that

dreadful canteen food I have to consume, usually on the trot. A clipboard in one hand and a sandwich in the other. Sometimes I don't know what I'm eating.'

Matthew was replying, but she wasn't listening.

His son. It was difficult to believe Jeth was Matthew's father. Yet there was a resemblance in the curving mouth and the jutting chin. But whereas Matthew's honed good looks were classic and timeless, Jeth Arnold was hewn out of granite. His dark hair was cropped short and the lines of his face were from character, not age. And those eyes . . . Lyssa avoided them. They were like laser beams, boring into her.

'Matthew tells us you have a daughter,' he said later, handing her a jug of cream to go with the latticed apple pie which Aunt Sarah served out in generous portions. It was ages since Lyssa had smelt real home-made apple pie. She hoped she would be able to eat it. She had only picked at the roast chicken and garden-grown vegetables, pleading a large breakfast, which was a lie. She'd only eaten half a slice of toast and marmalade on the run.

'Bethany. Yes, she's five years old, nearly six,' said Lyssa, hoping she was on safe ground now.

'And your husband died?'

'A car accident,' she said, not elaborating. She

had not told Matthew that the accident was before their wedding. It had no relevance now, all these years later. She felt as if she had been married to André and he lived on in his dark-haired daughter.

'How do you manage to bring up your daughter and still cope with this busy job? Locations manager, did you say?' There it was again, that tinge of disapproval. Jeth Arnold was obviously one of those men who thought women ought to be chained to the kitchen sink, especially those with children.

'I work on the road,' she said, instantly regretting her choice of words. She sounded like a call girl. 'That is, I'm rarely in the office. I pick up a few files, go to a meeting or two to discuss scripts, then I'm out on the road looking for locations. It can take five minutes or five days to find something really special. And I have to keep finding new places. We used a particular stretch of Thames tow-path twice in different shows and some eagle-eyed viewers spotted it. They wrote in, of course.'

'It sounds terribly important,' Jeth mocked. The angles of his face were sharply defined. He looked at her in a cold, calculating way which made her feel under dissection.

'It is important to viewers who are stuck at home, mothers, invalids; people who are too old or frail to get out,' said Lyssa defending all television, mindless and worthy. 'The box is their lifeline. OK, so some of the programmes are awful. But there's also a lot that is very good. British drama is excellent. Perhaps you never watch anything.'

She had noticed a big television set in the sitting room and some programme magazines strewn about.

'Rarely,' he said. 'I prefer to catch up on some reading or walk the South Downs in my leisure time. When I get any, which is rare.'

'Jeth spends more time in the air than with his feet on the ground,' said Aunt Sarah. 'He flies all round the world. He's got a flying office, fax and all. I doubt if he'd know how to switch on a television set. I'm the television addict here. What programme are you working on now, Lyssa?'

'It's a new ten-part series of *Inspector Dutton Investigates*. This is the third series. The ratings are really good. The Inspector has been seconded to a new station so I'm looking for fresh locations. I like to think that the places I find have a visual connection to the storyline.'

'A new series? Oh, that's good. I like Inspector Dutton. He's so natural and never pompous. I'll note the locations in future and think, ah, yes,

Lyssa found that place and set up the arrangements.' Aunt Sarah smiled with pleasure at the thought.

'So what happens to young Bethany while you do all this rushing around the countryside?' There it was again, that tone of masculine disapproval.

'She goes to school and I employ a sitter who collects her and looks after her till I get home. Sometimes I'm home in time to collect her myself. Each day can be different. If I find what I'm looking for quickly, I can take the paperwork home.'

'What if she's ill?'

'Oh, she's hardly ever ill.' The lie stopped uneasily on Lyssa's lips. She caught Matthew's glance and half-smiled back at him. She did not want to explain about RAS now. It was too early and too complicated. People sometimes thought she was making it up, turning the disease into a drama. 'Not childhood things, and she never has a cold. She's a very healthy little girl . . .' Her voice trailed away and her eyes pleaded with Matthew not to say anything about RAS.

Lyssa forked a mouthful of apple pie. It was delicious. Her tastebuds curled round it. She lived on half-cold cafeteria food and plastic-wrapped location sandwiches. Bethany fared better: Lyssa made sure she had plenty of protein and fresh fruit and vegetables, but often she was too tired to eat herself.

'And school holidays? What do you do about them?' It was Jeth again. He was tipping his chair back, regarding her with half-closed lids.

Lyssa bridled. This was getting to be the third degree. She shot a look of resentment across the polished dining table but the big man had abruptly stopped looking at her. He was helping himself to another slice of pie. She felt a fleeting moment of sympathy for all the plated airline food he had to consume, then withdrew it abruptly. He probably flew first class, and that was a different kettle of microwaved fish.

'Although I don't really think it's any of your business, I take Bethany with me. She enjoys coming out with me in the car, rushing around the countryside, as you put it. She brings crayons and books and the crew make a great fuss of her. She has a whale of a time.'

'Isn't that an unsatisfactory way for a five-year-old to spend her school holidays – stuck in a traffic jam?'

Lyssa opened her mouth to make a sharp retort then thought better of it. He was Matthew's father even if he was being objectionable. He could say what he liked. She knew Bethany enjoyed holidays with her. There was a moment of silence and then

Aunt Sarah rushed in to heal the breach.

'We don't mean to pry, my dear. It's been so long since there's been a child in the family. Your independent ways are so new. A little unorthodox. But we'll get used to them in time.'

'Better than being incarcerated in a boarding school,' said Lyssa, knowing what had happened to Matthew. He'd told her how unhappy and lonely he'd been, isolated deep in Dorset in a cold, grey stone building for seven months of the year. 'Bethany sees me every single day. She knows she's got a mother.'

She heard Jeth's sharp intake of breath and knew she had scored. Matthew's mother had left home when he was small. Lyssa did not know the circumstances but she could guess. Jeth Arnold would not be an easy man to live with.

'Perhaps you'd like to bring Bethany with you next time you come down,' Aunt Sarah suggested, smiling across the table.

'That would be lovely.'

'You could teach her to swim,' said Matthew.

'She'd love that. She's always wanting to learn.'

'Don't you take her swimming in a local pool?' Jeth asked, as if determined to pinpoint her failings as a parent. 'I thought children learned to swim much younger these days.'

'Our local pool is always very crowded,' said

Lyssa. And I can't risk her getting knocked, she added silently, letting the words soothe the raging feelings that were beginning to mount again inside her. She had to think of Bethany. She was thinking of marrying Matthew so that Bethany would have a stable home life. There was no point in antagonizing Bethany's future grandfather.

The venerable title was so absurd that Lyssa laughed aloud. This big, overpowering, attractive hunk of a man – her baby's grandfather?

'Sorry,' she said, her eyes twinkling with amusement. She looked round the group at the table, hoping they'd share her amusement. 'I was just remembering that Bethany thinks all grandfathers have long grey beards. Do you think you could manage to grow one in time, Mr Arnold?'

Lyssa looked at him, without fear for once, and the sparkle in her gold-flecked hazel eyes seem to ignite something in his own. There was a definite response from him, as if they were the only people in the room and Aunt Sarah and Matthew had faded into the blue flocked wallpaper.

'Perhaps if I tugged at the growth every morning,' he offered.

'Or hung weights?'

'Took extra vitamins?' Then, just as abruptly, Jeth's mood changed. He scraped back his chair and stood up. 'If you'll excuse me, I have some work to do in my study. It's been . . . a pleasure to meet you, Mrs Pasten.' The pause before pleasure was unmistakable and Lyssa felt her anger sharpen. He had no need to be so rude to her, even if he didn't like the idea of his precious son marrying someone with a ready-made family. She was sure that her daughter was the main reason for the antagonism – or was it herself? Was there something about her – her job, her personality, her looks – that he disliked so much?

'We'll have coffee in the sitting room,' said Aunt Sarah. 'You've hardly eaten anything, Lyssa. No wonder you're so thin.'

'I'm sorry,' said Lyssa. 'It was all delicious. My appetite seems to have fled.'

'Nerves,' Matthew whispered in her ear, looking pleased. He was such an uncomplicated soul. He thought she was suffering from bridal nerves.

'We've got things to talk about, Lyssa and I,' said Aunt Sarah, practically pushing him out of the room. 'Wedding things. You'll just be bored, Matthew. Why don't you have a swim? You looked jaded, all that living in London's fumes.'

'Get Father to move his head office to some more environmentally friendly place, then. He's the one who bought Arnold Place and stuck up a damned skyscraper block.'

Lyssa did not let her dismay show by one flicker

of an eyelash. She had once been thrown out of Arnold Place by security guards. Till this moment she had not linked the incident, many years ago when she had been rash and impulsive and learning her job in television. She had been trying to smuggle a film crew into the vast stainless steel reception area, with its indoor trees growing the height of three storeys and its silent escalators. She cringed now as she thought of her foolishness . . . all without permission. They had thrown her out. And quite right, too. It had been a standing joke for months. Don't go anywhere with Lyssa unless you want to get thrown out.

It had been a kind of turning point. It took a lot of living down and made Lyssa determined to be one of best location managers in the business. From then onwards she almost turned somersaults so that everything should be just right, perfection, with permission, and satisfactory to all parties. Her attention to detail was prodigious. That was why directors trusted her.

'This is a lovely room,' said Lyssa, as they settled to coffee in the sitting room. Aunt Sarah cleared away some magazines so that Emily could put the tray down.

'There's a more formal drawing room at the back of the house with patio doors that open out on to the lawns,' said Aunt Sarah, rearranging the cushions behind her back. 'It's very formal, with two grand pianos. Jeth sometimes has musical evenings to entertain business friends. But I like this room best. It's more homely and comfortable.'

Hardly homely, thought Lyssa, scanning the length. Her twelve foot by ten was homely. Lyssa began to wonder how long the Arnold family had been moneyed and successful. Some rumour floated into her mind, from long ago. Both Jeth and his sister had something very down-to-earth about them. It was Matthew who had all the polish of a young man used to money from birth.

'Have you no family that can help you with looking after Bethany?' Aunt Sarah asked, pouring the coffee into pretty floral cups. She offered a box of wafer mints to Lyssa.

Lyssa shook her head. 'No one. My parents split up when I was quite small. My father disappeared somewhere and my mother brought me up. Then she died when I was sixteen. Cancer. I've looked after myself since then.'

Aunt Sarah touched her arm sympathetically. 'I'm so sorry, my dear. That explains why you are such a good mother to your little girl.'

'Good mother?' Lyssa nearly choked on her coffee. 'Mr Arnold is almost having me strung up on the village green for neglecting Bethany.'

'Men and women look at things in a different

way. I could tell what you weren't saying. I can guess what a struggle it has been for you. Well, my dear, you've got us now. You aren't alone any more. And you'll have Matthew at your side. I wish I'd written to you sooner. I regret it now but I'm always so busy.'

'Why didn't you?' Lyssa asked. 'I thought you didn't want to know me, that I wasn't good enough for Jeth Arnold's son.'

'I think I *was* afraid you'd be a gold-digger. But I know now that you're not. You are going to be just right for Matthew. He's a lucky man.'

Lyssa felt tears come into her eyes at the older woman's honest words. Yet it wasn't Matthew she thought of as standing at her side. It was his father, that tallness, that overpowering strength. He was a tower, a rock, decisive, protective . . . She shook the alarming thoughts away and took a firm hold of herself. God, this could be destructive, could ruin everything. 'Yes,' she said in quiet voice. 'I'll have Matthew.'

'He's such a nice boy,' Aunt Sarah prattled on, taking another mint. It was obvious why she hid her waistline behind a loose, floppy jersey. 'He'll make a lovely husband. Now, about the wedding. Jeth's really set his heart on St Margaret's, Westminster. You see, he's got a lot of business friends he wants to invite.'

'A business media opportunity?' Lyssa suggested. 'A PR operation? Matthew is being a little premature about any marriage.'

'I know it doesn't sound very nice, but yes. If Jeth's going to pay for it, he'll want his various connections there. People do like to be seen going to posh weddings, and so do their wives. You can't blame him. And the reception at the Savoy? What do you think of that?'

'I'm not sure.' Lyssa felt the whole situation slipping away out of her control. 'Of course, I have friends too. Television people . . . only they're not quite so posh. In fact, you might class some of them as rough.'

'They'll be more than welcome. There's no question of freezing out your friends. Now about your dress, what have you in mind? Who is going to make it?'

'I don't know. I haven't thought about it at all. Perhaps I could hire one? Bethany wants to be my bridesmaid but . . .' Suddenly she thought of the crush, all the people crowding round her daughter, the possibility of her falling. 'But I don't know . . . it might be too much for her. This seems to be getting much bigger than I expected.'

'It has to be, Lyssa. Jeth Arnold is *somebody*. You can't just have the village church and walk across the green to Hollow House.'

Suddenly that seemed the perfect scenario. A marriage service in a small Sussex church and then to walk back across the green, her ivory skirts billowing round her feet, satin shoes becoming green-stained by the uncut grass, Bethany skipping alongside, picking daisies. Back to Hollow House . . . Emily and some other village girls serving drinks on the lawn, someone playing the grand piano, Aunt Sarah rushing around in her wedding finery, hair awry, fixing her ear-rings.

'What are you thinking about, my dear?'

'A small wedding,' Lyssa confessed.

'Oh, you can't have a small wedding, not if you're marrying an Arnold.'

'But I never –'

Emily came into the room. 'There's a call on the line for Mrs Pasten.'

'You can take it in here,' said Aunt Sarah. 'The phone is on the windowsill.'

Lyssa hurried over, her heart pounding. No one knew she was here except Maggie. And if it was Maggie calling, then it was something to do with Bethany.

'Hello. This is Lyssa Pasten.'

'Lyssa? It's Maggie. Now don't panic.'

'Bethany? Is she all right? What's the matter?' She tried to keep the fear out of her voice. Even after all these years, she could never get used to Bethany's condition.

'Now don't worry. She hasn't fallen over. Nothing's happened. I just thought you ought to know that she's covered in pink spots. I kept her in a different room at ballet; I don't want my entire class to come out in spots. Not good for business.'

'Spots? What kind of spots?'

'She's got a temperature too. I'd say it was measles, though it's a long time since my lot had measles. I thought you ought to know as soon as possible because no doubt you'll want to make some sort of arrangements, get time off from work.'

Outside, a bird was bombing the lawn for grubs. The sun speckled through the trees in long, lazy rays as if the world was all at peace and nothing was happening. A small pink sucker from the creeper had found a tentative hold on a diamond window pane, hoping the gardener would not notice.

'Time off from work?' Her voice spiralled upwards. Lyssa held on to the phone, gripping the receiver till her fingers were bone white. Time off from work . . . that was a joke. The new *Inspector Dutton* series wouldn't wait. She had so much to do. She couldn't take time off. The producer would go berserk. Measles would mean nothing to her bosses.

'Thank you, Maggie. I'll be home right away. Will you be able to take her back to the flat? Thanks. Tell Bethany not to worry.'

She put down the phone and turned a wan face to Aunt Sarah. 'I'll have to go. My friend thinks Bethany has got measles. She's covered in spots. I never saw anything this morning but I must admit we were in a hurry and she can dress herself. Just when I said she was so healthy and never had a cold.'

'What will you do?'

'I don't know,' said Lyssa, almost wringing her hands like an actress. 'Nothing like this has happened before. I suppose we've been very lucky. I'll have to think of something.'

'Get her and bring her back here.' It was Jeth Arnold speaking from the doorway. His face was impassive. He had heard the last few minutes of conversation. 'We've plenty of room. She can have her spots in peace. Sussex is very therapeutic.'

'I can look after her,' said Aunt Sarah brightly, obviously longing to play auntie. 'Absolutely no trouble at all. I'll have Emily to help.'

'That's very kind of you, but I can't just leave her here. And I have to go to work . . .' said Lyssa lamely.

Jeth's voice was stiff, as if she ought to have jumped at the offer. 'We've a good train service to

London. You may have to get up at dawn and catch the milk train but it's quite possible.'

'I can't stay here.' She was looking at him now, wondering if he understood why she couldn't stay. Her skin was tingling just at the sight of him, her breathing constricted as if she had asthma strangling her air passages.

'Nonsense. Of course you can. It will be lovely having a house full of people. Jeth is away most of the time. Matthew will drive you home to fetch Bethany while Emily and I will get rooms ready for you both. The yellow room and the rose room are connecting with a shared bathroom between. It'll be ideal for you,' said Aunt Sarah, already bustling, planning flowers, finding toys.

'I can't, really,' said Lyssa helplessly. But he would be away. 'It's an imposition. You hardly know me.'

'A wonderful opportunity to get to know each other.'

'Of course you can,' said Jeth firmly, brooking no further argument. He came across the room to her in easy strides. It was as if the room emptied. He stood in front of her, willing some sort of adrenalin into her. It was like jumping from the plane again and he was the jumpmaster giving her a push in the middle of her back. 'Nothing will happen.' His voice was low.

'How can I be sure?' and the words were only between the two of them. No one else heard.

'Because I will make sure,' he said. The granite-grey eyes were letting her go with a kind of reluctance that she could hardly believe. She felt the world spinning. Oh, God, she had met him too late. She was somehow engaged to Matthew, dear Matthew, whom she could not hurt. Any moment now she would become hysterical, cling to this man's legs, stroke the long limbs, let the world know that her defensive shell was cracking.

'I'm away most of the time and Sarah will enjoy your company,' he was saying quietly, his eyes locked on to hers, a smile hovering on his mouth. Her plans for Bethany's happiness were falling about her in blackened ruins. How could she go through with the marriage? Only by putting a hundred miles between this man and herself and making sure she never saw him again.

But she had to get through the next few weeks until the wedding fiasco was sorted out.

'If you're sure it'll work . . .' she whispered.

'It will work,' he said firmly.

Lyssa collected her things, looked around for Matthew. He came from the pool area, rubbing his hair dry with a towel. He looked apologetic when he heard the news.

'I'm terribly sorry, Lyssa, but I can't drive you

to fetch Bethany,' he said. 'I haven't had measles. Men get horrid complications. I can't risk it.'

'But we have to talk,' said Lyssa, taking him aside. 'This has all escalated far beyond what I thought we had agreed. I have never said that I would marry you and yet you introduced me to your family as your fiancée.'

He grinned. 'Well, you are, aren't you? Very nearly. We've talked about it many times and we both know that it would work and it would be good for Bethany.'

'That's all we've done,' said Lyssa, wondering how she was going to get through to him. 'A lot of talk. But nothing was definite. Yet Aunt Sarah is already planning a wedding and zipping me into dresses and making guest lists. It's terrifying.'

'She's just enjoying herself.'

'But it isn't a game, Matthew. I'm not getting married just to make Aunt Sarah happy. It's a serious decision and I'm not ready to rush into it.'

Matthew closed his arms round her and rocked her. He smelt nice and clean and young. Lyssa closed her eyes, wishing it had all remained simple. 'But it would make me happy,' he said against her hair. 'And I know I could make you happy.'

'Then why didn't you ask me properly, somewhere when we were alone together, instead of announcing it to your family first? I could hardly deny it, in front of them.'

'Sorry, sweetheart.' He sounded rueful. The enormity was coming home to him at last. 'I guess I was carried away, having you there and you looked so at home, so glowing, so perfect. But measles is catching, you know. Men get a particularly nasty form of it. And if I'm getting married . . .'

'That's mumps,' said Lyssa, amused. Sometimes Matthew was like a small boy. 'OK, I'll get the train. Your father said there was a good train service.'

'I'll drive you to the station, though. Oh, no, heavens, sorry, Lyssa . . . do you think *you're* contagious?' His face registered real shock.

She laughed, but it was not genuine. 'I doubt it, but don't you worry about me. I'm used to making my own way.' It was a mite feeble that a grown man was afraid of catching measles. Suddenly she felt a hundred years old and almost as tired. 'Just point me in the right direction.'

She said goodbye to Aunt Sarah and thanked her for lunch. Jeth was nowhere to be seen, which was as well. She didn't want to see him, didn't want him to shake her hand, to feel the warmth of his skin, the pressure of his fingers.

'Where's Matthew with the car?' asked Aunt Sarah.

'Waiting along the drive somewhere,' said Lyssa, not wanting any fuss. They'd find out soon enough that he had let her go by herself.

She began to walk along the driveway, regretting her silly shoes, hoping the station was not too far. It was not even a proper station, apparently, just a halt, the other side of the village green. You can't miss it, Matthew had told her. Part of her brain wondered if she could use the small, deserted platform for *Inspector Dutton.* They needed a bare and windswept station, with peeling paint and a few bedraggled weeds with litter blowing about. She made a mental note to look at its possibilities.

She heard the low vibration of a powerful engine behind her and stepped on to the verge to let the car go past. It was a silver Mercedes coupé, roof closed against the cooling autumn weather. It stopped alongside her and the driver's window rolled down.

'What the hell do you think you're doing?'

'I'm walking to the station,' she said as coolly as possible in the circumstances.

'I thought Matthew was driving you back to London.'

'He's allergic to spots of all shapes and sizes,' said Lyssa, unable to resist a joke.

Jeth said something unintelligible under his breath. He leaned over and opened the passenger door. 'Get in. I'm going to London. I've some papers to pick up from my office, some figures the fools have forgotten to fax me. I can get hold of them while you pack for your daughter and yourself and cancel the milk or whatever else you have to do.'

'I'm not going with you,' said Lyssa feeling her high heels sinking into the soft grass verge and threatening to topple her stance.

'Don't be difficult, woman. I said the train service was good but not at the weekends. You might have to wait an hour for a London train. We can be there by then.'

He saw the look of reluctance on her pale face and her floundering confidence despite the smart clothes. 'Think of your daughter, Bethany. Think what's best for her. You want to get there fast, don't you?'

'I can drive myself back,' she parried, thoughts leaping ahead. 'I'll need my car down here.'

'That's fine. I hadn't intended to return to Hollow House. I have a meeting in Geneva to-morrow at ten.'

She went round to the other side of the car, knowing he was watching her every movement, taking in the too short skirt, the muddy heels if he could see them.

'Cheer up,' he said. 'I won't bite you. And look, both hands on the wheel.'

The voice was the same, still stern and taciturn, but again there was that undertone of amusement.

'I'm glad you think my predicament is funny,' she said, taking off her sandals. 'I don't happen to relish it. The next two weeks are going to be murder, trying to work from here out in the wilds, looking after Bethany, the worry . . .' Her voice trailed off. She stared out of the window, only too aware of the closeness of the man sitting beside her in a bulky leather jacket, refused to look at the aquiline profile.

'You can stop worrying. Sarah and Emily will take good care of your daughter and I've already phoned Dr Carrington, our local doctor. He said he'd call in this evening and make sure it is measles. And you'll soon get used to commuting. Thousands of people do it.'

'I don't only work in London.'

'We've got a stack of folders at Hollow House, covered in red and blue and yellow lines. Recent invention. They're called maps. You can drive to wherever you've got to go. Sussex is not exactly off this planet.'

Lyssa tried to relax, to let the tension go from her shoulders. 'I'm sorry. I get so worked up about Bethany . . . She's been my whole life for so long.' She did not explain.

He did not probe further but switched on a tape

player and slotted in a tape. 'How about some music? I'm not good at talking while I drive.'

She nodded. She didn't want to talk either. 'That would be nice.' She wondered what he would chose. Aunt Sarah had said something about musical evenings and there were two grand pianos. But Barry Manilow's smooth voice came from the loudspeaker with a soft and gentle melody.

'Do you make a habit of taking off your shoes?' he added, glancing at her toes.

'I didn't want to be accused of muddying your light grey carpet,' she said, hiding the muddy tidemark on the heels.

'Carpets can be cleaned.'

He drove swiftly and competently, slowing down only when they reached the outskirts of London and the speed restrictions made him reduce his speed. Lyssa wanted to stay with him forever, for the drive never to end, to simply drive into the future. Just to be sitting beside him, watching his hands move over the controls, was enough living. His fingers were long and tanned, nails clean and cut short. There was a brush of dark hairs on the back of his hands. She longed to touch them, to feel their softness against her cheek. The crease in his grey trousers was sharp, his black shoes polished and tooled with a pattern. Everything about him was masculine and expensive. He would not be afraid of a few spots.

'You'll have to direct me now,' he said, breaking into her thoughts. 'I don't know where you live.'

'South side of the Thames, near Lambeth Bridge. We need to strike off right along here.'

She gave him clear, concise directions. As they neared the block of flats, gaunt and foreboding, she pointed them out to him. The sky behind was an uninspiring flat grey and the demarcation line was barely visible.

'That monstrous block of concrete?' he said grimly. 'That's no place to bring up a child. Not a blade of grass in sight. No playground.'

'A lot of people have no choice,' she snapped. 'The block is full of children and none of them have anywhere to play except the streets.'

'What floor are you on?'

'The seventeenth.'

He swore under his breath. 'God forbid. And I suppose the lifts are always breaking down?'

'Frequently. We walk.'

'Supposing there are no lifts today?' She could sense him battling with his conscience and those figures he needed to pick up so urgently.

'Maggie will help me carry Bethany. We'll make it somehow. Anyway, we don't know about the lifts yet.'

There was a newsagents and stationers on the corner of the small row of shops before the block of flats. Lyssa often used them when she rushed home from work. Jeth drew up outside and went in. He was only gone a few minutes but came out with a bulging carrier bag.

He got into the car and put the carrier on her lap. It was full of comics and crayoning books and from the top poked the ears of a cheeky-faced teddy bear.

'For the invalid,' he said.

'That's very kind,' said Lyssa.

'I'm practising being a grandfather,' he said with a sudden, wicked smile that almost destroyed all her returning composure. 'I gather there are certain obligations, like slipping extra pocket-money and defending requests to stay up late and watch unsuitable programmes on television.'

'I can see I'm going to have trouble with you,' said Lyssa, her eyes dancing.

She thought for a moment that he was going to lean across and put his hand over hers. But he didn't. He seemed to be gathering his thoughts, pulling up the drawbridge, regretting his momentary lapse.

'Quite the reverse,' he said sharply. Then he wrote something down on a piece of paper with a gold biro pen. 'This is my telephone number if those damned lifts are stuck. I'll carry her down.'

He left her on the pavement outside the block of flats, accelerated with a roar and drove away as if the devil was after him and his flash car.

CHAPTER 3

Bethany travelled down to Hollow House wrapped up in blankets in the back of Lyssa's car, hot and feverish and spotty, clutching the new teddy-bear, not really aware of what was happening.

'Can you carry her?' said Aunt Sarah hovering anxiously at the front door.

'I can manage,' said Lyssa. 'She not very heavy.'

'Hello, Bethany,' said Aunt Sarah, peering at the flushed face, half touching the tousled hair.

'Lo,' said Bethany obediently.

'The yellow room is all ready for her. I'll show you the way. Come along. Mind your head.'

Lyssa might have said her daughter was not heavy but the twisting stairs nearly defeated her. They rested on the turn and then set off again. Aunt Sarah took them along a picture-hung corridor to the far end, where she opened two doors and put on shaded lights.

'This is Bethany's room and this is yours, Lyssa, right next door. Emily is bringing up your bags. I'll leave you to settle in and put Bethany to bed. Just let me know if you want anything. Anything at all.'

'Thank you. You're being very kind,' said Lyssa.

The yellow room was lovely. It was decorated in the soft clear yellow of spring and the wild primrose theme grew on the patterned curtains and duvet cover. The furniture was white with gold handles and there were watercolours of seascapes on the walls. Of course, they were near the Sussex coast. Lyssa had forgotten. She loved the sea and its wildness. Perhaps when Bethany was better they would get a chance to walk on the pebbled beach and hunt for baby crabs.

She put Bethany to bed and unpacked their few clothes. Emily had brought up the bags. Lyssa only had soft airline travel bags; she had never owned a suitcase. Suddenly their few possessions looked pathetic.

'Are we staying here?' Bethany asked, tossing about, her hair lank and sweaty. She was not taking in much, though Lyssa had explained. 'Will Matthew be coming to see my spots?'

'No, I don't think so. He's not into spots. But he'll come as soon as you're better. And yes, you're staying in this pretty room till your spots have all gone.'

'Is this a hospital?' Bethany asked drowsily.

'No, it's Matthew's father's house.' It sounded awkward. It was awkward. 'He lives here.'

The connecting door opened to a shared bathroom. The room was a corner space with cross beams and a sloping ceiling. Perhaps it had been a walk-in cupboard but now it was fitted out as a luxurious bathroom with floral tiles and thick aquatint carpet, plants on the deep windowsill and wicker fittings holding towels and every kind of bath toiletry.

Lyssa had not thought before that she might marry into money. Matthew earned a good salary, his flat was bigger and far more comfortable than hers, but Hollow House spelt real money. She dared not compare this bathroom to the utilitarian white tiled bathroom in her flat on the seventeenth floor . . . though she had done her best with pearlised emulsion paint and plants and amusing cartoon pictures.

Jeth Arnold was seriously rich. Hollow House had been extensively modernised without spoiling its old and unique qualities. She had glimpsed the gardens but knew the grounds stretched into a bleak and misty distance that were the South Downs and then the sea beyond.

Her pink bedroom was an extension of the rose garden: roses everywhere. Aunt Sarah had let her imagination run riot, starting with beautiful limed oak furniture and a deep rose carpet. The curtains and duvet and comfortable arm-chair were all in a rambling-rose-patterned fab-ric. She hung her few clothes in the wardrobe. Someone had thoughtfully moved in a small desk, lamp and chair so that Lyssa could work by the window. Aunt Sarah again. It was a raft in an ocean of luxury.

She looked outside at the slope of verdant lawn lit by security lights and drenched with shadows. Bill and Ben, the Great Danes, were romping about, chasing each other like mad things, tails thumping, not doing much to deter intruders.

Matthew had already gone back to London, fearing the coming plague. Lyssa would have Sunday to settle in, then back to work on the Monday. It was so strange and different. Aunt Sarah and Emily were being very kind but Hollow House was not home. Lyssa longed for her flat in the bruised skies, then she realised it was a juvenile bout of home-sickness and that Bethany had to be cared for while she worked.

'Damn *Inspector Dutton*,' she said, but didn't really mean it. *Inspector Dutton* was her bread and butter and sometimes their jam and cream. She occasionally got a bonus when she pulled off something spectacular.

She would have to phone Greg Wilson, the director of the series. He ought to be aware of her change of circumstances and that she would be working from deepest Sussex for a couple of weeks. He might make a few allowances, though he was not domesticated in any sense. Children did not exist except as small-sized extras.

Dr Carrington arrived, the tweedy image of a rural doctor, and said that Bethany had a classic case of measles: cough, runny nose and sore eyes and a temperature.

'Your spots are coming out nicely,' he said, peering behind Bethany's ears. 'They'll spread to the body and legs later. Try to keep Bethany from scratching them, Mrs Pasten. She's much too pretty to have scars. There's no specific treatment, but I'll prescribe something soothing for the spots. Keep the lighting shaded and no bright sunlight. Sponge her down with tepid water and make sure she drinks lots of fluid.'

'Water?'

'She can have anything she fancies. Don't over-heat the room. Some parents think that keeping their child in a hothouse is the answer to illness. She'll still be infectious until four days after the rash appeared.'

'It only came out today.'

'Then she'll be all right about Wednesday or Thursday. Don't hesitate to call me if you have any problems.'

'What sort of problems?' Lyssa felt the old rise of panic. 'What should I look out for?' She did not mention RAS. Bethany would at least be safe from danger, safely tucked up in bed. She would put a chair either side so that she did not fall out.

'Refusing to drink, fast or noisy breathing, earache, headache, those kinds of things. These are very rare complications. I'm sure Bethany's measles will run the normal course.'

'Will my new teddy catch the spots?' said Bethany, coughing restlessly.

'Quite probably, especially if you squeeze him that tight,' said the doctor, packing up his case.

Lyssa stayed with Bethany all evening, sponging her down, reading to her till she dozed off, reassuring her when she woke up and wanted to know where she was. Emily brought up a tray with some cold supper, chicken salad and fresh fruit salad. But Lyssa still did not feel like eating. Aunt Sarah appeared with a selection of drinks for Bethany, orange juice, lemonade and blackcurrant cordial.

'We'll get whatever she likes tomorrow. There's bound to be one of those Sunday shops open somewhere,' she said, in her element with two visitors. Lyssa realised that Aunt Sarah was probably lonely with Jeth only appearing occasionally at Hollow House between transatlantic flights. She gathered that Aunt Sarah drove an old Riley erratically and Jeth wouldn't let her go any further than the village. 'There's one on the road to Worthing.'

'I'm sure this selection will be quite enough,' said Lyssa. 'She likes all of these.'

There was quite an age difference between the brother and sister. Lyssa thought Aunt Sarah must be in her late fifties whereas Jeth would be about forty-four. She could not imagine him getting married and siring Matthcw in his teens.

The thought struck her to the bone with a coldness. An image of Jeth making love to some youthful and beautiful girl . . . and how many women since? He was darkly attractive and so eligible that the local beauties must be queueing from here to the White Cliffs of Dover. She knew how they must feel when they met him, imagined their eager faces in the light of the bedside lamp, saw their wrecked eyes when he passed them over for a new fancy.

Six years was a long time without being in a man's arms, but loving Bethany and looking after her had been enough for Lyssa. Or she'd thought it had been enough till she had met those granite-grey eyes across the room. She could still feel the way the air had trembled with the possibility of love. That old across-a-crowded-room syndrome. It still worked, but she didn't trust the message from her body, did not want to hear its clamouring.

When Bethany fell into a deeper sleep, Lyssa went downstairs with the tray, found her way to the kitchen. It was a dream country kitchen, with pine cupboards and fitments, tiled counters, high-level oven and microwave, fitted shelves hanging with fresh herbs and garlic ropes and dried flowers. She could not help thinking of her cramped kitchen where she could hardly turn round without banging her elbows.

'You haven't eaten much,' said Emily, stacking a dishwasher. 'Can I get you something else?'

'I'm sorry, I'm not hungry. Perhaps I could take some coffee and join Sarah . . . Miss Arnold, for a few minutes.'

'She's in the front sitting room. I'll bring it through, miss.'

Lyssa chalked up the 'miss'. Emily had noticed the lack of a ring, but it was not unusual these days. A high percentage of children were born out of wedlock. Only the older generation found it difficult to accept.

Aunt Sarah was watching a noisy television

panel game but she turned it off as soon as Lyssa arrived.

'Absolute rubbish,' she said. 'I don't know what makes them think it's entertainment. Sit down, my dear. You look dead beat. How's your little girl?'

'Sleeping at last. I thought I'd come down and thank you for everything. And I'm afraid Dr Carrington left a prescription.'

'Emily will take it to the Sunday rota chemist. Heavens, it's the least we can do, especially as you are going to be one of the family.' A strange look crossed Aunt Sarah's face. 'I hate to pry, Lyssa, especially when I hardly know you. But you are sure, aren't you? Matthew is a delightful young man but . . . you seem so independent, so mature and sure of yourself . . . and . . .'

'And so much older?' Lyssa finished for her. 'I'm four years older than Matthew, though sometimes it feels like forty. It's because I've been fending for myself for so long.'

'Only four years, is it? Well, that's nothing these days. You have this very self-contained look and lead such a busy life. But I suppose you'll give up work when you get married?'

The words were a shock. Lyssa had never thought of giving up work. She could not live without the challenge and excitement of television. Apart from Bethany, it was her whole life.

She had never countenanced for a moment the possibility of giving up.

'We haven't discussed it,' she said, smiling her thanks to Emily as she came in with a tray of coffee and a plate of home-made cakes and flap-jacks. 'I think Emily is trying to fatten me up.'

'We can't have you fainting halfway down the aisle,' Aunt Sarah laughed. 'Oh, this is such fun. A wedding and a new little girl in the family, both at once. My dear, you must forgive my enthusiasm, but nothing has happened here for years. Jeth comes and goes and I rarely see him. Matthew went to Oxford and then straight to London. Another non-appearing member of the family.'

'But we shall live in London,' Lyssa put in quickly. 'At Matthew's flat. It's plenty big enough.'

'But you'll be down every weekend, surely?' The older woman's face clouded momentarily. She dangled bait. 'There's the garden and the pool . . .'

'Of course,' said Lyssa quickly. 'I know we shall. I love it here, and so will Bethany.'

Lyssa stayed talking to Aunt Sarah until her coffee was drunk and she had forced down half a slice of moist coconut cake. Then she went upstairs, looked in at Bethany who was sleeping fitfully, had a therapeutic bath in the pretty bathroom, put on pyjamas and a robe and took her duvet and pillow into her daughter's room.

She slept on the floor, wrapped up like a parcel.

Someone came into the room in the early hours of the morning, but Lyssa thought it was Bethany stirring and stumbled to her feet, falling over the duvet, disorientated. This woke Bethany, who then wanted a drink. They were unaware of the figure outside and still in the corridor.

Lyssa could not understand the sudden current of air. She was so tired from the events of the day, all the driving, the impact of meeting Jeth Arnold and her inner struggle against his magnetism. It was a wonder that she did not sense it was him, standing there, watching them, dark in a navy dressing gown, soft mules on his feet, stubble on his chin. He, too, was tired from driving back to Hollow House after he'd found and absorbed the figures he needed for his meetings in Geneva. And he had set his alarm for five a.m in order to be at Heathrow in time for his flight.

'Don't be alarmed,' he said quietly as Lyssa caught sight of him. 'I was concerned. I came back to see if you were both all right. Sarah didn't seem to know when I phoned.'

'You frightened the life out of me,' Lyssa whispered, her hand at her throat. 'I thought you were a burglar.'

'Bill and Ben are around.'

'Softies, both of them, according to Matthew.'

'The cameras are on and anyone climbing the wall will get an electric shock. How's Bethany?'

Lyssa smiled slightly and nodded. 'She's sleeping again. And she's doing all right. Dr Carrington thought it would be a straightforward case of measles. Would you like to see her? I don't think you've met my daughter.'

This time the big man hesitated, then nodded. He came into the room and peered at the small, sleeping form, caught his breath at her smallness. Bethany was a lovely little girl, despite the spotted face. Her lashes lay like dark fans on her cheeks; her open mouth was a rosebud, her dark hair tangled on the pillow.

'As pretty as her mother,' he said, so softly that Lyssa was not sure what she heard.

'She's dark like her father.' Lyssa emphasised the word 'father', giving André life, a man who had lived, breathed, taken her in love. 'I'm pale and blonde.'

'But she has your fragility,' said Jeth, still to himself. 'I can see the resemblance. You're very lucky to have such a child.'

'You have Matthew. He's a fine son, young, talented, handsome. You must be proud of him,' said Lyssa, amazed that they were talking about the man she was engaged to in this way. She suddenly felt remote from Matthew and it was Jeth's fault. Matthew seemed like another child. She supposed the generations were getting mixed up in this very odd twenty-four hours. It would straighten itself out . . . some time . . . it had to, or nothing would make sense.

'I am. He has a good brain, applies himself to his work. But the best thing he has done in life is choose you for his wife.' Jeth sounded regretful, and his attitude towards his son was not exactly fulsome.

'But today . . .' Lyssa could hardly find the words in her sleepy dormouse state, suddenly aware that she was in striped pyjamas. She pulled her robe tight, feeling its silkiness against her skin. 'You hauled me over the coals, criticized my work, as if I were the worst mother alive.'

'Bad mothers don't sleep on the floor when their child is ill,' he said slowly.

His hand was on her arm. It was the lightest of touch but the electricity ran through her veins. The old house was so quiet and dark, breathing its own timeless song as the night wore on. The rooms had other inhabitants, people from years long gone, living and dying in dramas from other centuries. But now Lyssa and Jeth were quite alone, apart from the sleeping Bethany.

If Jeth came any nearer, Lyssa knew she would be lost. There was a stunned acceptance about her weakness. Not exactly a weakness . . . but the most natural thing in the world would be to move into his arms, yielding, and take comfort from his closeness. To forget Matthew. She half turned towards him and then his face, saturnine and forbidding, stopped her. He had thrown up a wall between them.

'You're going to Geneva tomorrow?' she said, stumbling over confused thoughts. 'How nice.'

'Don't worry, I'll make it. I don't need a lot of sleep. But you do. You're worn out. Get back into your own bed. I'll stay with Bethany.'

'No, please,' said Lyssa, a small bubble of mirth lifting her soft mouth but it burst just as quickly. 'You'd frighten the life out of Bethany if she woke up and found you here. Heavens, what would she think? She'd think you were a pirate or a bandit. It's the influence of watching too many old films . . .'

He raised his hands in mock surrender.

'Pirate in retreat,' he said. Then he bent and placed a small, light kiss on her luminous forehead. 'Goodnight, future daughter-in-law.'

Future daughter-in-law. That was what he labelled her. It was so final.

Lyssa watched him walking back along the

corridor, then out of sight round a corner. Her heart contracted. She could still feel his cool lips like rain on her skin. God, this was a disaster. She must never be alone with him again. She must keep out of his way.

'Was that Father Christmas?' asked Bethany, slightly delirious. She already had Christmas on her mind. It was the shops' fault, with their advertising months in advance.

'Too early for Christmas,' said Lyssa, pouring her some juice. 'Here's a drink.'

'But who was it?'

'The man who gave you your new teddy.'

'Oh,' said Bethany, satisfied. 'That's nice.'

The man. Not grandfather. She couldn't say it. Nor father-in-law. Jeth Arnold, business tycoon, owner of some huge empire. He had a name of his own. A man who was a man. This gun-slinger, a man who would look at home with a rifle slung on his hip. There was a case of rifles, some of them very old, polished, gnarled, in the hallway. Not a man who worked at a desk with columns of figures. This man worked with money, with deals, with influential people; he didn't play left field, he knew what he was doing.

Lyssa sank wearily on to the floor, wrapping the duvet round her. It was all too late. She was marrying the wrong man. But she had to go through with it and learn to love Matthew. Do the best for Bethany. The best for Bethany . . . the words were a lullaby as she drifted into sleep, taking the stars with her, taking her dreams into a facing wind.

By Monday morning Bethany's small body was a route map of spots, but she was feeling better and taking an interest in her surroundings. Lyssa's lively daughter required constant attention and Lyssa swore she had been up and down the main staircase at Hollow House a hundred times. She looked forward to going back to work for a rest from Bethany's demands.

'Don't let her wear you out,' Lyssa said to Aunt Sarah as she grabbed a cup of coffee in the kitchen. It was a cold dawn. She was leaving earlier than usual to get to London in time for the first script meeting of the week.

'There you go again. You worry too much. I can cope with one small spotty girl, and Emily will help,' said Aunt Sarah, noting the frugal breakfast.

Lyssa had not seen Jeth since his late-night visit to the primrose bedroom. And she was very glad. She wanted to forget him, to fill her mind with work and put him firmly out of her life.

She drove to London through the dim and forlorn lanes, wet leaves brushing the windscreen, meeting an early milk float and a post office van. She wondered what Greg Wilson would have in store for her. He was a deceptively bluff man, whose amiable exterior hid a sharp and well-organised intellect. He did not brook fools . . . or excuses. If he said he wanted a Norman castle wall with a oak tree on the right and a watermill on the left, then that was what he wanted, and an approximation of the scene was just not good enough.

Lyssa had gone to work for the television company as a secretary. Her typing skills were not wonderful and her shorthand even less reliable, but they had soon discovered she had a flair for digging out unusual props and impossible artefacts. She had moved on from objects to places by degrees. Her main talent was for spotting exactly the right location, for mentally indexing places and scenes from years back, for knowing where to go and remembering if there was parking space, public toilets and a good pub nearby. She was also very good at negotiating with testy landowners and putting right anything that had been accidentally damaged – film crew were notoriously careless where they put their feet.

'I'm down in Sussex for at least two or three weeks,' Lyssa reminded him, although she had already told Greg on the phone. 'My daughter has measles and needs looking after.'

He nodded, taking the address she offered, not really listening. 'Any good locations down there? We need a railway station and an old house.'

The first episode of the new *Inspector Dutton Investigates* series had a whole lot of new locations for Lyssa to find. She could see she was going to have a busy week and they wanted to start filming the outside scenes in seven days. They were filming interior shots now. She had to keep cost in mind and not transport the entire crew to the Outer Hebrides.

She got back to Hollow House well after eight o'clock. She'd found a telephone kiosk on a deserted crossroads where the body would be found, slumped, phone hanging, a air of menace about the neglected kiosk that was perfect. She'd found an estate agent's on the verge of going bankrupt that didn't mind being filmed and being paid for it; and she'd found an old blacksmith's cottage with an anvil pitted with age that she knew they would use time and time again in different episodes.

'How's Bethany?' she asked, coming straight to the point as she walked into Hollow House.

'No problems at all. And as soon as we told her that the farm cat has had kittens and when she's better she can have one, she's been as good as gold.'

'I can't have a kitten in a high-rise flat,' said

Lyssa, shedding her anorak and her briefcase and sitting at the kitchen table, too tired to move. 'Please don't promise her things that she can't have.'

Aunt Sarah looked pleased with herself. 'Don't worry. I've told her that the kitten is a country kitten so it has to live here but she can see it when she visits us.'

'So we'll be down every weekend,' Lyssa groaned, thinking of Jeth being around. 'And every half-term.'

'Won't that be nice?'

'Very.'

'I know you and Matthew are going to be happy,' said Aunt Sarah complacently. 'Perhaps you'll be looking for a weekend cottage around here? There are a couple of delightful places for sale in the village.'

'We haven't talked about it,' said Lyssa. They hadn't talked about anything, it seemed. It was extraordinary. Matthew had phoned her on her car phone, enquired after Bethany. There were Interflora flowers at Hollow House from him and chocolates for Bethany. All very thoughtful but easily done. Ordered by phone, paid for by credit card, delivered by a local firm.

But it meant nothing, and chilled the warmth from her heart.

Lyssa changed into jeans and a loose check shirt, chased some scampi and rice round a plate, then spent the evening doing a jigsaw with Bethany. She knew the farmyard view by heart, every shade of feather on every duck. They had done this jigsaw at least three times already.

After giving Bethany a good wash-down, reading her a story and tucking her up for the night, Lyssa went downstairs to the sitting room and sank thankfully on to a sofa.

'I could sleep for a year,' she sighed, stretching her hands out towards the fire.

Aunt Sarah offered her an opened box of Black Magic. 'My favourites,' she said. 'I like the coffee ones best, then the toffee mallow. So I eat all those first. But then there's the others to eat up before I can buy another box.'

'Force yourself,' said Lyssa taking a hard caramel and chewing it slowly. It would be her luck to break a tooth.

Aunt Sarah settled back to watch some television soap. She'd bought some pink wool in the village and a pattern. 'I'm going to knit Bethany a jersey. I hope you don't mind. Look, it's got a white rabbit on the front. Do you think she'll like it?'

'She'll love it.'

'I'll measure her later,' said Aunt Sarah, confidently casting on.

Lyssa was dozing off when they heard a car arrive in the drive. It was a low, powerful sound, purring to a halt outside the porch. Her heart lurched. She was starving for sight of him. But was it Matthew or Jeth? She longed for it to be Jeth but would prefer the safety of Matthew . . . and that was some crazy mixed-up woman. She'd lose her job if she was that indecisive about work.

She did not move. She did not want to know. There were lots of staircases at Hollow House, Matthew had said. Perhaps she could find a different way up to their end of the corridor bedrooms, avoiding whoever it was altogether.

Suddenly the sitting room door burst open. Jeth was standing in the doorway, still in his overcoat, with Bethany in his arms. He was ashen-faced. Bethany was lying all limp and lifeless, her cheeks deathly white, her lips blue.

'She's dead,' he gasped, his voice shocked, desperate. 'I found her at the bottom of the stairs, all crumpled up . . . and Lyssa . . . there's no pulse . . . she's not breathing . . . oh, my God, I think she's dead.'

CHAPTER 4

'She isn't dead,' said Lyssa, stamping down the rising terror in her heart. She knew it was important to appear calm. Jeth and Aunt Sarah were astounded at her composure, but it was something she had learned was always necessary. 'She's unconscious. I know it looks like death, but she's suffering from a form of shock.'

'I'll phone for an ambulance,' said Aunt Sarah anxiously, rising quickly from her chair. 'And Dr Carrington. She needs a doctor. He'll be here in no time. He doesn't live far away. And I'll phone 999.'

'There's no need,' Lyssa persisted. 'This state is temporary.'

Jeth laid Bethany's limp body on the rug in front of the fire and knelt beside her. She looked so small and helpless, her hair fanning out. 'But she's not breathing,' he said, with a stricken look. 'Oh, God, what's happened? Kiss of life . . . I know how to do it.'

'No . . .' Lyssa put a restraining hand on his arm. 'Please don't do that. You might make her choke and that would only make things worse. All we can do is put her in the recovery position, keep her warm, and wait for her to come out of it.'

'Come out of what?' he said abruptly. He took off his jacket and wrapped it round the still figure. 'Would you please tell us what is going on? Bethany looks at death's door, if she's not already dying, yet you are not in the least worried. You're a very unnatural mother. Heavens, woman, don't you care? What's the matter with you? Or is your daughter getting in the way of your marriage to Matthew?'

Lyssa whitened, flinched at the cruelty of his words. He was trying to manipulate her again but she wasn't having it. There'd been enough difficult producers to deal with in the past. She wanted to hurt him in some way, but how could she, with Bethany lying there between them? She shuddered that she had become capable of violence. This was not her true nature. Jeth was destroying more than her composure.

'I'll forget you said that,' she said, her voice level, low with anger. 'Bethany is the most precious person in the world to me. If Matthew didn't like her, I'd drop him in less time than it takes to show someone the door. You may be rich and powerful and famous, Jeth Arnold, but that doesn't give you the right to speak to me in that cruel and malicious way.'

'I was saying what I saw. An uncaring mother –'

'Stop it, the two of you. This is no time to be arguing. What's the matter with Bethany?' Aunt Sarah said, her hands fluttering. 'Can't we do something? It doesn't seem right to just leave her.'

'We're wasting time. Phone for an ambulance.'

'I know what I'm doing. This has happened before. She must have bumped herself . . .' Lyssa began, going down on her knees. 'Even a little bump will start it off. Sometimes it's no more than a tap. In another child it would produce no more than a bruise.'

'She fell down the stairs, obviously,' snapped Jeth without apologising for his anger. 'You were down here drinking coffee, not sitting with her as you should have been, and she came looking for you. She tripped on her nightgown and fell,' he glared. 'You left her alone. Typical.'

'I'd only just left her upstairs sleeping. I've been with her all evening. And you might note she's wearing pyjamas. Andy Pandy pyjamas.' Lyssa frosted, barely polite. 'I can't be with her every single minute, night and day. Now, if you would kindly stop fussing and let me deal with Bethany.'

Aunt Sarah was quick to defend Lyssa. 'Lyssa

has only been here a minute; she came down for a break. Bethany was asleep. There was no harm in leaving her for a few moments. But we have got to do something now. She's not breathing.'

Lyssa took a deep breath and felt all over her daughter's body. 'Please believe me. She didn't fall. There are no injuries and she hasn't hurt herself. She probably just bumped her leg as she swung round the banister post. It's a form of shock or trauma. It only takes the slightest bump . . .'

'Dammit, I'm not listening to any more of this nonsense. It's serious; she ought to go to hospital,' said Jeth, rising. His profile was stony, his mouth a thin line of displeasure. 'If you won't let us phone for an ambulance, I'll get the car out and take her. This is wasting valuable time.'

'She's been to hospital a dozen times,' said Lyssa, her strawberry-blonde hair falling across her face as she bent over her daughter, the fire's reflection turning the strands to a fiery flame. 'Believe me, I used to take her every time this happened. She must have been to hospital around thirty times. I try not to panic so much now but it's not easy. The doctors say it doesn't help Bethany to wake up in a strange hospital ward or in an bumpy ambulance, hurtling through the night. When she wakes up, she'll be happier to find herself here with us.'

Jeth and Aunt Sarah stared at her with different degrees of hope. 'Wake up? Are you sure? Are you positive?'

'She has a very rare condition. It's called RAS or reflex anoxic seizure,' Lyssa said slowly so that they could take in the new medical words. 'Some people call it the Sleeping Beauty syndrome. Bethany gives every appearance of being dead, even looks like it, her heart stops and she becomes unconscious for a period of time from two minutes to an hour. Her heart actually stops beating. The seizure leaves her clinically dead before she starts to breathe again.'

'Then she comes round? Every time?' Aunt Sarah asked, retrieving her knitting from the floor, stitches hanging loose. 'Are you sure, Lyssa? How do you know? It seems wrong not to do anything.'

'Yes, she will, and it's not after a hundred years. It just seems like it, especially for me. Sometimes it's only a minute. But it's the longest minute of my life. Her teachers know what to do and so does my neighbour and friend, Maggie. The main thing is to protect her from any further bumps or falls. Even the slightest knock . . . look, I think she's coming round. Bethany, darling . . .'

The small body jerked, lashes fluttering.

'Don't worry,' said Lyssa, pushing the sofa

away. 'This is difficult to watch. She's going to convulse as her muscles go into spasm and her heart starts beating again. What was it this time? Three or four minutes . . . it always looks worse than it is.'

'I can't stand this,' said Jeth. Aunt Sarah covered her mouth in horror.

Bethany's arms and legs began to jerk and Lyssa hurriedly put cushions round her body to prevent her from hurting herself. Aunt Sarah handed her more from the sofa, glad to have something to do. But the convulsion was over in moments and Bethany opened her eyes.

'Don't cry, Mummy,' she said sleepily. 'I'm back now.'

'That's lovely. You're safe with me.'

'Thank God,' said Jeth, rising off his knees. His voice was still harsh. 'How often is this going to happen?'

'Not often if I can help it. I wrap her in cotton wool as it is, but I can't keep her from living as natural a life as possible. If you think about it, surely you'll agree with me? She's a little girl, full of beans. She probably woke up upstairs, feeling better and thought she'd like to explore the house. You like this house, don't you, darling?'

'S'lovely.' Bethany's lashes fluttered and she settled to sleep in Lyssa's arms.

'Does Bethany know about this . . . this illness?' He ran his hand down his angular face, bone weary.

'She's bright enough to have gathered that something happens to her and that I get worried. But I haven't told her exactly because she's naughty enough to use it, perhaps bump herself on purpose if I told she had to do something that she didn't want to do or she didn't want to go to school. So I'm not taking that chance. She doesn't go out into the playground at break time; she stays indoors in a classroom and colours or paints. The school playground is a jungle,' Lyssa brooded, remembering her constant worry and concern.

'She ought not to go to school. She ought to have a home tutor, a governess.' Jeth was standing back in a superior, masculine stance, aiming to dominate, his face grim. He wanted to take over, organize everything for Bethany's life from now on. He went over to the drinks cabinet and poured himself a whisky.

Lyssa tried not to think of her own thirst.

'Definitely not. I'm not stopping her from having a normal life, especially at school. She needs friends.' Lyssa turned to Bethany, holding her close, stroking her hair.

The convulsions were over and as Bethany's heart began to beat normally so her colour returned and her lips regained a rosy hue. She was beginning to look her old, spotted self.

'Thank goodness,' said Aunt Sarah. 'Is she all right now? What a relief. I think we all need a cup of tea. I'll go and make it. What about Bethany? What would she like?'

'A soft drink will be fine,' said Lyssa, hugging her daughter. 'Then I'll put her back to bed.'

'Where am I?' said Bethany, waking. 'Mummy? I woke up in bed and you weren't there.'

'That's what I said. You weren't there,' Jeth growled under his breath, prowling the room with long fluid strides. He was unnervingly powerful in everything he said and did. Lyssa was tired of his accusations. One more and she would tell him straight that he didn't know what he was talking about.

'You were having a lovely sleep so I came downstairs, sweetheart, and I've been talking to Aunt Sarah.' said Lyssa, lifting Bethany up on to her lap. 'She's been telling me what a good girl you've been today.'

'Yes, I have,' said Bethany smugly. 'And I've got a lot more spots. Look, hundreds and hundreds.' She pushed up her sleeve. 'I've got proper measles now.'

Everyone laughed and the tension eased. Jeth shrugged and sat down heavily at the other end of the sofa. He looked tired, his face drawn by the drama. He sat forward, his hands clenched. Lyssa remembered that he had flown to Geneva, worked at meetings, driven to Heathrow this morning and back again to Sussex since she had last seen him. Hardly an easy day.

'You ought to have a driver,' she said without thinking. 'At least someone to take you to Heathrow and pick you up. That M25 is a killer.'

'How very astute,' he said bitterly. 'Are you volunteering to be my driver?'

'Sorry, my family loyalty doesn't stretch that far. Besides, you haven't sampled my driving. Sorry, that was supposed to be a joke. I drive hundreds of miles every day with my work.'

'Your future loyalty, you mean,' he corrected grimly. 'You are not part of this family yet.'

It was like a slap of cold water in her face. Lyssa jerked back with the force of his words, clutching at Bethany. But he was scanning a financial newspaper as if he had said nothing of any consequence.

'That's true. Matthew and I have no more than an understanding,' she said, barely audible. He was playing a game and she didn't like it. There was only the two of them. Bethany and Aunt Sarah had become shadowy images. It took an iron will to remain calm.

'A lot can happen in a short time.'

'I might change my mind.'

'I can't see that happening. You are in a strong position. Matthew is crazy about you.'

'There's a difference between love and his kind of heady infatuation. Matthew could fall out of love just as quickly. It could happen.'

'I think you have far more to gain than Matthew realises. I can see why this marriage is attractive to you. It's obvious that he's a catch. Few single men would take on a ready-made family and you need the security he can offer.'

Lyssa cradled Bethany in her arms. She couldn't get away. His words stuck in her throat with the taste of truth. She knew he was right. He had seen right into her heart.

'That's not fair,' she said vehemently, but numbly. 'I love Matthew.' She could not look at him in case her eyes gave away the truth. 'We're going to be very happy. He's a wonderful young man, kind and considerate . . .'

'Do you love him? Are you sure?'

Bethany fidgeted, grown bored with the adult argument. She scrambled along the sofa and snuggled up to Jeth.

'Will you read to me?' she said beguilingly.

'Of course,' said Jeth, forgetting to look stern. 'What would you like? Sports page or financial news?'

'Sports,' said Bethany. 'I like dancing best.'

'I'll see if I can find any sports stories about dancing,' he said, hiding a sly grin as he rustled through the pages. He had changed suddenly. It was amazing and heartening. All trace of aggression disappeared, as if Bethany herself had wiped it away with one of her smiles.

Lyssa watched the big man reading to her daughter and her bones melted. Something was happening that she could not understand. This man was generating an overpowering emotion in her. The child was leaning against Jeth's chest, so trustingly, and the scene burned into her memory. Lyssa felt lined with pain for what André had missed.

Bethany hung on to every word as Jeth read sports reports on ice hockey, golf and racing. He was spicing up the stories to suit Bethany. Racehorses didn't normally talk back to their jockeys and golf balls couldn't tap dance. Bethany didn't seem to mind what he read, was mesmerized by that deep voice, and she only succumbed to boredom when he began on the quarterfinals of the European Cup Winners' Cup. Her eyes fought against closing but eventually she fell asleep leaning on his arm.

'You've a little charmer here,' he said, looking down at the flushed and sleepy face. He could see

Lyssa's features in the soft, moist mouth and long lashes.

Lyssa said nothing but she could not take her eyes away from the cameo they made. A dangerous emotion was surging through her, making her limbs ache with longing. She wondered what it would be like to feel the hard strength of Jeth's hands on her body, running through her hair, to let him melt the ice that crippled her emotions.

'I'll carry Bethany up to bed,' he said, moving carefully so that he did not disturb Bethany or wake her. He picked up her easily as if she weighed no more than a feather.

'And I'll tuck her in,' said Aunt Sarah. She had forgotten all about making tea. 'We'll leave you in peace, Lyssa. You look worn out, my dear. It must be a worry. Never mind, you have us now. Help yourself to a glass of sherry and relax.'

Lyssa could not watch Jeth carrying her daughter out of the room. She knew the sight would mangle her heart-strings. She let her head fall back on a cushion and closed her eyes, collecting her scattered wits. What a day . . . what a weekend, and now this. Matthew's unexpected announcement of their engagement had thrown her. She didn't know if she was strong enough to cope. The room was warm and Lyssa knew she might fall asleep if she was not careful. Then she would get another lecture from Mr Jeth Arnold telling her she was overdoing it, taking on too much, stretching her resources, being a bad mother.

All of which, except the last, was partly true, but she was certainly not going to admit it and least of all to Jeth.

She pulled herself awake, hearing his returning footsteps down the staircase. But he went elsewhere, to the seclusion of his study perhaps, to make more money, clinch more deals, working at putting the ty into tycoon.

A clap of thunder woke her. She had dozed off on a comfortable sofa, the cup of tea gone cold beside her. The thunder rumbled and rolled overhead and Lyssa immediately thought she had gone back in time to the October storm in 1987. She had been so alone that terrible evening while the trees in London parks crashed to the ground in their thousands. She had watched from the window, tears in her eyes, as the wind tore along the street, racing dustbins and lids and litter, flinging severed branches across the road.

'Bethany?' she said, sitting up. 'I'd better go to her. She'll be frightened.'

'She's all right,' said a voice from the sofa opposite. Jeth was sitting in rolled-up shirt sleeves, surrounded by books and files, tongues of scrap paper hanging out of pages where he had marked a place. 'I've been up to check on her. She's fast asleep.'

'She hates thunderstorms.'

'Don't we all?'

Lyssa sat up and tidied her clothes, aware that Jeth must have been looking at her in sleep. What a gruesome thought. Supposing her mouth had fallen open? 'It must have been awful in that storm. Did you lose a lot of trees?' Lyssa asked cautiously.

'About a quarter of all the trees. It was like a swathe cut through the woodland. You could see the path of the storm, almost uncanny, like a giant's hand decimating the land with great sweeps of a scythe. And we lost half of our roof, slates sliding down everywhere. My car was smashed by a falling oak. What a mess. But you can easily replace a car. You can't replace a century of ancient trees.'

'It was a nightmare.'

Jeth nodded. 'Sarah and I were up most of the night. Bill and Ben were terrified, cowering under chairs and tables. It was strange the way they acted as if they knew something we didn't, something primeval. I've heard lots of tales about the way animals reacted.'

They were very aware of each other, visual

fencing, watching intently. They were testing, circling like riders, getting under each other's skin, their words really saying something quite different. Lyssa forced a smile but he was staring into the fire.

'I don't think there was much sleep for anyone.'

Lyssa looked across into the now dying, flickering firelight, logs glowing with red pricks of light. For once Jeth looked relaxed and comfortable, a dark shadow of stubble appearing on his stubborn jaw. A tumbler of golden liquid stood on the small table at the side.

He followed her gaze. 'Would you like one? It's brandy and ginger ale. A good brandy, not firewater, made by the worthy monks. Great for winding down after a rough day.'

Lyssa shook her head, teasing her shaggy mane with her finger tips, could not prevent a yawn. 'I rarely drink. A nice wine sometimes. Is it very late?'

'One a.m.'

She shot upright in dismay. 'Oh, heavens, and I've such an early start tomorrow. Everything's programmed, arrival times, etc. I've got to see everything goes right, be there first on site if possible. How could I?'

'But you've had three good hours of sleep down here. We didn't like to disturb you. Sarah went to bed ages ago. She likes to read in bed. You looked like . . . well, I was going to say like a Sleeping Beauty but those words can never be used in jest again. They're too potent.' Jeth was staring at her, making it an intimate imprisonment.

'Why did you stay?' she asked, barely audible. 'It wasn't necessary. I don't need a baby-sitter.'

'I stayed in case the storm woke you up; in case you were confused suddenly and disorientated. It's easy to get lost in Hollow House. There are some rooms *I* haven't found yet,' said Jeth, trying to sound casually indifferent. His dark eyes held hers, leaving her floundering.

'And I expect you have a ghost.'

'Oh, yes, we have a ghost. Several.'

But he was laughing at her. She could see the amusement, playful and warm, a kind of reluctant caring. His granite eyes were glinting in the fire-light, bright as gems, his mouth curved into a smile, the musky smell of his aftershave mingling with the wood smoke. She could not let him see the devastating hunger that was causing her body to ache. It was time she went. He was dangerous.

'I'll say goodnight, then, and leave you to your books.' Lyssa tried to stir but she was frozen to the soft cushions with the magic of the moment, the promise of something tantalisingly new. All she wanted to do was keep looking into his eyes. This man was an expert in reaching into a woman's heart. She wondered how many woman there had been in his life since Matthew's mother.

'Finished,' he said, clapping the book shut. He moved over and sat down beside her, his hand brushing hers by accident. His closeness was only a breath away. Lyssa felt trapped, locked in time. This must not happen. It was too close to reality. It could inflict a terrible hurt. His eyes darkened as they looked into hers. He carefully drew her into the curve of his arm and she found herself trembling.

'I have to go . . .' she said, dazed.

'Not yet,' he said, aware of the power he wielded. It was half calculating, half instinctive. He believed himself to be a fair man, but more than anything his son's future was paramount. The empire he owned was vast but Matthew was more important than any of it. 'Don't go.'

'Please . . .'

'Lyssa, we have to talk. It's important.'

'Please don't . . .' Her voice was broken with glimpses of what might have been. Thunder rumbled in the distance, scudding across the skies, and took her pain with it. This man was everything she had ever wanted, ever longed for. Their sides touched and it was like an electric shock.

'Don't what . . .?'

She did not know who reached out for whom. Their identities vanished, senses began to swirl like a mist coming down. It was *Brigadoon* for one complete moment. Lyssa's resolve collapsed as his mouth touched hers, and his lips moved with such tenderness that the price suddenly lost all meaning. He leaned his weight on her and crushed her against the back of the enveloping sofa, and her surrender was so total that she was beyond rational thinking or caring.

She forgot how uncomfortable it was on the sofa as he silently pulled her hard against him, devouring her sweetness with pent-up hunger, igniting the flame inside her. There was only the feel of him, the muscles in his long thighs, the warmth of his body, the smell of his skin, the boldness of his arms, the moist invasion of his seeking mouth. She did not know if she heard more thunder or if it was simply the crashing of her heart.

He let her go and her body went limp with rejection. A chill crept into her bones. She did not know where to look, what to say. The enormity of her grief was unbearable. And she felt pinioned to his body by her own wantonness, could not move, could not leave him. She had wanted that kiss, had been waiting for it for years, and yet those few moments of passion had ruined everything.

Matthew's father. And there was still Matthew.

'But I love Matthew,' she whispered, her eyes were closed, lashes fanned and vulnerable. His breath was still warm against her face and then he moved back. 'Why did you do this . . .?'

'That kiss proves that you don't love him.' His voice was hard, grating, and she gasped with defeat. He had been testing her, had kissed her on purpose. 'I don't want my son marrying a little flirt, a gold-digger, an opportunist,' he went on, his hands now hard and strong, gripping her arms in a vice. 'And that's what you are. Matthew's quite a catch, isn't he? Hollow House, acres of Sussex countryside and eventually the control of my business. A long way from a council flat.'

The shock was humiliating.

'Don't you dare say that,' she began, tight with emotion, gathering the tattered rags of her pride. She wondered if she could pretend that she had thought he was Matthew in her half sleepiness, but knew he would not believe such a flagrant lie. And it would have been a lie. Jeth was no one but himself. Kisses were different. Matthew kissed her differently, almost too gently, his enthusiasm boyish, not mature. Jeth had been all man, all demanding, yet with an unexpected tenderness that had been at the same time forceful and caring.

She groaned aloud, clenching her fists to her

forehead. 'Oh, God, Jeth, why did you do that? You bastard. You don't understand. Why couldn't you have left me alone? I didn't want that to happen . . .'

'Really? I think I do understand.' He was mocking her now, rolling down his sleeves, fixing gold cufflinks, as if to mark a return to civilized behaviour. 'You seemed quite an eager participant. Was I mistaken? Or is that how you normally fight off a man?'

'I don't know anything any more . . .' she said brokenly, like a wild horse suddenly tamed. 'It shouldn't have happened and I couldn't be more sorry. I'm not a gold-digger. I want to marry Matthew for all the right reasons . . .' Lyssa could not bring herself to say because she loved him again. Suddenly she was not sure any more. 'Nothing like this has ever happened before. There has been no one at all those years before I met Matthew, since Bethany's father. I didn't go out, I didn't date men – I wasn't even looking.'

'You expect me to believe that?' he glared. 'With your stunning, princess, fairy-tale looks? Every red-blooded man in the block must have been canvassing at your door.'

'How dare you?' she said angrily, tossing back her tangled hair. 'If Bethany wasn't ill, if there wasn't a storm, if I knew where the hell I was in

Sussex I'd go home right now. This isn't hospitality, this is a third degree, an inquisition. Am I going to be marched out and ducked in the village pond?'

He gave a short, derisory laugh. 'Is that what you want? Something wet to cool you off?' He looked mad enough to tip his drink over her. 'You've certainly bewitched me. I suppose Matthew is under your spell, too.'

'Matthew knows exactly what he's doing.'

'But does he know you? That's a completely different question.'

'I'm going to bed and I hope I won't see you in the morning,' Lyssa muttered, rising unsteadily. 'I suppose you'll have to be around but pardon me if I don't say more than a courteous hello. I don't think I could bring myself to speak to you.'

'Not even thank you for paying the bills?'

'I don't want a single penny of the Arnold fortunes to pay for my wedding,' said Lyssa acidly. 'I'd rather have a registry office ceremony and a bangers-and-mash knees-up at a local pub.' Lyssa was deliberately crude.

'Is that what you did at your last wedding?'

'It's none of your business what happened,' she said, her eyes as impenetrable as stone. She wasn't telling this damned man anything.

'Oh, yes, it is,' he said, starting to pile up his

books and files in a tidy manner. 'I want to know everything about the woman my son is going to marry. And if you won't tell me, then I'll find out myself by some other means, and there are plenty of those. I seem to have discovered a lot about you this evening already.'

'This is unforgivable. You're not being fair. But it's what I should have expected. Big men in the money world don't usually play fair. It's a dirty tricks trade, isn't it, at the top? That's how you stay there, isn't it? Stepping on anybody who gets in the way.'

She was beyond caring what she said. She hated this man. Jeth had encroached on her life in a way she could not comprehend, manipulating her in a disastrous manner. She stared out of the window at a moonlight that added a sheen to the sky. Dark rags of cloud moved across the moon as if washing out the light. No one had ever treated her like this before. Somehow she would have to stop him to survive.

'Two can play at that game,' she said smoothly. 'I can be a tough cookie. You've taken on a woman who can fight and forget there were ever any rules. Don't imagine that I'm going to go away and weep in some corner. I haven't cried since André died, and I have no intention of starting now.'

CHAPTER 5

It was the weekend before Lyssa saw Jeth Arnold again. He had flown to Japan to a major sales convention in Tokyo and was returning via the States. The man was never at home. She needed the time to regain her composure and decide what she was going to do. Somehow she had to fight her way out of this situation. Her first instinct was to escape, go straight back to the flat and barricade herself in against all comers.

But Bethany was so happy at Hollow House, spoilt rotten by Aunt Sarah and Emily, full of tricks now that she was feeling better. She was skipping in and out of bed, eager to explore every room and find out everything about Hollow House.

'Is this Matthew's house?' Bethany asked, bouncing up and down on the bed, her hair flying.

'No, I've told you a dozen times. It's his father's house,' said Lyssa patiently. 'Jeth is his father.' She repeated the words silently: Jeth is his father.

If only he were someone else. Some stranger, a man she'd met on a train, a writer, a designer, an actor on the set. Anyone but Matthew's father.

'Did he read to me when I was spotty and tell me stories? Is he going to be my grandfather? Are we going to live here?'

'No, we are not,' said Lyssa firmly. 'We are going to live in London with Matthew at his nice flat.'

'But we'll be able to come here, won't we? Aunt Sarah is going to give me a kitten. We're going to choose it as soon as I'm better. It's a farm kitten and they live in the barn. There are four kittens, one black, one grey and two stripy ones . . . I don't know which one to have,' Bethany prattled on, making Lyssa quite tired listening to her.

Lyssa turned her face away from her rapturous daughter. Bethany had no idea what a strain life could be. She was a child and every day was rosy. And today had been no exception for Lyssa. She felt shredded, minced up.

It had been a fruitless kind of day. Lyssa had been searching frantically for a sixteenth-century farmhouse that was untouched by time, somewhere in Kent or Essex, for background shots of a dawn chase. She'd looked at a dozen properties but they all had modern dwellings too close which could not be painted out or disguised or demolished. The scene was a short but important one and the house had to be right.

But she had decided that the local station halt in Sludbury was perfect for the Inspector's lost briefcase scene, and she'd organised the crew to come down early tomorrow to shoot background and a brief scene. British Rail had no objection as long as the name of the halt did not appear on the screen or customers were not inconvenienced. But she was always anticipating disaster. The station-master had only to forget a crucial key to the side gate and she wouldn't work for Greg Wilson, the director, again.

'We don't want vandals descending on the place and wrecking it,' warned a BR official. 'They go for anything that's on the telly. God knows why. Morons.'

Matthew phoned every day, sent florists' flowers, Belgian chocolates and a giant panda. Bethany did not like the panda. It was too large and bulky to hold, so it sat in a corner of her room in disgrace, getting told off for various misdemeanours. Lyssa felt quite sorry for the creature.

'That panda is so naughty,' said Bethany, crossly. 'Today he threw his dinner out of the window.'

'I hope you ate yours,' said Lyssa, washing a sticky face with a wet flannel. 'No grumbles.'

'Of course. Aunt Sarah makes lovely puddings. Especially chocolate.'

'I can see that,' said Lyssa. 'You've got it round your ears.'

'So you're doing all right at Hollow House?' Matthew said for the tenth time on the phone, his voice full of possession. Lyssa resented the tone.

'We're fine and everyone is very kind. Bethany is having a great time. But, Matthew . . . we have to talk.'

'Yes, we do. There's so much to arrange and to plan for our wedding. Have you started any lists? Oh, Lyssa darling, everything is going to be wonderful. I'm so pleased that Aunt Sarah and my father took to you. I knew they would.'

Talking over the phone did not achieve much, Lyssa knew that, but she had to try. Matthew only saw what he wanted to see, heard what he wanted to hear. What lists? She had to convince him that their engagement announcement had been premature. A terrible ache filled her. She had once been vibrating with joy, meeting Matthew and hoping he would fulfil her dreams of security.

'Matthew, I didn't say anything in front of your father or Aunt Sarah when you introduced me as your fiancée – I didn't want to embarrass you – but I do think you should have said something to me before announcing our engagement. After all, it hadn't been decided. I was thrown, totally thrown.'

'I had decided. We'd done enough talking. I knew you would still be dithering in a year's time if I didn't take the initiative. You will marry me, won't you? Believe me, it'll work. I love you both so much.'

Dithering? Lyssa objected to the feeble word. Was that how Matthew saw her? A frail and feeble little woman? Marriage was a serious step and she had to be sure. She had been one hundred per cent sure about André. 'I think you're marrying me for my daughter,' she challenged.

'What could be better? A ready-made sister for our son.'

Their son . . . she felt a Judas flap of fear. Lyssa hadn't thought about lovemaking with Matthew. Kisses, yes. Somehow she had expected intimacy to grow as they got used to living together, but now she was uncertain. She could not imagine herself naked in his arms, longing for his youthful body heavy on hers. He would sweat, fumble, apologize, leave her in the air and staring at the ceiling, unfulfilled and crying silently for André.

There was only one man who could make her forget André.

'It wasn't fair,' she insisted. 'You should have warned me. I could hardly say, Hold on, folks . . .

Matthew hasn't even asked me yet. You sprung it on me.'

He didn't sound at all sorry. 'Don't spoil it, Lyssa. Everyone is so happy for us.'

'Are they? Really?' Lyssa thought of Jeth's reaction, the derision in his eyes. He had not been happy about the situation at all. He'd be happier if the entire episode could be erased from history. That bruising kiss had been his way of proving it. It had been a terrible mistake and they both knew it.

She closed her eyes, trying to deny the memory, wishing it had never happened, wishing she could turn the clock back and act out that first meeting again. How differently she would have behaved, dressed, and conducted the introduction with a decorum that would have fooled everyone.

'Why didn't you tell me what your father would be like?'

'I don't know what you mean. What he's like? He's my father, a workaholic, never around, stern, difficult to approach. Would any of that have helped you?'

'Cold, disapproving, hypercritical, sexist . . .' Lyssa added.

Matthew chuckled. 'I'm glad you two have really hit it off. He'll get used to your modern ideas and grow to love you as much as I do. You'll see, he's really a caring man and he'll love Bethany.'

Lyssa knew that already. Jeth had been amazing with Bethany. The image of him reading the sports pages to her daughter was indelible, Bethany curled up against him, her eyes on his face. Jeth had a soft and secret side, but she would never see it for herself. It was locked in the custody of his eyes.

'He thinks I'm a fortune-hunter.'

'But I haven't got any money. OK, I earn a more than adequate income for the three of us, but it's hardly a fortune.'

'He thinks it's *his* money I'm after.'

'What nonsense. Jeth's only forty-four, fit and in his prime. He might remarry if he stopped travelling long enough to find someone. Dozens of women would jump at him. He's a catch. Darling, we must do a little matchmaking. Have you got any nice friends?'

Lyssa caught her breath. Jeth married to someone else would break her. How could she live through it? The hurt would be transparent to the world. She would have to hide the pain but eventually it would destroy her, split her into fragments.

'I'm sure Jeth can find his own women,' she said lightly.

'Look, darling, I have to go. Everything will

work out all right. Don't worry. Love to Bethany. Did she like the panda?'

'Loves him,' said Lyssa. 'He's being kept in strict isolation.'

Lyssa was becoming good friends with Aunt Sarah. It was not difficult, Aunt Sarah was the easiest person to get on with, but Lyssa did not want anything to happen which would tarnish this friendship. There was no way of knowing how Jeth would use his powerful knowledge of her body's frailty. Surely he would not tell Matthew that his fiancée had accepted his father's arms and returned his kisses with abandon?

Her face flamed at the memory of their passion. That would be too cruel. Or was he expecting her to break off the engagement and disappear back into suburban obscurity? Surely not? He had tricked her into that kiss and she would never forgive him for that, the same way that Matthew had tricked her into the engagement in the first place.

She showered and changed into clean jeans and a sweatshirt, ready to spend a pleasant evening with Aunt Sarah after putting Bethany to bed. The fever had gone and the spots were fading, and Bethany was ready to sleep at her usual time.

Aunt Sarah was dismayed by Lyssa's lack of interest in the wedding plans. She had wasted no time and produced suggested sit-down menus from the Savoy Hotel and a dozen dress designs from several of London's top bridal designers. The frothy virginal creations were unpriced.

'This is all much too soon,' said Lyssa, careful not to say anything which might incriminate Matthew. 'We haven't really decided on anything.'

'You only have to make an appointment and they'll dream up anything you want, Lyssa. Don't you like any of them?'

'On the contrary, I like them all. They're beautiful. That's the trouble. But this is all so sudden; Matthew hasn't really given me any time to think, to make plans. Yes, they are quite wonderful dresses. Any one of them would do. I don't mind.' Lyssa knew she ought to show more enthusiasm.

'Lyssa, really – that's no way to choose a wedding dress. You're doing it with a pin. Please look at them again and decide which designer you'd like to go to for talks and a fitting and I'll make an appointment.'

'How about ready-made? Or hired? It would save a lot of time.' Lyssa pushed up her sleeves, feeling warm in the heating of Hollow House. Every room was thermostatically controlled. Her flat was not so well insulated. Even the windows rattled and she swore that sometimes the building swayed. The economic thought of hiring a dress soothed her wretchedness. It could be a last-minute thing.

Aunt Sarah shook her head in despair. 'What a reluctant bride. We *could* look at ready-made dresses, I suppose. There are some lovely shops in Knightsbridge and South Kensington. We'll go together. I don't trust you to chose a proper outfit. Jeth would have a fit if you appeared in a white trouser-suit.'

'I'm not marrying Jeth. Perhaps Matthew might like it. What does it matter what Jeth thinks?' asked Lyssa, her face wearing a shut-down look. 'A trouser-suit sounds ideal. Or white jeans and designer T-shirt? I could have them dyed navy afterwards.'

'Don't you dare let your daughter down,' said Aunt Sarah. 'She's longing to wear a long dress and has appointed herself your chief bridesmaid. It's all decided, pink apparently with roses and bows and frills and masses of petticoats.'

'Sounds wonderful,' said Lyssa drily. 'A bit like a crinoline lady tea-cosy.'

'She's at least taking more interest than her mother, for sure,' said Aunt Sarah, delving into a tapestry bag for her knitting.

'She's only five and a bit. She doesn't understand. Weddings are fairy-tales,' said Lyssa. 'And she's never even been to one. Have you measured her yet for that jersey?'

'I'll do it later,' said Aunt Sarah, knitting with confidence. 'It's bound to fit. My knitting always fits.'

Aunt Sarah's confidence was catching, and Lyssa hoped that her future would fit whatever great cosmic plan was in store for her. She couldn't help laughing.

'That's it, dear. Nice to see you laughing.'

Lyssa slept well that night, spangled dreams chasing her worries away, like an afternoon saturated with light and dragonflies. Her bedroom at Hollow House was warm and comfortable, and it was such a luxury to come back to a hot meal all cooked and ready to eat. Some of her appetite had returned and she realised that her lack of interest in food was due mainly to continued weariness. Her job was all stress, the level of anxiety deceptive. If she didn't come up with the right locations, no producer would employ her. She wouldn't work again. Most people, particularly viewers, thought her work consisted of VIP flights abroad and wandering about sun-drenched beaches checking palm trees. She smiled to herself at how wrong they were. Traffic jams, crowded trains and damp locations were more normal.

She did not hear Jeth's Mercedes sweeping

along the drive in the early hours of the morning. He let himself in quietly, spent some time on paperwork in his study before retiring to his bedroom at the other end of the house. He was pie-eyed with jet-lag and fell into a deep sleep. He didn't wake when the rest of the household stirred around seven.

But Lyssa was up at six. She crept round the house, getting ready, making a quick cup of instant coffee, enjoying having the empty kitchen to herself. She had arranged to meet the crew at the Sludbury halt and show them which areas they could film and which were off limits. It was going to be an easier day and about time she coasted.

The timed arrival of crew, cast and catering was choreographed down to the last minute. They couldn't all arrive at the same time, blocking roads, monopolising parking space. The Unit signs were up. They'd got clearance from the police, council and British Rail. She'd checked Gatwick flight paths for sound interference, any military movements, the weather and temperature prospects as far as anyone could predict.

'I have to go now, sweetheart. I'll be home early,' Lyssa promised Bethany in a whisper in the still dark bedroom, giving her a kiss. 'We'll play some games.'

'I'll look after Pudding while you're gone,' said Bethany, hugging the cheeky-faced brown bear which Jeth had given her. 'And he'll look after me. I've called him Pudding after Aunt Sarah's lovely puddings.'

Lyssa remembered to turn off the alarm system before letting herself out. The morning was chill with remnants of the night still in the vaulting halls, the sky the colour of dark slate. The house slept like an old lover in the arms of the countryside.

The film crew were late, arrived grumbling and frozen, flapping their arms, huddled into anoraks and base-ball caps. They couldn't find the damned place. They didn't spot the Unit signs. Weren't there any signposts in this God-forsaken part of the world? Sludbury where? Had catering arrived? Where was the nearest café? They needed gallons of coffee. Now.

'Is there a McDonald's?'

'Where is this? Siberia?'

'There's no café but I'll see if the pub will lay on some coffee,' said Lyssa, just thankful that they had arrived. A wasted day cost a freakish amount of money.

'Looks good,' said Greg Wilson, striding round the near-deserted halt, kicking litter. He was a short, wiry man with gold-rimmed glasses and unruly grey hair that rarely saw a comb. He used his fingers. The station was still functioning but there were few early trains and only a handful of curious passengers stood about. The crew had the place to themselves and began setting up their equipment at the far end of the platform.

'Like it, Lyssa. Like it. Look at this angle. And the light. I like it. Great. OK, let's get moving.'

Filming was a chaotic business at the best of times and the day's shooting was no exception. Lyssa laid on non-stop sandwiches and coffee at the pub as the catering van never arrived, and the pub owners made a bomb. They told her to come back, any time. Would she like the pub as a location, too?

'I'll remember your offer,' she laughed.

The scene was simple one in which Inspector Dutton's briefcase was expected to fly open and its contents spill over the platform. The briefcase was rigged.

Lyssa hid her amusement when the case refused to fly open. Take after take was fruitless. The gadget man was red with embarrassment, took the object away to fiddle with.

'I'll fling it on the bloody line soon,' said Gareth Warwick irritably, using language which would have ruined Aunt Sarah's good opinion of the character Gareth played.

'Just don't go after it. That line's live,' said Greg. 'Lyssa couldn't get the power turned off.' Easy to blame it on Lyssa. 'It would be inconvenient to have to replace you halfway through the series.'

Lyssa was grateful when the briefcase worked but by then the wind had sharpened and Gareth's scarf kept blowing across his face and across the contents of the case.

'Take that scarf off,' said Greg. 'We can't see the money in the case.'

'No,' said Gareth. 'The scarf is part of Inspector Dutton's image. It is him. I'd feel naked without it.'

Greg groaned and turned to Lyssa. 'Can't you do something about the wind?'

The crew and cast were all getting irritable. The chill factor of the wind was biting and she had been standing around for hours with ice-cold feet, her hands deep in the pockets of her anorak, her hair flying, ears frozen, wishing she could borrow the despised scarf.

Her body was still keening for Jeth. It was ridiculous. She had to get him out of her system. She was going to marry Matthew, the sweetest of young men who would make a perfect husband. She was doing it for Bethany and Matthew would create a happy home, she knew he would. She would be happy in a low-key way, not delirious, but more ordinary and enduring. And she would settle for that.

'Take twenty-eight.' The clapper-board boy dodged down.

The last hour of filming background shots was an agony. Gareth Warwick had gone home in his Porsche, pleading frostbite in sensitive parts. Lyssa was cold and overstretched. Her head ached with exhaustion. How many hours had she put in recently? How many hours a day? Not counting working at night at that little desk with the melting view of the South Downs, her daughter dozing in the next room. All weekend she'd spent planning and costing ahead. She hoped the avid fans of *Inspector Dutton Investigates* would appreciate her hard work.

They wrapped up the last shot of the halt, finally packed equipment into trucks. But when Lyssa came to start her car, she found the battery was flat. In her haste, parking in that dark mottled morning, she had left the side-lights on.

'Sugar,' she swore. She would need her car in the morning. It was London tomorrow for a pre-production meeting. She could walk back to Hollow House, though that meant a lot of inconvenience the following morning. 'Has anyone any jump leads?' she called out hopefully.

No one was listening. 'You gonna do another jump?' someone asked, mishearing.

'No fear,' she fumed, annoyed at herself. 'My car won't start. I need to borrow some jump leads.'

'I'll drive you back,' said Greg. 'Get in. You can collect your car tomorrow.'

'But I need it early. You know there's a meeting.' Lyssa sighed. Greg didn't understand how difficult it was, living as a guest in someone else's house. He knew nothing about measles or children or domestic arrangements. He lived permanently in some small Bayswater hotel. Now she had the car to add to an overladen day. She'd have to phone a local garage and hope they could organise something.

'Thanks,' she said, getting into his battered Ford saloon, knowing its springs were on their last bounce. He was in a good mood after the day's filming.

They talked generalities as he followed her directions to Hollow House. They drove along the wooded drive without comment but Lyssa did not trust Greg. She knew him too well. He was always one jump ahead of her. She did not like the way his attention began to flicker around the looming trees.

'Where is this place, Lyssa?' he asked. 'I thought you said you were staying at a friend's house, somewhere local?'

'I am. This is the drive. It's quite a big house, right off the beaten track and very difficult to find. People are always getting lost.

'Creepy trees,' he commented.

'Definitely haunted.' Lyssa tried a laugh. 'It must be cursed.'

Lyssa wished she had kept her mouth shut and walked, sorry now that she had accepted the lift. Greg was absorbing the dense trees, the secret paths, the hidden hollows, filing them away in his magpie brain.

'Some house,' said Greg on a long breath as Hollow House floated into view. It looked even more old and mysterious in the fading light, the patchwork brick patterns like tapestry, the chimneys' twisted fingers rising to the sky. A bat swooped on cue across the lawn.

'Sixteenth century?' he asked, looking closely at the farmhouse end, seeing his actors on site. 'But you've been looking for sixteenth century, haven't you?'

'No, not this house,' said Lyssa firmly. 'I won't let you. You can't use Hollow House. These people are my friends, my future family.' She could read his mind. 'Please, Greg, they won't want their home televised for a murder case, crew and actors swarming all over it. They don't even watch much TV. The owner wouldn't want his privacy disturbed.'

'It's perfect. Who's the owner? It's only an outside shot; a chase across the front lawn. No one could object to that.' Greg was making mental notes of shots, angles, which aspects of the ancient farmhouse could be used without showing glimpses of the two adjacent cottages. There was a lot he could use. He had a strong gut feeling that their long search was at an end.

'The owner is Jeth Arnold. But don't you dare approach him,' Lyssa said defiantly. 'Please, Greg, Hollow House is off limits. I'm living here for the time being with Bethany and I'm going to marry his son. They are my hosts, my in-laws. What a way to repay their kind hospitality, a crew tramping over their lawns. Just be patient and I'll find somewhere else.'

'Time costs money. You know it's only outside shots,' said Greg, brushing aside her objections. 'We'd replace any damaged turf, the odd tree. But if this is the Jeth Arnold, the industrial tycoon, then he can afford it.'

'That's not the point, Greg. For heaven's sake, this is a private family home. Don't you think of anything except your precious programmes? Things are difficult enough for me here as it is. You'd ruin everything.' Lyssa fought against a surge of anger.

Greg set his mouth into a determined line. 'The

show pays your salary, doesn't it? Have you forgotten that? I presume you like your job and enjoy doing it? And want to go on doing it?'

'Of course I do. Don't threaten me.'

'And you want to keep your position?'

Lyssa flushed. 'Are you trying to blackmail me?'

Greg patted her arm, all paternal. 'Just testing, Lyssa. Sorry if I alarmed you. Don't worry, we won't use Hollow House. The station was perfect. We've had a good day. It's all in the can.'

Lyssa got out of the car, her legs weak with relief. For a moment she had thought that crazy crew was going to descend on Hollow House, creating chaos. She did not ask Greg in for a coffee, but gave him directions for the best way back to the M25 *en route* for London.

Bethany was happily tucking into her tea in the kitchen at the pine-topped kitchen table, wrapped in her dressing gown. She had a kitten hidden on her lap, a small bundle of fluffy tabby fur that was patting a button with velvet paws.

'I've borrowed him from his mummy for a few minutes,' she explained, sensing Lyssa's concern. 'He's going back soon because his mummy has to feed him.'

'That's sensible,' said Lyssa. 'He's too young to be stuffed with scrambled egg and toast and chocolate biscuits.'

'You look cold, dear. Why don't you have a swim?' asked Aunt Sarah, handing her a cup of tea. 'There are spare swimsuits over there for visitors, all clean, and the water is lovely and warm.'

'What a wonderful idea.' The thought of a swim was enticing. To get away from everyone. 'That's just what I need,' said Lyssa gladly. 'A quick swim.'

Bethany sighed with relief as Lyssa hurried across the courtyard to the stable complex. Now she would have the kitten on her lap for an extra ten minutes. Aunt Sarah winked at her. They were already bonding in a way that would last for years.

A wave of heat met Lyssa as she let herself into the stable complex. The outer room was fitted up with exercise equipment, rowing, bars, presses, weights. It looked as if Jeth took his health seriously. She went through the connecting doors and switched on the overhead lights, flooding the pool area. The water was a still, aquamarine sheet of colour, reflecting the silvery lights.

She found the changing rooms and a cupboard with a supply of big towels and spare swimsuits. She chose a plain black one-piece with narrow straps.

It was new, the price tag swinging from a shoulder strap. Macy's, New York. Jeth's visitors had expensive tastes. But of course they would. All his visitors would be well-heeled, smooth, groomed, sleek, not working girls.

The swimsuit fitted perfectly. Lyssa plaited her hair and clipped it up on top with a butterfly clip. She always carried a spare one in her bag.

She dived cleanly into the pool, surfaced and watched the ripples breaking the smooth enamelled surface of the water. It was breathtakingly beautiful. No one had truly captured that essential moment on film yet. She swam the length, a lazy unstressful breast-stroke, bobbing her head under the water every second stroke, the warmth relaxing the stiffness in her neck. The silence travelled with her. Time rolled away.

It took her back to those halcyon days swimming with André in Minorca, in the azure blue of the Mediterranean. Life had held no problems then. They had spent the days walking and swimming, the nights in amazed wonder in each other's arms, their bodies discovering the heights of passion. So young, so trusting, deeply in love, believing that life would be all roses. But the roses had shrivelled and died, and only Bethany bore the bloom of that love.

She still mourned for André in her subconscious, her love for him arrested and distressed. She had a great well of love, unused and waiting, sick and hungry for love. A grief clouded her eyes. That time with André had been so short but so special. But she had made a life for herself and Bethany, knowing that was what André would have wanted.

Her thoughts were taking her back in time and she was unaware of someone joining her in the pool until the water cleaved and arms sliced through it like paddles, cutting cleanly, ploughing the length.

She didn't need to look to know who it was. It could only be one person. Her face went expressionless, her thoughts tucked away in an instant. She couldn't bear the idea of meeting Jeth in the pool; she didn't want him looking at her. She ought to have chosen the wide-strapped school-regulation-style blue swimsuit.

Jeth surfaced beside her, water falling off his face in a shower of glistening drops, brown shoulders close and intimidating, the dark hair on his arms and chest plastered to his skin. He shook his head and grinned down at her.

'Hello, mermaid,' he said amiably. 'I see the suit fits.'

She flung her arms swiftly across the plain black swimsuit that barely covered the soft swell of her breasts. She pulled at the straps as if to cover herself from his gaze as he towered potently over her. A wave of apprehension splintered all her enjoyment of the swim. He had no right to look so pleased with himself.

'Fits?' she hesitated.

'I bought it in the States for you. Took a chance on the size. Told them you were about this size.' He waved his hands over an imaginary figure. His glance was penetrating, burning into her. He blocked her way to the steps. 'A fairly accurate guess. And it looks wonderful.'

'How did you know I would have a swim? I might not be able to swim.'

'But you can. Bethany told me you loved swimming but the council pool was always crowded so you couldn't take her.'

'I can't take Bethany to a public pool,' said Lyssa. Jeth might not understand the implications. She wriggled out of his way and stepped back, dipping down under the water to cool her head. 'She might get knocked.'

'She could swim here without coming to any harm. Do you like the pool?' he asked when she surfaced.

'Worth every million,' she said coolly.

'A hundred thousand.'

'Peanuts, then.'

She couldn't take her eyes off the dusting of dark hair on his broad chest and the vertical line of hair than ran below his navel. He was wearing tailored navy swimming briefs that hugged his lean hips. Her wanton thoughts wondered what it would be like to wrap her legs round that muscled body. She shivered, her supple flesh tingling with desire.

His face clouded over, taking her silence to mean another criticism of his wealth.

'You disapprove of money, don't you? Yet you don't object to marrying into it. Shall I close down the pool? Give the cost to Angola, Bosnia, Sudan? If I gave away every penny I have, it wouldn't make that much difference.'

'I know you can't right the world's wrongs,' she said, wondering how on earth they had got on to the subject when her heart was pounding like a hammer. She was fighting a fierce desire to touch him, to slide her wet skin against his. 'None of us can as individuals, and governments are just as helpless . . .'

'Then why that disdainful look again? Look at me, Lyssa, let's see those beautiful green eyes. Tell me what you're thinking.'

Something in his tone made her look up in dismay. His voice was arresting, powerful, compassionate. This was different. He was showing an interest in her as a woman, not as his son's fiancée. Perhaps it was another test, but this time she was warned.

'I'm thinking that it's time I got dressed and

went back to my daughter. Matthew will be phoning soon and I want to be there for his call. We've a lot to talk about. Arrangements and everything.'

She was furious with Jeth for affecting her, for being so attractive, so desirable. It chipped through her veneer of coolness and sophistication, that barrier which had served her so well over the lonely years.

'Don't play games, Lyssa,' he said curtly. 'That's not what I mean. I want to know what you're really thinking. What you feel in there . . .'

He briefly touched the region of her heart. It was like a searing of fire through the thin stuff of the black swimsuit. Her eyes widened in shocked disbelief that he had dared to touch her again.

'You're impossible,' she glared. 'Why can't you leave me alone? I don't want anything to do with you. OK, you're Matthew's father and I can't completely ignore you, but that doesn't mean that I have to see you any more than necessary. It would be more sensible if we kept a distance.'

'Is that how you want it?' he growled.

'Yes, it is,' she said.

'Then that's what you'll get.' His voice was laced with scorn and disapproval. Rain smeared the windows and daylight drained from the pool. It was as if someone had turned off the sun.

He turned away abruptly and plunged under the water, not surfacing till he reached the other end of the pool. By then, Lyssa was scrambling up the shallow steps and wrapping her starved body in a towel. It wasn't what she wanted at all. But she knew she couldn't have what she wanted and never would.

CHAPTER 6

Lyssa was awoken by an appalling noise. It sounded as if some part of the nearest farm cottage was being demolished, as if the grounds were being invaded by a horde of workmen, busy with hammers and chisels.

She staggered to her window, wrapping her robe round her shoulders as she drew apart the curtains. It was still gloomy but she could see dark shapes moving about. At the same moment the security lights flashed on outside and the scene in front of her was all too familiar.

They were building a camera ramp and track at the point where the drive widened out into the sweeping courtyard in front of Hollow House. There were trucks and vans, a jeep and a dozen cars parked askew, strewn all over the place as if part of the aftermath of a motorway pile-up.

Her heart shrank and sank. It was the film crew. They were preparing to shoot Hollow House for the dawn scene. She peered out, recognising the bulky figure of Greg Wilson in a padded combat jacket and baseball cap. She would kill him.

She pulled on some jeans and a jersey, pushed her feet into sneakers and hurried downstairs as quietly as she could. Though she couldn't believe that the rest of the household would not be wide awake by now. The noise was deafening.

The cold air of the coming dawn hit her face like a slap with a wet flannel as she let herself out of the front door. She had remembered to de-activate the alarm system before opening the door. She hurried over to Greg Wilson, who was directing operations in what he thought was a tactful whisper.

'What the hell do you think you're doing out here?' she hissed as loudly as she dare. 'I told you not to come to Hollow House. Get out quickly . . . and quietly.'

'Put that over here, chaps. Ah . . . Lyssa, you're awake,' said Greg quite unnecessarily.

'And are you surprised, with this racket going on? This is unforgivable, Greg. You've no right to be here. I told you yesterday that Hollow House is not available. Jeth Arnold is my host and I'm enjoying his hospitality. And he'll be down any minute now, throwing you out and probably me as well.'

Her voice shook with anger and her body with

the cold but she knew that her rage was nothing compared to Jeth's when the noise reached him at the other end of the house. 'You'd better pack up and get out while you've still got a chance,' she snapped, her eyes blazing.

'For heaven's sake, Lyssa, we just need a few dawn shots,' said Greg unperturbed. 'They won't take long once we're set up. Those roof slopes and twisted chimneys are fascinating . . . just the angles I want. A bat's eye view. The shadows even look like an intruder. We'll be gone before Mr Money-Bags is up for his early morning swim.'

'Don't you bet on it,' said Lyssa darkly, aware of lights flicking on in the house behind her, upstairs first, then downstairs. 'He's probably calling the police right now. I'd better go in and reassure Aunt Sarah and my daughter. Have you any idea of the trouble you're causing?'

Aunt Sarah was wandering about in a burgundy-coloured velvet housecoat and fluffy slippers. She looked bewildered and half-asleep, her hair like a nest.

'What on earth's going on?' she asked as Lyssa came in. 'I saw you outside, talking, so I thought you must know all these people.'

'Don't worry, Aunt Sarah. I'm doing my best to get rid of them. They've no right to be here.'

There were fast footsteps coming down the main

staircase, two at a time, and Jeth burst on to the scene, face distorted, a black tracksuit obviously thrown on, heavy torch weighted in his hand. He shot a fierce, disgusted look at Lyssa, then pointed an accusing finger at her.

'Am I seeing what I think I'm seeing? A television crew? Get those so-called friends of yours out of here, at once, Lyssa, or I'll call the police,' he said dangerously. 'So this is how you repay my hospitality. I should have known you'd be up to something. You're just out for all you can milk from the Arnold family. Never mind loyalty or consideration.'

Lyssa took a grip on herself. She refused to be frightened by him, though she knew there was little chance of him believing her. At least she would try.

'I've told Greg to pack up and go. I did *not* arrange this, Jeth. I didn't invite them down here. It's nothing to do with me. They had no permission to use Hollow House, I know that. It was Greg's own idea,' she said coldly. 'He arrived without my knowledge. I am as surprised and horrified as you.'

'Am I supposed to believe that?' he cut in with equal frost. 'You must think I'm stupid. I saw you come back with your boss yesterday. I suppose you thought I was still away but I came home early.

Perhaps you planned to get your filming done while I was out of the country.'

'No, it wasn't like that at all. True, Greg brought me home from filming the station yesterday. My car wouldn't start; the battery was flat. Go and look. It's still there; it's been by the green all night. I was going to phone a garage when they opened this morning. I've nothing to do with this invasion. Aunt Sarah, tell him. You know I couldn't do this.'

Sarah looked dismayed. 'Well, I . . . er . . . we know how devoted you are to your work.'

Lyssa groaned. How was she ever going to convince Jeth? Her desperate defiance was having no effect. 'I knew nothing about it, believe me. I was just as surprised and furious when I heard all that noise and I'm trying my best to get rid of them.'

'You . . . furious? Furious that your little plan has gone astray, you mean,' he glowered. 'That's the more likely story.'

'It wasn't a plan. Why don't you listen to me? You think you know everything but you don't. You don't really know anything about me.' Lyssa was losing her patience.

'True. I don't know anything about you, who you are or what you get up to. I'll sue your company for trespass,' he shouted, his dark brows knitted with fury.

They stood glaring at each other, both breathing heavily. Jeth turned on his heel and stalked out of the door. Lyssa could not bear to listen to the confrontation on the front lawn. She did not want to hear what he said to Greg Wilson, for she knew the older man could be just as stubborn and awkward.

'I'm so sorry,' said Lyssa, turning helplessly to Aunt Sarah. 'I didn't mean this to happen, truly.'

'I'm sure you didn't, my dear. But you should have asked Jeth first. It would have been polite.'

Even Aunt Sarah didn't completely understand. Lyssa took a long breath, wishing she had thought ahead. If only she had walked home. That had been her big mistake.

'I didn't ask Jeth because I had no intention of allowing them to film Hollow House,' said Lyssa wearily. 'It was Greg's idea. That racket woke me up, too. If it had been my idea I would have been out there with them now, timing arrivals, organising parking etc. Anyone with any sense could see I had nothing to do with that chaos. I'd better go and see Bethany.'

'Since we're all up, I might as well make a cup of tea,' said Aunt Sarah, taking comfort in the old calming ritual. 'I'm sure we could do with one.'

Bethany was up at her bedroom window, kneeling on a chair, hair bobbing wildly.

'Are they filming here?' she asked excitedly. 'Can I go down? Can I be an extra? Please, please, Mummy. And Pudding too. He'd like to be in it.'

'No, you can't,' said Lyssa, more sharply than she had intended. 'It's all a mistake. Greg is packing up the crew fast and they're going. There isn't going to be any filming.'

'No, he isn't. Look, Jeth and Greg are talking.'

Lyssa pulled her daughter close, knelt beside her and peered out of the window. It was true. The two men were deep in conversation. It didn't look like a fight. In fact, Greg was waving his arms about and pointing roofwards. Her pulse started to descend. There was no fight going on; no blood to mop up. What had happened? Had Greg offered Jeth a lot of money? Some amount even he could not resist.

'Back to bed, scamp. It's too early to get up. I'll get you a hot drink and then you must sleep a bit more.'

'I don't want to sleep,' Bethany protested.

'Look at a book, then, or do some crayoning.'

'Crayons. I'm doing a picture for Aunt Sarah.'

Lyssa hesitated outside the kitchen, wondering about her reception. Would she be ordered to leave? Pack her bags and go back to where she belonged?

Aunt Sarah had returned to bed with a tray of tea. But the pot was on the counter, covered in one of Aunt Sarah's many knitted cosies. Lyssa heated some milk for Bethany in the microwave, poured herself a cup of tea. Perhaps if she went on her knees, apologised again, pleaded, Jeth would let them stay a few more days. Bethany wasn't well enough to go back to school yet. She was still coughing but the rash was fading.

Suddenly she realised she had not missed Matthew once in the last two days. She sank on to a stool at the counter and cradled her head in her arms. Everything was going terribly wrong. A draught touched her shoulders. She did not know it was the door opening and Jeth standing in the doorway, looking at her, taking in the slender shoulders couched with despair.

He stared at her fall of burnished hair, wishing he had met her in another time, another place, long before Matthew. She was all he had ever wanted and she was going to marry his son. And he was acting badly, he knew that. He couldn't help it. The anguish was like a knife in his guts. It made him angry, mad at himself, knowing he was almost out of control. And he had never acted like this before. It was unnerving.

Lyssa raised her head. 'Have they gone?'

'Nearly.'

'What does that mean? I saw you talking together, all chummy. Has Greg offered you a cheque with an irresistible row of noughts?'

Jeth's face stiffened. 'I don't know what you mean.'

'Money, my friend. You do everything for money, don't you? They can take pictures of your house if they pay for it. Isn't that right? I don't hear them moving out.'

He slammed a mug on the counter, poured himself some tea and drank it without milk, spilling half of it. She could make him so angry.

'It's none of your damned business, madam, but Greg explained that many of the crew are paid on a day basis. If they don't get the shots, they lose their pay. So I said they could take some of the roof and chimneys, parts of the lawn – nothing else – and then get out, fast. I've given them till eight o'clock. Then anyone or anything that is left on my premises will be confiscated and or prosecuted.'

Jeth didn't elaborate on what else Greg had said would happen to the crew or, in particular, to their pretty locations manager for blocking necessary shots.

'I suppose you negotiated a fee?'

'Yes, I did.' He wasn't going to lie about that.

'What will you buy with it? A new car for Aunt Sarah?'

'She's not safe in anything mechanical. Have you seen Sarah driving? She meanders at ten miles an hour like a drunken caterpillar. I don't think she has ever found second gear.'

He laughed and all the anger melted as if the sun had lanced it. He came swiftly round the counter and pulled Lyssa into his arms.

'Don't let's fight,' he whispered into her soft hair. The cold dawn scented every glowing strand. 'This is hard enough as it is. I'm not going to be able to cope if you stay on here.'

'I don't know what you mean,' said Lyssa, lost in his closeness, distressed by her desire for him, wanting him out of her life, yet in it forever. 'Leave me alone. Let me go . . .'

'Is that what you really want?' he said, shaking her.

No, it wasn't what she wanted. She wanted Jeth to carry her upstairs and make love to her all day and all night, for neither of them to go to work, to forget the world, to forget Matthew. But that was impossible, a pipe-dream, a fantasy.

'I'm marrying your son,' she whispered, forcing out the words, her throat constricted. 'Matthew.'

'I think of you every minute of the day,' he groaned. 'Sometimes I think I'm going out of my mind.'

'I can't hurt him. I love him . . .' Her voice trailed off.

'What kind of love are we talking about?' he said, his mouth moving over her skin. His face was only an inch away. She closed her eyes, waiting for something to happen. It was a dangerous trap. His arms were a haven and she was drowning in her need to be close to him, savouring the sweet joy of his words. She could no longer fight him, driven by responses that could not be denied.

The colour went from the day. It changed with the acknowledgement of her need, of her desire. Dawn was stencilling the sky, drawing lines on the shadows, the curtain of darkness lifting from her heart. She knew she loved him.

The knowledge stabbed her with its ferocity. She gasped and drew back from him, seeking to imprint his strong face on her mind in case she never saw him again. The emotion was more intoxicating than wine. A grief descended on her as if day had changed its mind and night was coming all too soon.

'Why aren't you old and bald?' she whispered.

'I could try,' he said, tugging at a few hairs.

She traced the lines on his face, the surprise furrows on his forehead, the deepening grooves from nose to mouth.

'Plenty of lines,' he said. 'The marks of Cain.'

'You work too hard,' she murmured.

'Who else is there to run the company?'

'Don't do this, Jeth. Let me go . . .'

Lyssa pushed Jeth away with a force she did not feel. 'I'm taking Bethany some hot milk.' It had cooled but it was hot enough. Lyssa felt as if she was dying as she walked away from Jeth. She was walking away from life itself, denying herself happiness. Why was she doing it? She only had one life. This was no rehearsal.

'Do you know what you're doing?' he said, his eyes burning like a brand.

'No, I don't . . . and I don't understand anything,' she breathed. 'But I'm doing it just the same. Because it's right. Because we have to. And you know that, too.'

She did not go in to work that day. She phoned in and said she was sick. In part, that was true. She did feel sick, sick at heart. It was emotional not physical. She heard Jeth's Mercedes roar away down the misty drive sometime before eight. Jeth had not spoken to her again. The film crew were packing up and leaving. She was too angry to say goodbye to Greg.

'I'll see you tomorrow,' she said curtly at the door. It was a pity it was too heavy to slam. Greg grinned. 'I've got to get my car back.'

'Well done, Lyssa. Great location. Wonderful girl.'

'Get lost.'

She spent the day repairing fences by talking to Aunt Sarah, playing with Bethany, planning her work for the following week. It was not easy. She had to force herself to sit and work. There was a lump of ice wedged inside her and it hurt.

A local garage said they would fetch her car and give it a long-overdue service.

'I'd be very grateful,' she said.

She wrapped up warmly and went outside to tidy the driveway, raking over the gravel to remove all the churned up wheel marks. The holes in the lawn from the ramp were more difficult to cover over but she stamped down the turf as best she could. Bill and Ben romped around, looking on with interest. They were used to her now, especially as she often threw sticks and balls for them to retrieve.

'And where were you this morning, guarding us from intruders?' she accused them. They looked sheepish and wagged their tails.

She kept remembering Jeth's saturnine face and the force of his anger. And then suddenly that amazing tenderness as he touched her in the kitchen, all the fury gone . . . a revelation. As if some primitive message had reached his stony heart. And she couldn't believe that. He was too much of this earth, of this world. A man among men. Foolish, call her foolish, but she had fallen over the edge of loving him.

Love at first sight. People did not believe it could happen but it could. Jeth had an extraordinary pull of personality and character. But it wasn't only a magnetism; there was something else. A feeling that she had already known him for a very long time, that he had been a bright star waiting all the time to come into her life.

She remembered when she had first seen him, so tall and dark . . . that moment was engraved on her mind for ever. Her whole body had recognised the possibility of loving him.

She would have to leave Hollow House. As soon as Bethany was better, they would go home. Lyssa could not risk being alone again with Jeth.

Bethany was well enough to get up and dressed now. The gardener brought the kitten from the farm and she spent the day playing endless games with balls of silver-foil and pieces of string and wool or carrying it around fast asleep in her arms, wrapped up like a baby.

'Can't I take him home?' she pleaded, putting on a plaintive face. 'Mummy . . . please?'

'You know we can't. A flat is no place for a cat. They grow up, very quickly, and then they want to go out and climb trees and chase things.'

'Couldn't we have an indoor tree, put up our

Christmas tree again and keep Tipsy in a box at night?' She'd heard Aunt Sarah say she was going to make a tipsy pudding.

Lyssa clasped her head with her hands. 'Children,' she moaned. 'They always let you down. I suppose you think a plastic green Christmas tree is absolutely the pits.'

'Credit me with more sense,' said Aunt Sarah. 'I can remember Christmases when we couldn't afford any tree at all.'

Lyssa stopped in the middle of making a Victoria sandwich. She liked making cakes but never had the time at home. It gave her pleasure to know that she could still cook when she wanted to. She knew that Bethany would enjoy licking out the sticky bowl with a finger.

'Couldn't afford . . . haven't you always lived here at Hollow House? I thought this was your family home, for years and years. You could have dug up a tree from the wood.'

'Oh, yes, but we haven't always been able to live here. There was a time when I was a small girl, before Jeth was born, that we had to leave Hollow House. My father, David Arnold, was in financial trouble and we moved to north London and lived in an ordinary suburban house. Hollow House was leased to another company and used as a head office. They turned the place upside-down and ruined it. Then they went bankrupt. Jeth worked night and day to get Hollow House back to its former giory and put the firm on a sound basis.'

'Offices? How awful.'

'It was dreadful. They made a real mess of the place. You wouldn't have believed what they did. It took Jeth years to get everything straight again. You should have seen this kitchen. Years of smoke and grease ingrained in the beams.'

Lyssa listened to Sarah describing the state of Hollow House and everything that Jeth had done before they could return, working to get the family firm back on its feet. All the improvements and modernisation as well as having the old buildings preserved. She was seeing the man in a new light. The small boy from north London, dreaming of a return to the family home in Sussex. And somehow being strong enough to make it come true.

No wonder he was protective of Hollow House and the family . . . so what had changed his mind that morning? Money? Surely not? Surely he had enough for everything.

She kept out of his way that evening, not risking a swim, sitting in the room with Aunt Sarah until she was sure he was locked into a stack of work in his study. Lyssa had got into a routine at Hollow House and enjoyed the quiet evenings with no housework or cooking and only some hand washing or ironing to do.

'I like to see things nicely ironed,' said Aunt Sarah approvingly as Lyssa smoothed out some panda-patterned pyjamas. 'I can't stand this modern habit of crumpled undies.'

Lyssa hid a smile, knowing how many of her clothes were drip-dry or crease-resistant and had never seen the flat side of an iron. She had to buy time.

She was lunching with Matthew between script meetings the following day. It was over a week since she had last seen him, and, although they had spoken on the telephone, she felt she was drifting in some sort of open boat and was afraid of losing touch. She did not want to hurt him but there was no chance of seeing him in the evenings now that she was living in Sussex.

He looked fresh-faced and eager as he came forward to meet her outside the exclusive restaurant. Lyssa was glad she was wearing her apricot suit again and a pale silk shirt. Her strawberry-blonde hair was plaited high on her head and fastened with a pearl clip that matched her earrings. She had taken a lot of trouble with her appearance, as if somehow to make amends for her neglect of him.

'Darling,' he said, bending to kiss her cheek

under the canopy. 'It's lovely to see you again and you look marvellous.'

'I'm being spoilt at Hollow House. It's your Aunt Sarah. She does so much for me – I reckon I'm putting on weight.'

'In all the right places, I see,' he teased.

'I'll lose it as soon as we get home and I have to do everything again.'

He took her arm and led her into the theatrical restaurant. They went down the white marble steps like film stars.

'I hope you'll like this place. It's very different, the in place to be seen. And I want to know everything you've been doing. I'm very jealous of my father,' he joked. 'He's had more of your company than I've had recently.'

Lyssa hoped her face would not betray her feelings. Matthew must never find out just how they had spent that time together. She lowered her eyes because they would give her guilt away, and she could not hurt him.

'Your father has been . . . considerate,' she murmured.

Considerate. Those kisses. She felt weak at the thought of them and her wanton response and was glad that a waiter was showing them to a table, moving a chair for her to sit down.

It was a large showy restaurant, on two levels, all

chrome and silvery glitz but with an undercurrent of superb efficiency. Dozens of waiters in black waistcoats weaved through the tables, trays held high, laden with delicious-looking food. A long promenade bar ran along one side of the room on a higher level where quick luncheon snacks were served.

Lyssa chose some cucumber and radish soup, which sounded unusual, followed by plain grilled sole. She desperately wanted Matthew to convince her that they were doing the right thing and that their marriage was going to work out.

She waited until the waiter had poured out a glass of chilled hock and left them alone. Matthew was delighted to see her again, as if they had never been apart.

'Is everything all right?' he asked, spreading a roll thickly with butter. 'You seem a bit quiet. Is my father being a pain in the neck? I know he can be an awkward cuss.'

'No . . . really, he's being quite pleasant. Of course he's not used to having a child around the house, but he's very good with Bethany. I'm the one who gets on his nerves.'

'I don't believe it. He likes you, I'm sure. How could anyone not like you?' His eyes were full of the warmth of love and Lyssa flinched from their honesty.

'He doesn't like my work.' What an understatement.

'So what? You don't have to take it back to Hollow House with you, do you?' Matthew was in a good mood.

He obviously hadn't heard about the film crew invasion, and was Lyssa was thankful for that. At least she didn't have to explain to him; she was tired of explaining.

'I think we'll be moving back to London at the weekend. Bethany is much better now. She'll soon be back at school.'

'That's great news. Then everything can return to normal. I want you back. I've missed you, darling.'

Lyssa summoned a smile but it was not her usual big smile. It didn't reach her eyes. Back to normal. How could that ever be now? She couldn't even think what normal was. How was she ever going to get Jeth out of her system and remember she was marrying Matthew?

'Wouldn't it be nice to live abroad?' she said out of the blue. 'The States or Australia. We could be free, our own people, out of the shadow of your father and Arnold Consolidated Industries. I'd like to start afresh.'

'My dear girl, we couldn't do that,' he said decisively. 'We both have good jobs here and good prospects. Unless, of course, my father offered me an overseas post. There are subsidiaries. We couldn't just uproot ourselves and start afresh without Consolidated behind us.'

'Why not?' Lyssa asked, searching his face for reassurance that being together was more important than his job.

'Because I like working for my father. It's what I want to do. What I've always planned to do. He needs me. I'm being groomed.' He tried to laugh that one off.

And Matthew liked being the heir to the company. It was not surprising. He had been brought up to expect to inherit, in training for the day when he would take over.

'It was just a wild thought,' said Lyssa, chasing a shred of radish with concentration. 'Forget it.'

'Let's talk about us. Do you want to go and see a show soon? I'll get some tickets. Would Maggie babysit or have Bethany for the night?'

Lyssa nodded. 'I'd like that. A musical. Nothing too heavy. Matthew . . . about us. Do you still feel the same about our marriage? There's no need to rush things.'

He took her hand and squeezed it. 'Of course I do, darling. I can't wait for the great day, our wedding. It's going to be marvellous. Are all the arrangements in hand?'

What arrangements? Lyssa thought with despair. So far she had not done anything, only gone along with whatever Aunt Sarah hinted.

'Aunt Sarah is having a great time making suggestions,' said Lyssa, which she knew was no answer but it was the best she could do without lying. 'This is lovely soup,' she added.

She had only half a mind on her work that afternoon. They needed a small, unusual-looking general store which wouldn't mind being downgraded with a lot of local produce. The lunch had not clarified anything about her marriage, only confirmed that she was important to Matthew. He was like a small boy who had been promised the greatest treat in the world.

Jeth was home early that evening, and he followed her car slowly along the drive. She kept looking into her mirror, watching the silver Mercedes close on her tail. He parked beside her and switched off the powerful engine.

'Aren't you even going to pretend to be grateful?' he said darkly, catching her arm as she locked her car door. He was daring her to deny his charitable action in letting Greg stay. But she refused to allow him that luxury.

'Have you banked the cheque yet?' she asked drily.

'Yes, I have,' he said, taken aback. 'How did you know? Who told you?'

'It didn't take a genius to work that one out. You'd do anything for money.' She went indoors and through to the kitchen, tried to resume her visitor's manners. Aunt Sarah was not around. She filled the electric jug kettle. 'I'm just making a pot of tea. Would you like a cup?'

He shook his head, losening his dark tie. 'You've got pretty hands. I noticed them before.'

It was so casual, throw-away. Her heart-rate shot up and all sense went out of the window. How could he say things like that? She was his son's fiancée. It wasn't right.

'Two weeks at Hollow House have eliminated my dishwasher's wrinkles. I have Emily to thank for that.'

'Do you have to go back to your flat?'

'Of course. Bethany is much better now and it's an imposition to expect Aunt Sarah to look after her any longer.'

'What about half-term?' He shot a quick look at her under his dark brows, leaning against a counter, relaxed. 'What are you going to do then?'

'Take Bethany with me,' said Lyssa firmly. 'That's what I usually do. She likes coming out with me in the car. It's fun.'

'More fun here with Bill and Ben and her kitten.'

'No, thank you,' repeated Lyssa simply. 'She's

staying at home. We are going to be together again. We don't need you, Mr Arnold.'

He took his mug of coffee and made to leave the kitchen. 'Perhaps we need you,' he said as he went through the doorway.

CHAPTER 7

Bethany shrieked with delight and splashed her mother in the face. She was having her first swimming lesson in the pool but there was more larking around than serious instruction. Lyssa wanted Bethany to gain confidence in the water and to have fun before learning to float and paddle.

They were going home at the weekend so there were only a few days left to use the pool. Lyssa reckoned they could fit in three lessons before they left. She took care to pick times when Jeth was not around. He had flown to Amsterdam that morning, so she felt sure he would not be home till late. Two flights in one day, though Jeth would call it commuting.

'Now, let's be serious for a moment,' said Lyssa, shaking the water out of her eyes and pushing back strands of wet blonde hair. 'I bought some arm-bands today. We'll blow them up and you can try them on for size.'

She could not stop herself glancing towards the entrance, always wondering if Jeth might come in, knowing there would be no understanding and welcoming smile for her. He had made it perfectly clear what he thought of her. She was an unsuitable match for his son and he was going to sabotage the marriage.

But she could not deny Jeth's magnetism. He made Matthew look young and insignificant by comparison.

'Mummy, is Jeth coming? I want him to see me swimming,' Bethany cried, slapping her small hands over the water, making noisy waves.

'So you can swim already, can you? That didn't take long. The Junior Olympics next, is it?' Lyssa grinned.

Lyssa knew when Jeth arrived without turning round. She was towing Bethany up and down the pool, aware suddenly of his presence. She had misjudged the time of his homecoming; he was early. For a second she faltered and her head dipped below the water, seeing rivers of blue. She did not want to see him. She did not want to speak to him, to have to fight him on any level.

'Time to come out,' she said as they reached the shallow end. 'Mr Arnold will want his luxurious pool to himself.'

'Did I say that?' he called out, resonant and

ringing, before diving into the deep end and swimming under water the whole length. She felt a painful surge of happiness as the strong, lean body arrowed towards her with powerful strokes. She could just see the outline of his shape, like a big gleaming machine.

He surfaced beside Bethany, lifting the little girl into the air. She clutched his hair, wriggling and squealing like an otter.

'I can swim, Jeth. Look, I can swim,' she told him excitedly. 'Watch me!'

'That's my girl,' he said with approval.

'She's my girl, not yours,' said Lyssa, suddenly possessive. 'Come on, Bethany. Time for bed.'

Jeth lowered Bethany into Lyssa's waiting arms. For a moment they were very close in the water, all three of them, skin against skin, bare and wet, like a primitive family standing in some rushing, jungle-clad river. Father, mother, child. Steam heat rose from the water. Without the sophistication of clothes, Jeth was all backwoods muscle. He was tanned and fit with this dusting of dark hair; broad shoulders that could heave wood and stone, height that could command, steely eyes that would scheme and plan and fight to save her from all marauders.

'I hear you're leaving soon,' he said suddenly, letting Bethany go.

'Yes, at the weekend. You'll be glad to see us go. We've taken advantage of your hospitality for long enough.'

He made no comment but ran his hand through his cropped hair. 'I want to talk to you,' he ordered. 'It's important. Find me when you've put Bethany to bed.' He turned and dived under the water, to surface into a fast, angry crawl that took him to the other end in less than half a minute.

It was an order, not a request. Lyssa was incensed but said nothing to provoke him. She had had enough of fights with Jeth Arnold.

Bethany was happy to go to bed. She had seen Jeth now and that had made her day. Lyssa knew how her daughter felt about him. It was something they shared.

Lyssa looked at herself in the mirror. There was an intenseness about her face, making her eyes huge, that revealed the strain of living at Hollow House. It was not easy, seeing Jeth every day, knowing how she felt. She did not know now if she would or could marry Matthew. How could she, when every thought, of every day, was dominated by his father?

She stood in the shower for ages, as if stranded in time, putting off the moment when she would have to see Jeth. Then she dressed casually in crimson tailored trousers and a loose navy crocheted top. Shoes? No shoes. Her bare toes had matching red nails. She made up her face in an understated way, as if preparing for her execution. It was as if she was going to her doom.

She moved her hand down the banisters, wondering if a small boy had ever slid down them on visits to the family home, thinking of how he had worked and fought to get Hollow House back and make it into a family home again. Had he brought a woman upstairs to his room at the other end of the house? Had he loved her, cleaved his body to hers? Where had he lived with Matthew's mother? Who was she and where was she now? No one ever seemed to mention her. Had she ever existed?

The tormented thoughts rushed round her mind as she forced herself in slow motion herself towards his study. He was waiting for her, scalpel in hand.

Summoned to the headmaster's study. She almost knocked.

'Jeth?' she called instead, steadying herself.

'Come in.'

He was working at his desk, changed now into a black polo jersey, casual dark trousers, his hair still wet. She had not seen this room before. It was lined with books: company law, trade regulations, Hansard, encyclopaedias, and a smattering of modern hardback thrillers. His desk was piled with files and newspapers. A briefcase lay open and spilling more paper.

'Sit down,' he said abruptly.

'I'm glad I don't work with paper,' she said, pulling up a leather-backed swivel chair. 'I like working with something more tangible and real, like buildings and places and people.'

It sounded impertinent the way she said it, but it was not what she meant. He didn't take offence.

'All this paperwork *represents* money and people and buildings, though I don't actually do the manual work myself.

'That I understand. I don't make the films.'

'Let me just finish this fax, then I'll be with you.'

'You asked me here. I could go.'

'No. Stay.'

Another command. A log fire flickered in the hearth throwing shadows across the room. A tray with coffee in a flask and a covered plate of sandwiches were on a low table. Hadn't he eaten yet? He would die young at this rate. A stab of pain hit her ribs. She did not want him to die. He was precious to her, even if he was not hers. She looked at the dark, grey-flecked head bent so studiously over his work. If he touched her heart, there was nothing she would not do for him. Her lost happiness was so acute, she could hardly stand another moment being in the same room.

'Sorry, Lyssa. These figures had to be finished.'

He got up and fed the papers through the fax machine. Was he apologising to her? It was unbelievable. Yet from his expression he was going to bawl her out again.

'Shall I pour you some coffee?' she offered politely.

He gave a short, mirthless laugh. 'Coffee? I suppose so. Let's at least be civilised.'

Lyssa poured out some coffee, pushed it in his direction. She felt disapproval flowing from him. Yet every part of him was pulling her towards him, mentally and physically, as if he did not care that she was less than worthy to be his son's bride. Hunger hung in the air.

Her body was reacting to his nearness. Her breasts were firming and glowing, demanding that he touch them, that he bring them to a voluptuous peak. The arousal crept down her body, firing her thighs, melting her with need, knowing she wanted him more than she had ever wanted any man.

She leaned back in the chair and swivelled it round to face the fire, feeling the warmth on her face, wondering what he was going to say.

He took the deep armchair opposite her and

drank some coffee slowly, as if trying to find the most wounding words. His silence was more ominous than anything he might say.

'I cannot believe you were so stupid,' he began in a low voice, his eyes flashing chips of granite in her direction. 'Call yourself a mother? A real mother? Risking life and limb for the sake of a few thousand pounds? Tell me what the hell do you think you were doing, jumping out of an aeroplane at two thousand feet? You could have been killed.'

So that was it. He'd found out about the parachute jump. A minute breeze of excitement prickled her shoulders as her mind remembered the ecstasy of floating. She could not even raise a murmur of protest. Somehow she managed a hoarse response.

'You've been snooping around my private life,' she accused, not looking at him. 'How dare you . . .?'

The coolness of his tone filled her with a hopeless kind of guilt. He was right, she had risked her life, but at the time it had seemed like a good idea.

'Isn't that what you do all the time? Snoop around for locations, snoop around other people's houses to film?'

Lyssa felt colour rise in her cheeks. 'That's my job,' she said acidly. 'It's a form of field research.

Scheduling the use of my locations is an art form all of its own.'

'And is parachute jumping an art form?' he bawled at her. He had a rare talent for getting under her skin. 'Supposing you'd been killed or badly injured?'

'Well, I wasn't.' She clenched in her stomach. 'How did you find out? What business is it of yours anyway?'

'Everything about you and Bethany is now my business.'

'No, it isn't. I look after Bethany and I look after myself pretty well, too. We don't need you.'

'RAS,' he said, and the acronym took her totally by surprise. 'I made it my business to find out more about reflex anoxic seizure after seeing Bethany that other evening. I was appalled to see her so ill and so helpless and wanted to do something useful. It was a shock and I had to know more. Now I know about her illness and a lot more about you.'

'RAS is a good cause,' she said, swallowing. 'Don't you dare degrade it.'

'I should like to remind you that you were quick enough to jump down my throat when I accepted payment from Greg Wilson for filming Hollow House.' It was on the tip of his tongue to repeat Greg's veiled threats. 'Yes, he paid me and I took the money. But the cheque was made out to RAS research as a donation. When I contacted the national group that funds the research, saying that the donation was to be in Bethany's name, they told me about your jump and the sponsorship. Though I can understand your motivation, I can't believe that you were so foolish.'

Jeth's eyes were riveted on her. His command of the situation was draining her resistance.

'Thank you for the donation. It will be put to good use. But *I* couldn't just write a cheque. I did it my way and raised a lot of money,' said Lyssa in a thin, taut voice. It was starting to rain again. This was becoming a very wet October. She could hear the pattering on the windows like little feet wanting to be let in.

'Supposing you'd been hurt, killed even? What help would that have been to your daughter then?'

A flood of indignation swept over Lyssa. 'I had no option. I don't have stacks of money at my disposal, nor do I have an excess of spare time to run coffee mornings and garden fêtes. Sponsorship is a very quick way of collecting money. I did some practice jumps beforehand in the jump shed, had lessons from an instructor. I knew what I was doing.'

She saw him flinch. Jeth was seeing her on the ground, crushed and crippled from the fall. He was shaken by his own horror of her being injured. She was as fragile as wind-blown blossom, like a dusting of wild flowers.

'Everyone was very generous,' Lyssa went on. 'That research is needed now, this year, if Bethany is to benefit. Ten, twenty years ahead might be too late for her.'

'Your concern is admirable but to jump out of a plane, thousands of feet high . . .' He ran a hand over his face as if trying to blot out the thought of her flying through the air, only a silken canopy between life and death. His expression changed minutely, his eyes smouldering.

'It was frightening,' Lyssa admitted, remembering that terrifying moment before she actually jumped from the plane. 'But once the canopy had opened and I was floating, it was a wonderful, glorious feeling, like flying.'

He leaned forward and pushed her arms back in a punishing grip. 'Promise me you'll never do it again,' he said, forcing her to sit still.

His voice was passionate with concern. Again Lyssa had this ridiculous feeling of attachment, of belonging to this big man. She drew in a long breath, as if life had slowed down. His eyes were burning with an intensity that flowed into her with strength and purpose. Their minds fused into a warmth and closeness that took her by surprise.

Lyssa had a sudden clarity of thought. Surely . . . Surely Jeth didn't feel the same way? No, she was being ridiculous . . . he was only thinking of his son's welfare, of Bethany.

'I can't promise anything,' she faltered, with unconscious bitterness. 'And you can't make me.'

'Can't I?'

She began to shake her head but he cupped her chin, stopping the movement. She stamped on a fierce desire to be touched by him. The firelight flickered on his dark hair, finding the few glinting strands of grey, painting them with silver. Without thinking, her hands ran over his head, her fingers relishing the softness of the shorn hair. It was like velvet. She wanted that softness against her breasts, to feel that velvet on her naked skin. Her mouth opened softly.

The moan she heard came from nowhere. There was no way of telling if it was from Jeth or herself. The rain was a chorus in the background, relentless and persistent, drowning the clamouring of her heart.

He framed the shape her face, fuelling the fire within her. She wanted to cry out: this isn't fair. But part of her begged him to go on, to kiss her, to touch her, to do whatever he wanted. His fingers were skimming the translucence of her pale skin, tracing the curve of her rosy lips.

Just when she thought she could not stand a moment more, he moved closer and his mouth descended on hers, pulling her off the chair and on to the rug in front of the fire. He covered her body with his and he was big and heavy. She gasped for breath and he took his weight on his arms, never leaving her mouth, the thoroughness of his kiss so sweet and heady that Lyssa had no thought for anyone but Jeth.

He cradled her shoulder in the hollow of his arm, threading his fingers through her hair, grappling for some sanity that was leaving him rapidly. Jeth longed to take her closer, to slip silkily between her legs, but he knew he must not. The stakes were too high. His fingers invaded the softness of her breasts and he shuddered at the flame that threatened his control. So many years since he had felt this way. It was like being reborn. He had completely forgotten Matthew. His mind was absorbed by this fragile woman in his arms.

Lyssa floated in a haze of passion, seeing the flickering shadows on the ceiling, drinking in the pine-drenched smell of him, moving this way and that under the feel of him, her own cautious manoeuvring beneath him. She did not care what happened. She would reach for him and guide him. She wanted to draw him in, thrash brazenly against his bare hips, cup those tight buttocks with her hands . . .

Their passion grew, fuelled by nature's fire. They knew what they were doing promised pain ahead but recklessly did not care. He ignored the panic in her eyes, then the intense fear receded and he knew she wanted him too.

But not a garment shifted. They were both still fully dressed. There was no way of pushing aside her trousers or tearing off her top, of their bodies merging. She was safe. He fell away from her, breathing heavily, trembling with suspense.

'Jeth . . .' she said, too dazed to offer or deny. She shook her head, trying to clear her thoughts.

'Lyssa . . .' he breathed. His hands spread down to her waist, stroking the willowy curves. 'I'm sorry. You're so lovely. It's been a long time . . . I haven't wanted to make love to a woman for years.'

'Don't say that,' she said, trembling. 'Don't apologise.' She felt a sudden wild need to pour out the contents of her heart, but he was already shifting his body from her, leaving a chill of separation between them.

She tried to make him stay, pressing her mouth to his ear, smoothing his lean hips with her palms, reckless with need, but he was determined to go. She yielded to his departure with a single, surrendering sigh and turned on her side, shielding her face with her arm.

'Please don't cry,' he said shakily, unable to stand her distress.

'What am I supposed to do,' she replied, her words muffled. 'Jump for joy? Shout hurrah, I'm saved?'

'Think of how I feel,' he said darkly, wrapping his arms round his knees. 'This situation is beyond anything I've had to deal with before . . . I'm out of my depth. Think of me.'

'I do, all the time,' she said, her voice choked. 'I only think of you.'

'Then you can't marry Matthew.'

'I can't hurt him.'

'Dammit, woman. Marrying him without loving him is the same as hurting him. Haven't you any sense?'

'Absolutely none at all. You've managed to rob me of any sense or sensibility that I ever had. I never want to see you again.'

'Do you really mean that?' He had gone cold, as if their passion had never existed, as if their kisses had been a mere frolic.

She had no strength left. She could not fight him. She could not endure the constant tidal waves of feeling that engulfed her every time she saw him.

'Yes, I do. It's the only way.'

Anger flashed across his face. 'Then I'll be gone in the morning, as soon as the rain stops. You can stay till the weekend, then take Bethany home. There's no need for us to ever see each other again. I won't come to your wedding. How could I? But, damn you, make my son happy or I'll kill you.'

His gaze was remote, as if she was a stranger he had only just met. She tried to gather her composure, to find strength. She did not know how to pass the next few minutes, let alone the next few weeks or years.

'I will make Matthew happy,' she said brokenly. 'I promise you that. But I'll make him happy because he's your son.'

CHAPTER 8

It was raining heavily when Lyssa awoke the next morning. She looked out of the window, surprised to see a surface of water glinting on the untenanted grass like an ice rink. She turned on her radio and the news was all about the unprecedented October rainfall and widespread flooding in the Home Counties. Kent and Sussex were the worst hit, with rivers bursting their banks.

She put on a grey pin-striped trouser suit and white polo-necked jersey. Bethany was still fast asleep, her hand curled under her cheek. The last few days had seen the return of colour to her cheeks. Gone was the London pallor and she was beginning to look like a healthy country child.

Lyssa drew back, an unaccountable hollowness inside her body. She had to get Jeth out of her system, regain some balance in her life so that she could marry Matthew and give Bethany the stable home life she needed.

Sarah was pottering round the kitchen in her dressing gown, intent on making a big pot of tea.

'Do you think you're going to work?' she asked briskly, noting the clothes. 'You'll be lucky. Emily can't get up from the village unless she comes in a boat. The roads are flooded.'

'I'll make it,' said Lyssa with more confidence than she felt. 'Your drive doesn't seem too bad. I can drive through a few puddles.'

'It's more than a few puddles, girl. Have you looked outside recently? Jeth's out in the barn now, filling sandbags. He's really worried. Amos – that's the gardener – and his eldest boy are helping. I'm just making them some breakfast.'

So Jeth was still around. Lyssa shrank at the thought. She had hoped to avoid him.

Lyssa opened the door that led out on to the courtyard and a blast of rain hit her in the face. The paving stones were awash with water, the overflowing drains unable to cope. The sky was black with rainclouds and she could hardly see the chimneys, lost in a mantle of rain. She shivered and drew back into the shelter and warmth of the kitchen.

'Sandbags. Why sandbags?' Lyssa repeated numbly. 'That's a bit extreme, isn't it? Surely that's not really necessary? Are you expecting Noah's flood?'

'There's a good reason why this house is called Hollow House. It was built in a hollow of the Downs and all the water drains down from the hills towards us. Normally the ground can cope and the surplus flows into the River Slud, but if the level of the river is rising then we'll be in trouble. Jeth went down early this morning and it's risen several feet.'

Sarah looked out of the window, her pleasant face troubled. 'I think I ought to take up the carpets,' she added to herself. 'Especially the Chinese in the drawing room.'

Lyssa made up her mind instantly. It meant another day off. At this rate she would get the sack but at least she had a valid excuse. No one could argue about the weather if it was on the news.

'I'll stay and help,' she said crisply. Greg Wilson would go berserk; they were already behind schedule. 'Give me a minute to change and I'll take that tea out to the barn.'

'Bless you. There's a pair of wellington boots by the back porch that might fit you. Jeth will be glad of an extra pair of hands.' Sarah smiled approvingly.

'In an extra pair of boots.' Lyssa threw on some cords and an extra jersey, pulled on thick socks. Her intention was to take the tea to the workers and then come straight back and help roll up carpets. Filling sandbags was hardly a second career.

But she could see the size of the problem as soon as she went outside. Hollow House was becoming stranded in the middle of an inland lake. The rain was torrential and in moments her waterproof was streaming, her lashes heavy with droplets. Head down, she splashed across the yard to the barn, wading through puddles, water sloshing over the feet of the big wellingtons. She hugged the flask to her chest, carrying a basket of mugs and cheese rolls covered in plastic.

The barn door was half open, propped with a barrel. She could see three figures inside, shovelling sand into hessian bags. Jeth's face was glistening with sweat as he plied the shovel rapidly, using his shoulders to lift the sand in a rhythmic progression. She couldn't bear to look at him.

'Here comes Little Red Riding Hood,' she called out more cheerily than she felt. 'Breakfast al fresco. Tea and rolls . . .'

Jeth stretched up and she knew from the movement that his back was beginning to ache. She'd seen a lot of actors with bad backs. He wiped the sweat off his brow and leaned on the spade. He took in her bedraggled appearance and nodded curtly.

She saw the pile of bags they had already filled. They must have been at it since dawn. The young boy looked almost done in, his face drawn. He glanced at the basket with relish.

She set the basket down and poured the tea into blue striped mugs. 'I hate to tell you but I think some of those bags ought to be hauled into place immediately. Like now. The water's already lapping round the step by the front porch.'

'Dammit. I thought we might have more time to get them up to the house. We'll move this lot in the barrow,' said Jeth, taking a deep drink of tea. He put down the mug and the two men started heaving bags into the barrow while the boy kept it steady. Lyssa felt absolutely useless and in the way. What she could do?

She did not know where Jeth found the strength. He started wheeling the laden barrow outside, leaving her with the boy. The downpour had not abated. It was getting worse, lines of rain sheeting across the garden like a wave of arrow fire at Agincourt.

'I can hold the sacks open if you shovel the sand in,' she said when the boy had finished his tea and started on a cheese roll. The food was improving his spirits.

'Have you seen the river, miss?' he said cheerfully, his mouth full of cheese. 'It's burst its banks. Reckon I'll have to swim home. No school, thank goodness.'

'Shouldn't you be at home, helping your mother?'

'Our house'll be all right. We live in the Lodge at the end of the lane. It's on higher ground than Hollow House. It won't reach us. Well, not for a long time.'

Jeth and the gardener returned with the empty barrow. They were both soaked to the skin; they looked as if they had fallen in the river, hair plastered to their heads, clothes soaked.

'Thanks for telling us,' said Jeth. 'I didn't realize the water had risen so fast – we were just in time. We'll do the front door first so that Sarah needn't worry so much. Then there are a dozen other doors and the stable block.'

'You won't want your precious pool contaminated with river mud, will you?' she said without thinking. 'And that expensive car of yours. Play hell with the batteries.'

'I've put the car up on bricks,' he said. 'We did that first. No point in being marooned later. You take the next load with your father,' he said to the boy. 'Some fresh air will do you good. You'll probably think it's fun at your age.'

Lyssa felt like a hostage. She was being left alone with Jeth, wishing she could blot out the memory of the last time they were alone. She wanted to disappear but there was no way she could get out of helping. Her nerves were stencilled raw, unwillingly aware of him.

But Jeth was not talking to her beyond the odd snapped command to open out another sack, tie that one up, move this, move that. Her nails broke; the dust from the hessian was making her sneeze. There were smears of sand on her face from where she wiped her hair out of her eyes.

'Don't look so scared,' he said suddenly. 'I'm not going to leap on you. This is a barn full of cold, wet sand, not bales of sweet-smelling hay in the middle of an idyllic Sussex summer.'

'I'm not worried,' she replied, smarting from his scorn. 'You wouldn't stand a chance. Last night is not going to happen again, ever. I'll make sure of that. It was despicable. I'm going to marry Matthew, your son. Hasn't that sunk in yet? The sooner, the better.'

'Tell the truth for once, Lyssa. You wanted it as much as I did. I don't remember you struggling, yelling blue murder, kicking me on the shins or worse.' His face was grim, his mouth a hard line as he shovelled piles of sand into the bag she held open. He would not look at her but that was no protection against the accusation in his voice.

Lyssa knew she was equally to blame. She bit her lip to keep back an angry retort. It was an exquisite pain, as if the touch of his lips was happening all over again. Her bones were melting. He was nowhere near, yet she was responsive simply to the thought of him kissing her.

'You . . . took me by surprise,' she floundered. 'I didn't want to wake the house . . . Aunt Sarah . . . Bethany.'

'Don't talk like a foolish virgin. You wanted it as much as I did.' He was glaring at her. There was no love in his eyes, only distaste. 'Don't lie.'

'That's not true,' she choked, her voice charged with emotion. 'I didn't want you. I don't want anything to do with you and I wish I'd never met you. I wish I could turn the clock back and tell Matthew that I never want to meet his father. That letter from Aunt Sarah – I wish it had got lost in the post and I'd never received it.'

He threw down the spade and turned on her, gripping her shoulders roughly. Electricity flashed between them – or was it a wild echo of the storm outside? She could no longer differentiate between reality and fantasy.

'Why? Why didn't you want to meet me?' He didn't wait for her answer. 'It's because you know as well as I do that Matthew isn't right for you. But I am. I'm right for you. I'm damned right.'

The tension broke and swallowed its own echoes as thunder clapped overhead. Gusts of rain slashed fiercely at the garden, blowing into the barn, drenching them in needlesharp spray.

She hadn't stopped falling, hadn't grounded yet from his words. She kept hearing them. But I am, he'd said, I'm right for you. And she knew he was. Jagged zippers of lightning rent the sky, punctuating his words, bursting apart the dark clouds.

'Don't say any more,' she whispered. 'This isn't the time or place. Please, Jeth, leave me alone. I've enough problems. Let's save Hollow House first.'

'We must sort it out,' he said darkly with an expression that hid his longing for her. 'It can't be left like this. You won't make Matthew happy. Think about him. He deserves more than a half-hearted love and a tepid marriage.'

'Don't you dare say that. I shall make Matthew happy,' she insisted. 'I know I will. I want to make him happy.'

Jeth twisted round like a man in agony. 'And will he make you happy?' he hissed.

'So what is this thing called happiness?' she argued, disturbed by his forthright questions. 'Does any of us know? And do we have a right to happiness? I don't know. It's all too complicated for me. Can't we just fill sandbags?'

Amos and his son were returning with the empty barrow. The work had to go on. They had to keep

Hollow House safe and dry. Jeth picked up the spade.

'Let's fill sandbags,' he said.

By mid-morning Hollow House looked as if it was ready for a Third World War siege, sandbags piled knee high at every point of entry. Lyssa was exhausted, her pristine white jersey soaked with sweat, her hair straggling, plastered to her head, aching for a hot bath.

Bethany was beside herself with excitement. Pudding the bear was installed on a windowsill so he could watch the water rising and report back. Panda had been banished to a cupboard because he wasn't helping. Lyssa felt quite sorry for the panda. He did not look very happy. Perhaps she ought to rescue him, take him to bed for a cuddle, two unhappy people in one family staying together, consoling each other.

Matthew phoned from the dry warmth of his high-rise London office. He had just been well lunched by a new customer.

'Hello, darling. How is it? Launched the lifeboats yet?'

'I haven't time to talk to you now,' said Lyssa. 'I'm rolling up carpets. We've been sandbagging all morning.'

'I understand it's pretty bad down there. It was

on the news. Roads flash-flooded.' He had difficulty with the double 'f's.

'I hope Greg Wilson saw it, because I haven't even had time to phone him. He'll be hopping mad. I had a script meeting this morning about a story change. The scheduling will be up the creek. We're pushing for time.'

'Give me the number; I'll phone him and explain. He won't yell at me. You know, man-to-man. It might work.' Matthew sounded confident and helpful, his 'bailing out the little woman' act.

Lyssa laughed softly. 'Thank you, Matthew. Here's the number.' She reeled it off. 'Tell him anything you like. I'll be in as soon as I can drive through a river.'

She put the receiver down. Typical Matthew. Always so kind, so helpful, so dependable – except in the case of spots. A rush of affection for him leapt into her mind. Affection. The word was bone-stripping with its intensity. That was what she felt for Matthew. For a moment she was unable to speak or move, although Aunt Sarah was calling from the kitchen that there was home-made soup ready. Bethany was laying the table, putting spoons on the wrong side of place mats.

'Soup. Lovely,' Lyssa said, making slow tracks for the kitchen. 'Just what we need. Gallons of soup.' She knew she was talking rubbish, putting off the moment when she would see Jeth again.

He was sitting at the kitchen table, buttering a roll. He had taken off the wet layers down to a check workshirt that was darkened with patches of sweat, sleeves rolled up his muscled arms so that his skin could dry off. He had dried his face roughly and moisture clung to his roughened chin. He had not stopped to shave that morning.

'Can you two cope with the carpets?' he asked brusquely, spooning home-made vegetable soup. 'I'm going down to the village; they're in a bad way down there. Several of the cottages are flooded.'

'Of course,' said Lyssa. 'We can manage. Bethany is as strong as a horse now. You'll help Aunt Sarah and me, won't you, love?'

'Shall I have a swimming lesson today?' Bethany asked. The flooding was something that was happening just outside the window, nowhere else around Hollow House. The consequences had not sunk in for her. She thought the pool was reachable.

'Sorry, love. Not possible unless you fancy a long, cold paddle first.'

'But we're going home soon,' said Bethany indignantly, waving her spoon. 'I must have another lesson,' she said earnestly to Jeth. 'Mummy says I must learn to swim. It's important and I can't learn at school because it's so crowded and I could get pushed.' She was mature enough to understand that she mustn't get knocked or bumped.

'Come down at half-term,' said Jeth quickly. 'You get a week off, don't you? You could swim all week.'

Lyssa shot him a look of desperation. He was undermining her responsibility, hot-wiring straight to Bethany. He'd been making enquiries again, or else how would he know that her half-term was a whole week?

'We've made other arrangements,' said Lyssa, avoiding his eyes. He always knew when she was lying.

Matthew phoned again. 'Greg Wilson wants to know if he can take pictures of Hollow House with sandbags. It would make sense in the hostage scene.'

'Tell him to take a running jump,' said Lyssa, furious. 'Preferably into the river.'

'He was keen.'

'I bet. Tell him there's a two-foot ton of river water between here and the nearest main road. What does he intend to do, swim the crew to the house? Rent a barge? Make another donation?'

'Hey, Lyssa. Don't be angry with me. Don't shoot the messenger.' Matthew was bewildered by her outburst. He knew nothing of the film crew's dawn descent on Hollow House.

'Sorry, Matthew. I've been working hard since early morning and I'm dead tired. And there's still so much to do.'

'Don't let Jeth act the slave-master. He can be a big bully. Tell him I want my girl all in one piece.'

Lyssa held the phone away from her ear, panic surging through her. My girl, he'd said. The situation was getting worse, minute by minute, and here she was marooned at Hollow House with the bulky figure of Jeth only a few feet away from her and Matthew a planet away in London. How could she cope without locking herself in her room?

Everything stopped, laughter, movement, time. She ceased to know where she began and ended.

'Tell Greg anything you want,' said Lyssa putting down the receiver. 'As long as it's no.'

All coherent thought was driven from her mind. What could she do? She curled her feelings into a ball, to protect them from the real world.

'Your soup's getting cold,' Aunt Sarah called out.

'Coming,' she said, but it was not her voice. It belonged to some strange woman who was fighting all her natural instincts, trying to find shreds of loyalty to Matthew, stifling her own search for happiness.

'Pudding is keeping watch on the steps,' said Bethany confidently. 'He'll tell us when the water starts coming in.'

'I'm glad we've got such a reliable look-out,' said Jeth with a sidelong wink. 'Now I feel really safe.'

Bethany knew he was teasing her but she sensed the underlying care and did not mind. Jeth meant a lot to her. He was the first consistent male figure in her life. Matthew had been around but as an escort for her mother, and if he spent an evening at the flat then she was usually in bed by then.

'Perhaps Pudding will give us a hand with the carpets,' said Aunt Sarah, ladling out more soup.

'He could manage a small rug,' said Bethany, and they all laughed, the atmosphere lightening.

A quick change of clothing and then Jeth disappeared down to the village, wading through the water in thigh-length fishermen's boots, heedless of his back. Lyssa thought she saw him swallow some pain-killers from a small bottle stored in a kitchen first-aid cabinet, but she might have been mistaken.

The rain clouds were so black and heavy that all the house lights were on by three o'clock. Rain relentlessly streamed down the windows; flowerbeds were submerged, only the heads of sodden flowers bobbing like waterlilies.

Lyssa and Aunt Sarah rolled up all the carpets and dragged them halfway up the stairs to the first landing. They did not know what to do about Jeth's grand pianos but Lyssa remembered the trick with the car, and together they stood them on bricks. Lyssa struggled out to the barn to fetch the bricks. Any furniture that was movable went upstairs. The big sofas were lifted on to bricks. Lyssa could see that Sarah was flagging and told her to go and make tea. They seemed to have lived on a conveyor-belt of tea all day.

It was difficult to tell if the water was rising or receding. It washed endlessly over the front step, buffeting the first high layer of sandbags, but seemed to come no higher.

But a disaster was in rehearsal at the back door. The sandbags had not been piled with such precision and at some point, unnoticed during the day, they slid down. The first sign was a yell from the kitchen.

'It's coming in the kitchen,' cried Aunt Sarah, panicking. And it was. A tide of water had seeped in from the outer utility area and was creeping across the kitchen floor. Bethany danced around in her bare feet, both frightened and excited.

'It's coming in, it's coming in!' she shrieked.

Lyssa kicked off her shoes and rolled up her trousers. She went out to the back door, the cold muddy water lapping over her ankles, and saw all the sandbags spilling into untidy heaps. They were much too heavy for her to lift but somehow she managed to drag enough sodden bags into place to stem the flow of water. Gradually it receded with a plaintive sucking noise. Gasping for breath, she shut the back door and leaned against it. She did not know where she had got the strength from.

'Look at it. My beautiful floor,' Aunt Sarah wailed.

'We must stop the water going into the hall. Shut the door and stuff towels against the door at floor level. Go away, Bethany, and stay upstairs. Don't open the kitchen door.' Lyssa knew she was shouting at her daughter but there was no other way.

'Mummy,' Bethany cried from the other side of the door, frightened now she was all alone. 'I want to be with you.'

'Take Pudding and turn the television on in your bedroom. Tell us what's happening on the news,' said Lyssa, calming her voice.

They began the mopping-up process. It was endless. There was a lot of water over a big area of floor and mops and buckets and cloths were a slow method.

'Thank goodness you were here,' said Aunt Sarah when they had managed to reduce the inch of water to a dirty slush of mud and river debris. 'I don't know what I would have done on my own.'

'Called the Fire Brigade to pump it out,' said Lyssa with a grin, longing to get out of her wet clothes.

'Only if that nice Greek station officer from *London's Burning* promised to come along,' said Aunt Sarah with a straight face. She fancied him even if she was fifty-plus. Half a century didn't mean half a heart.

It was getting late and darkening and no sign of Jeth. He had not returned. Lyssa began to worry. There were stories on the television news of people being swept off bridges, of cars tipping into rivers.

Aunt Sarah was feeding Lyssa tea laced with whisky now. She recognized the signs of physical exhaustion. They had managed rather well, the two of them; two women, one small girl and a bear to cope with the drying-out of Hollow House.

Lyssa was fast asleep on a sofa when Jeth finally returned home some time later that evening. He came in, face gaunt and hollow-eyed, his long back aching. He'd been on the go for eighteen hours. His clothes were soaked, hair flattened. He was not the same man who ran the empire of Arnold Consolidated from a big mahogany desk.

He fell on to the other sofa without removing his boots. Sarah took them off slowly, covered him with a rug, and then ushered Bethany upstairs to bed. Everyone was tired beyond words, bone-weary.

At some point in the hours just before midnight, Jeth rolled over the space between them and clamped his long body against Lyssa. They fitted as if they had been made a matching pair. She tried to push him off her sofa in a daze of sleep but it was hopeless. He was too solid.

'I'm going to have to tell Matthew that you're not married and never have been,' he said sadly, against her dewy cheek. 'I'm sorry, Lyssa, I want you and I have to fight dirty.'

'What do you mean, not married?' she sighed.

'I'm going to have to tell him that you are not a widow, but an unmarried mother. That you were never married to André. That you lied.'

But she barely heard. The words were simply a dream.

CHAPTER 9

Matthew was planning an engagement party and inviting all his business colleagues and friends. It was an odd decision when a celebration had not occurred to him before and the wedding was being arranged. Perhaps he felt that Lyssa was slipping from him and wanted to consolidate their commitment publically.

'But not at Hollow House,' said Lyssa quickly before her face could betray her feelings. 'Aunt Sarah and Emily have their hands full clearing up after the flooding. It wouldn't be fair to give them extra work.'

'I thought a private room at the Connaught or the Dorchester would do. Just a few friends,' said Matthew, patting her hand. 'Nothing special.'

Just like that. Nothing special for her, just a private room at the Connaught Hotel or the Dorchester. Book it, pay for it, no washing-up to do. So easy, Lyssa thought drily.

'My flat is no way big enough for a party and yours, well . . .' he went on, oblivious to her feelings. 'There'll be fifty or sixty people at least.'

'No, a council flat is hardly a suitable rendezvous for all your posh friends,' Lyssa finished for him with a touch of irony. 'And besides, their Jaguars and new BMWs might get vandalized.'

'Hey, sweetheart,' he grinned, taking her slackly into his arms. 'That doesn't sound a bit like you. You're not usually bothered by such things, or so sharp-tongued. What's biting you?'

'Sorry,' said Lyssa, appalled to find that she was unconciously leaning away from him. She tried to be more affectionate but her body would not move. 'I'm just tired. I haven't got over all that hectic driving and commuting, let alone the measles and the flood. Just too many things happening all at once.'

And meeting Jeth, she wanted to say. She would never get over meeting his father. And thinking about him night and day and not being able to get him out of her mind. It was no easier now that she and Bethany were back in London and he was out of sight. Bethany's enthusiasm didn't help. It was Jeth this and Jeth that and how was her kitten, and could they phone Jeth, and when were they going down to Hollow House again?

'Do what you like,' said Lyssa, trying to make

amends with Matthew. 'And invite who you like. Invite all your friends. I'll turn up and smile prettily at everyone.'

'There's a family ring,' Matthew said hesitantly, not knowing how to handle a difficult Lyssa. She was usually so even-tempered. 'I know you weren't keen on a ring before . . . I'd like you to wear it at the party but you might think that a bit old-fashioned. It was Grandmother's, I think. If you want something new and modern you've only got to say.'

He took a velvet box out of his pocket and opened it, watching her face closely for her reaction. She gasped at the sudden, luminous brilliance.

It was a deep, glowing ruby surrounded by a circle of diamonds, the old gold setting heavy and ornate, a dress ring from an Edwardian past.

'It's beautiful,' she breathed. But she did not want to put it on. It would be an act of insincerity, knowing how she felt, and to take the ring had a clang of finality. Like wearing precious handcuffs. She shook away the silly thoughts and slipped the ring on her fourth finger. Its weight made it slip round underneath her finger, out of sight.

'I'm afraid it's too big,' she said, taking it off quickly to hide the fact that her hand was shaking.

'I'll get it made smaller.'

'Sometimes you can't if the setting is really big and heavy like this one. The stones have to be supported, and if the ring itself is made too small then the setting can snap at the shoulder.' It came out sounding like a string of excuses.

'We'll take it to Garrard's in Regent Street and see what they can do. They'll soon say if its too tricky and then we can chose something new.'

'Lovely,' said Lyssa faintly. The wedding was coming at her like another flood, relentlessly creeping nearer, washing round her feet. She wanted to rush away and fill dozens of concrete sandbags and lock all the doors.

She had bought a dress from a big department store, in a lunchtime rush. Long, white satin, simple, more than just understated. It didn't say anything at all. Lyssa did not know if she even liked it.

She drove down a lot of roads the next day, maps strewn over the passenger seat, Post-it notes stuck on the dashboard to remind her of what she had to do and whom she had to call. She had her camera, mobile phone, a tape recorder to log directions for the crew and a pair of boots in the back in case she had to tramp muddy fields. She also had a flask of coffee and some tuna and salad sandwiches to keep her going, and an absolute deadline. There would be no time to stop for lunch.

She was looking for a dilapidated row of lock-up garages in a closed-off yard or cul-de-sac, and dared not go back without one. Something shabby and unhealthy. All the handy ones had been used before in *The Bill* or *Prime Suspect*. She didn't want their regular *Inspector Dutton* viewers recognizing an overused location again. They were very sharp and wrote to *Points of View*.

Lyssa had developed some odd driving skills, especially high-speed reversing. Her car could also cruise at a snail's pace. It could look suspicious at times. She often got stopped by the police, who thought she was up to no good. She usually carried a few complimentary tickets for television chat shows to hand out. It all helped.

It was turning colder and she was wrapped up in a sheepskin flying jacket, her feet in fur-lined boots. Bethany had returned to school and the old routine was back in line but nothing was the same. Lyssa knew she had changed. Some of the joy of life had gone out of her and she was far more irritable. She had no patience with fools. Once she had started the day with such enthusiasm, such energy, able to push time, rush her films through developers, persuade directors into agreeing locations, talking to the police, measuring parking space, planning the movement order, anticipating disaster with a smile. And sometimes all at the same time.

But now she was drained. Sleep came slowly or not at all. She began each day with a hangover of sadness. A person could only despair for so long. She longed for a Technicolor dreamcoat, anything to brighten the hours she spent apart from Jeth.

Now an engagement party to get through. She would have to find something to wear and practise her small-talk. The last end-of-series party she went to she wore jeans, sandals and a fringed tunic top, hardly suitable for the Dorchester. Bethany insisted on being at the party too, and Lyssa did not have the energy to argue with her. Perhaps having her daughter by her side would help Lyssa survive the occasion.

Matthew was making a point of seeing her every day, as if to make up for lost time. His insistence was becoming a touchy subject. She was often too weary after work to give him any attention.

'I can't see you tonight,' she said that morning on the phone. 'I'm too tired to cook. I must catch up on my paperwork and the chores. And I need time to myself to unwind. Please, Matthew, don't you understand?'

'No need to cook. We'll go out to eat.'

'It's too late to find someone to stay with Bethany.'

'Try, sweetheart. There must be someone. I want to see you.'

But there wasn't time to ring round to find anyone. She had to take Bethany to school. They threw on their coats and rushed out of the flat to the lifts, which were working for once. Lyssa stood in the stuffy, graffiti-decorated metal box as it travelled to the ground, holding Bethany's hand, and knew that Matthew's possessive love was suffocating her.

She was exploring the mews areas behind Knightsbridge when she thought of all the lovely shops and boutiques so close by. She parked the car and slammed the door. There was time to go shopping for a party outfit. She would buy the first thing that fitted. What did it matter what she wore or how she looked?

She never noticed the name of the shop but there was a long skirt on a lean, pasty-faced model in the window that she liked. Ankle-length, black grosgrain, buttoned-down the front with silver buttons but left open from the knee. She tried it on and it looked perfect, so sleek and sexy. She shuddered at the price ticket. All that for a skirt. Then she tried to remember that she was marrying a man who had a high-powered income, and a father who was made of money.

'I've a black silk camisole at home which will go with the skirt,' she told the salesgirl, thinking it was still summer.

'A bit cold for this time of the year,' said the sales girl, noting the pale cheeks and vague look of her customer. 'Might I suggest this jacket over the top?'

It was a swirling black raised velvet, nipped in at the waist, dipping at the back. It transformed the down-to-earth, hard-working locations manager into a beautiful and sophisticated woman. Lyssa could not believe how she looked. It was incredible, unbelievable. She blanked off the price, pulling up her strawberry-blonde hair into unaccustomed elegance.

For once, Jeth would see her looking beautiful. She bought it for him. It was a measure of her insanity.

Insanity. She knew it now for what it was. She could not hide her feelings from herself. Her heart responded with all the hurt and longing of a woman deep in unrequited love.

But Jeth was not for her. He was the father of her fiancé. Still she drank in the thought of him, nourished herself on daydreams. A different pain splintered her body. Her endurance was almost at an end. She feared reaching an unknown breaking point.

She was expecting an evening to herself, had cooked a Spanish omelette for herself and Bethany, faced a pile of ironing and then decided that it could wait. She had a lot of notes to write up, routes to check, expenses to make out. It was a full evening's work. She recharged the batteries for her car phone and checked that everything was organised for a quick take-off early the next morning.

The phone rang. She picked it up warily.

'Hello. Lyssa Pasten.'

'Is that Mrs Pasten?'

Lyssa frowned. She recognised the voice immediately but the tone was totally foreign. It was hard and held no warmth.

'Of course, Matthew. You know it is,' said Lyssa carefully. 'You sound funny.'

'I'd like to speak to my fiancée.' It was Matthew, distant and strained. He sounded horribly different. Something had happened and she was suddenly afraid. What had he found out? Had Jeth told him of their momentary indiscretion?

'It's Lyssa speaking. What's the matter?' she asked bluntly. 'Have I done something to upset your father again? I know I'm always treading on his toes, but I thought my stint with the sandbags had put me in his good books.'

'It's nothing to do with my father,' said Matthew coolly. 'It's to do with trust and us. My trust of you. What I've always thought of you, how you and I trusted each other. Mistakenly, it seems.

How we always told each other everything.'

It must be Jeth, thought Lyssa forlornly. Matthew has found out about us.

'I don't understand,' she said, waiting for the worst. 'What on earth are you talking about?'

'I've discovered your past, how you've been fooling me for months. You've never been married at all,' he suddenly burst out in a vindictive stream. 'Bethany is illegitimate, a bastard. You told me you were married to André but now I find out that you were never married. It was all a bag of lies. Why didn't you tell me? You've made me look a complete fool.'

Lyssa was bewildered by his outburst. Matthew went on and on, a jumbled torrent of accusations and indignation.

'I don't recall exactly what I said to you when we met,' she said, trying to gather her wits. 'But I don't think I actually lied to you. I'm not ashamed of Bethany. I was going to marry her father. It was all arranged but André was killed only days before the actual ceremony, literally days. But it was as if we were already married. We had felt married. There was nothing underhand about our relationship.'

'But you weren't, were you, deceitful bitch. And I've been telling all my friends about this charming, brave widow, battling on her own, bringing up her delightful daughter on her own.'

'So I have been bringing up Bethany on my own. It's been just as difficult, marriage certificate or not. Matthew, you're being ridiculous and you're not being fair. What does it matter, now, all these years later?' Lyssa was stunned by his vehemence, determined to stand her ground. 'It shouldn't make any difference. No one minds about single parents now.'

'It matters to me that you didn't tell me the truth. That you didn't trust me with the truth. I would have kept your secret. I don't know what to do now.' His voice was bitter and aggressive, as if he had been publicly cheated in some way.

'It's never been a secret,' she retorted. 'I wasn't trying to hide anything. And it was all so long ago, I just didn't think it mattered.'

'So everybody knew except me,' he said stiffly, twisting her words. 'That's nice. I'm your fiancé and yet I'm the last to find out.'

Lyssa closed her ears against the verbal abuse coming down the phone. She held the receiver against her shoulder so that Bethany should not hear. She didn't know what all this would mean to her and Matthew. Maybe this was the end. Perhaps he would call off their wedding. But at the moment she couldn't stand any more hassle.

'Call me back when you've come to your senses,'

she said, her voice defiant, her brain making her put the phone down firmly. She couldn't take any more. She lay back in the chair, her hand to her forehead, letting his accusations wash over in a private re-run. How had Matthew found out? It must be Jeth. She remembered his half-spoken threat in some sort of sleepy dream. He'd promised to play dirty and he had.

It was nearly evening two days later when she found herself parked near the towering skyscraper called Arnold Place. The London sky was creased with rain clouds. She remembered the time when she and a crew had been thrown out by security staff. She closed the door of her car and locked it. Matthew had not phoned back. She had to see Jeth and sort things out. She did not care how many secretaries she had to confront to get to him.

'I have to see Jeth Arnold,' she said at the reception desk. 'Please say it's urgent.'

'Your name, please?'

'Lyssa Pasten.'

'I'll phone through to his office,' said the receptionist. 'Mr Arnold is very busy.'

Even reception were surprised how smoothly Lyssa was met by his private secretary, a neat and presentable young woman in a grey skirt and white shirt, then ushered to a separate entrance. A private lift rose swiftly to the penthouse office.

Lyssa found herself shown through a carpeted hallway with panoramic views of the Thames. Somewhere she could hear a fax machine clattering out a stream of messages. Find the machine and she would find Jeth.

'This is a pleasant surprise,' said Jeth, rising from his desk. His desk was an acre of polished mahogany but it was covered in paper and files and did not look as if it was just for show. And, strangely, he did look as if he was pleased to see her. He was actually smiling, the warmth reaching his eyes. He put the top on his fountain pen and motioned her towards a burgundy leather chair opposite him. 'Is something the matter? How's Bethany? Is she all right?'

He had taken it for granted that she needed his help and that was why she had come. How did he know? How could he be so sure?'

'Bethany's fine. She's back at school.'

'And how are you? Still anticipating some disaster?'

'Every day. The pace gets worse with every programme. But I'm coping.'

'That's good. How can I help you?' He was looking at her closely, drinking in the pleasure of seeing her again. She looked worn out, eyes shadowed, as if she needed some time in the sun.

He longed to take her away somewhere balmy, warm and luxurious and take care of her.

'I don't want you to do anything for me,' she said. She was also drinking in how he looked, how he sounded. The dark suit, the white shirt and silk tie, hair slightly longer, ruffled where he had run a hand through it. She had not seem him for some time but it made no difference. He was exactly the man of her dreams and just as dangerous. 'I've come to tell you that you've won, that I'm not going to marry Matthew. You can find him a suitable heiress, someone who will be a credit to Hollow House and the old family name of Arnold.'

A range of emotions flashed across Jeth's face. Relief, surprise, anger, even bewilderment. He flung himself out of his chair, faced her with steely determination.

'I don't understand. What do you mean?' he said darkly, brows knitting. 'I've won? I haven't been waging a campaign. And I certainly won't feel a winner if the result is both you and Matthew being unhappy. You must have a low opinion of me if that's what you think.'

'But it's what you wanted, isn't it?' said Lyssa scornfully. 'To break it up between Matthew and me. Well, you've done it. It's worked a treat. Thank you for telling Matthew that I wasn't married to André. He was thrilled by the news, over the moon. So thrilled that he doesn't want anything to do with me any more.'

Jeth looked shocked, more bewildered. 'I didn't tell Matthew. Can't you believe me, Lyssa? I knew that André was killed before your wedding, it's all there, recorded at St Catherine's House, on Bethany's birth certificate. You used your maiden name, Pasten. And I traced the accident in which André was killed.'

'You looked up my daughter's birth certificate?' Lyssa was aghast. 'How dare you . . .?'

He raised both hands. 'Perfectly innocently. I wanted to know her birthday date. That's all. To buy her a birthday surprise, something special.'

'Quicker to ask me, surely?' she snapped. 'Didn't that occur to you?'

'I wanted to surprise *you* as well. But I never told Matthew. And I'm so sorry about André. Why don't you calm down, start at the beginning and tell me what's happened.'

Lyssa hesitated, then took a letter from her bag. She held the torn envelope still for a moment, weighing it as if calculating the hatred. That other letter from Aunt Sarah had been the beginning; now this one was the end.

It was the briefest of notes from Matthew, politely breaking off the engagement, saying that perhaps they had been too hasty in the circumstances, that he was going to the States to set up some new project for his father. Matthew wrote that he would miss her and Bethany and hoped that they would both be very happy, whatever the future held.

'Read this,' she said, handing it to him.

The note was loaded with accusations written between the lines. You told me you were a widow, said Matthew. You lied. You didn't trust me. You didn't tell me the truth about André, therefore I want nothing more to do with you.

Lyssa sat back in the chair, watching the December rain streaming down the big picture windows, listening to the drumming. Was the rain cleaner up here, when it had less distance to fall? London lay below, a sepia carpet of glistening roofs and church spires. It was a view she loved, even rain washed and muted with cloud.

'It's true, I suppose,' she said wearily. 'At the time it didn't seem to matter. I *felt* married to André. I was going to marry him. He wanted us to be a family. I never called myself Mrs Pasten but people assume the title. It didn't seem important to correct them. There's no harm in being a single parent these days. It doesn't carry the same stigma as a generation ago. I've always worked hard to look after Bethany myself, never been dependent on the State for any handouts.'

'You've done a great job. Bethany is a credit to you.' Jeth said gently, keeping his eyes fixed on her. He folded the note and handed it back to her without comment. 'So why are you blaming me?'

'But you told Matthew, didn't you? You must have. *Why*?'

Jeth went over to the coffee percolator. The aroma of fresh coffee filled her nostrils as he poured out two cups and brought one over to her.

'Firstly, I didn't tell Matthew. Secondly, Matthew will get over the shock. He has always been impetuous. He's very young, Lyssa, younger than you in many ways, more than in just years. And he acts young. He's still growing up really. You know that. He reacts violently to situations . . . but he'll get used to this. Do you want me to talk to him? I could change his plans for going to New York. It's not essential that Matthew goes.'

'No,' she said loudly and quickly. 'No, don't talk to him. If it's finished, it's finished.'

She didn't add that she would keep away, a very long way away, so that there was never any chance of meeting Jeth Arnold again, so that she could rebuild her life. 'I thought you had told him,' she added, her eyes clouded and cold.

'Believe me, Lyssa, I didn't tell him. It was for you to tell him. I don't know how he found out but it wasn't through me. I don't know how I can make you believe me.' He shrugged his big shoulders.

'By keeping out of my way,' she said bitterly, without thinking. 'And leaving me alone. I don't want any Arnolds in my life.'

'If that's what you want,' he said, standing up, turning his back. 'Then that's what you'll get. I'll certainly leave you alone. My secretary will show you the way out,' he added pointedly.

CHAPTER 10

Aunt Sarah was upset and so was Bethany. But Lyssa felt sure Jeth was relieved. He had got rid of his son's unsuitable bride, and good riddance to her. Lyssa put away her party outfit and wondered when she would ever wear such elegant clothes. Crew parties were always jeans-and-shirt affairs. She returned the antique ring to its antique box and planned to get it back to Matthew whenever he flew back from the States. He had gone to New York. She checked that with the office.

She returned the wedding dress to the store.

'Don't worry,' said the assistant, checking that it had not been worn. 'It often happens. People change their minds. But I'm afraid I can't give you any money back. We can only issue a credit note.'

'As long as I don't have to buy another wedding dress with it,' said Lyssa, thankful that no one made any fuss. She tucked the credit note in her bag and forgot about it.

Meanwhile there was a lot to do. She had got behind with things during her stay at Hollow House. Now she had time to catch up. She might decorate the flat. Bethany's bedroom had endured an artistic onslaught with plasticine and Blu-Tack and crayons. Lyssa needed to keep herself occupied, to stop herself from continually thinking about Jeth.

'Your mind is not on your work, girl,' said Greg, a few days later. 'You forgot to check parking facilities yesterday. We were all over the side streets, parking tickets like confetti. Cost us a fortune. I know you've had your troubles but sharpen up.'

'I thought I'd made arrangements with a nearby school that was still on holiday,' said Lyssa. Christmas had been very low-key, though she had done everything possible to make it a happy time for Bethany. They had gone to see a West End pantomine, to hear carols in Westminster Abbey, to see the 30-foot candle-lit tree in Trafalgar Square. Bethany was enchanted but kept comparing everything to her idea of festivities at Hollow House.

'Hollow House would have had a real tree,' she said. 'And Tipsy misses me. Aunt Sarah doesn't play with her much. She'll grow up dippy-rived.'

'The school car park wasn't on the schedule,'

Greg reminded her. 'You didn't make a note of it.'

Lyssa knew her work was suffering, and so was the reorganization of her home life. She forgot errands, appointments, invitations. Painting Bethany's bedroom was only half finished. She was going to pieces, and the rot had to stop before she did something truly awful. She was worried that she might forget an essential arrangement that involved Bethany.

'Mummy, why don't you do another parachute jump?' said Bethany wistfully as Lyssa served up baked beans on toast yet again. 'You were very happy then. It made you happy. Jumping is a fun thing.'

Lyssa *had* been happy then, back in the summer, going out with Matthew, knowing that soon they would be united as a family. It had seemed like magic. Then she'd met Jeth and the magic soared to the heavens . . . in the wrong direction. Just a mention of Jeth crippled her thoughts.

'Not now, love. Perhaps in the spring,' said Lyssa. 'I don't fancy landing in a puddle.'

The rain never seemed to stop that winter. Lyssa watched the news, saw photographs of the flooding in Chichester, wondered if Hollow House was under water again. Several times she almost drove down but could not risk seeing Jeth. But she did phone Aunt Sarah and they had a long chat.

'I miss both of you,' said Aunt Sarah. 'I hope you're not working yourself into the ground.'

'Into the mud, you mean.'

The location crew were waterlogged for several weeks and Greg Wilson concentrated on indoor scenes, which gave Lyssa time to catch up on paperwork and finish Bethany's bedroom.

'It's very nice,' said Bethany, inspecting the pink and white paint, the frieze of zoo animals marching round the wall. 'But it's not as nice as my bedroom at Hollow House. Can we go down and see Aunt Sarah soon? My kitten is missing me. She'll have forgotten me soon and she's growing. Mummy, please . . .'

'I'll call Aunt Sarah and drop a few hints,' said Lyssa, giving in. She missed Aunt Sarah's cheerful company too. Perhaps they could call in when Jeth was not there.

'Of course,' said Aunt Sarah. 'Come next week-end. I shall be on my own,' she added quite unnecessarily. 'It would be lovely to see you.'

Lyssa felt her heart pounding as she drove along the familiar drive, daffodils and crocuses coming up in lush carpets of colour along the side. A woman was picking daffodils, which was strange. Perhaps someone from the village. Jeth was everywhere in her thoughts. Amos leaned on his fork and waved at them as they passed.

Aunt Sarah was so pleased to see them. She hugged Bethany again and again. 'My goodness, you've grown, girl. I hope the jersey I've knitted still fits you. And so has your kitten grown. Go and find that naughty little cat. She thinks she owns the place.'

Bethany raced away to see what Tipsy was up to. She was sitting on the television set, wiping the screen with her fluffy tail. She jumped down and ran to Bethany, purring, pleased to see someone nearer her own age.

'I'm so glad to see you, Lyssa. I was beginning to think I would never see you again. You know, Matthew is all mixed up. And he's a fool.' Aunt Sarah bustled about making tea. 'Women have far more sense. I heard about you not being married but what does it matter? It's what you're like now that matters to me, not what happened years ago. And you've done marvels, bringing up Bethany on your own. He should be proud of you.'

'It's wonderful to be here again,' said Lyssa, fetching cups and saucers from the dresser, not daring to answer. 'You're easily our top favourite aunt. And you were so kind to both of us. It was one long holiday.'

'Heavens, my dear. All that sandbagging and rolling up the carpets! Hardly a holiday.'

Lyssa smiled back. In her mind she saw Jeth,

soaking wet, muscles bulging as he heaved bags on to the wheelbarrow, hair plastered with rain. Her flesh constricted. She was not sure what facts Aunt Sarah had been given, nor did it matter. She was so at home in this country kitchen. 'How is Matthew?'

'Fine, I think. We don't hear much from him, of course. Not a letter-writer. He's bought an apartment in Manhattan. Seems to go to a lot of parties, made a lot of new friends in New York.'

'Broken-hearted?' Lyssa had to ask.

Aunt Sarah considered this. 'Just a little bruised, and it's more his pride than his heart. No, Lyssa, I don't think he's heartbroken, though I'm sure he really loved you . . . in his own way,' she added carefully. 'A year of New York society, holidays in Florida, skiing in Colorado and I think our Matthew will be blessing his bachelor status. Does that upset you?'

'No, I don't think so. Not now, not any more. And . . . how's Jeth?' Lyssa heard herself asking. He seemed so close, vital. Lyssa almost expected him to walk in the door, tall, saturnine-faced, eyes glinting. She closed her eyes, thinking he might appear when she opened them again.

'He's away. Overworking as usual. Jetting here and there. I don't remember when I last saw him. He seems to be packing twice as much into every day. Was it Thursday or was it Wednesday that he last ate at home? I ought to write it on the calendar.'

'Mummy's going to jump again from an aeroplane,' said Bethany coming back with her kitten draped round her neck like a scarf. The cat was biting Bethany's ear, her tiny claws mauling her hair. 'She knows how to do it properly, you know.'

'Your Mummy's very brave,' said Aunt Sarah, warming fruit scones in the microwave. 'And off her rocker. Lucky I made these scones this morning. Give me more warning and there'll be your favourite chocolate cake too.'

'She does it to raise money for me,' said Bethany, getting out the butter and jam and putting them on the table. 'So that when I knock myself, I won't go to sleep any more.' She wandered off, so happy to be back at Hollow House, stroking the kitten's soft fur.

'Has Bethany . . .?'

'Only once,' said Lyssa quickly. 'At school, bumped into a desk. It was all over very quickly. The teachers knew what to do. I can't wrap Bethany in cotton wool, even if Jeth thinks I should.'

'Never mind both those Arnold men now. We can sit down and have a good gossip. I hope you're going to get into a habit of visiting me. We can't have that kitten growing up without Bethany's calming influence. It's climbing the curtains and scratching the chairs.'

Lyssa was only half listening to Aunt Sarah. She was pining for Jeth even more now that she was in his home. His presence was everywhere, his things were all around her; she could almost smell his clean after-shave and the tang of his skin. From the garden came the wonderful clean scent of spring flowers and fresh turf being turned. Hollow House was coming to life after the winter.

'I shall do another jump,' said Lyssa. 'When the better weather comes. It'll be good for my morale. I need to rebuild my confidence.'

'Be careful, my dear,' said Aunt Sarah, not sure whether it was right to be critical. Young people did what they liked. 'Bethany needs you more than anyone.'

'And I need Bethany. She's all I have in life now. I'd do anything for her.' Lyssa tried to put the man out of her mind. She did not have Jeth. He was not in her life. He was walking his own tightrope.

Lyssa went back into training for another jump. She signed on every Saturday morning at the airfield while Bethany was at her dancing class. It was back to basics again. She had forgotten a lot.

'I hope you're going to land with more accuracy

this time,' said the jumpmaster. 'Use the drop zone.'

Her second jump was planned for the first Saturday in March. Lyssa remembered how scared she had been the first time. It was no better this time. She fastened the top of her overall with trembling fingers, wishing her sponsors among the television crew had not been so generous.

'This is for you, Bethany,' she said, tugging on the parachute webbing. She clipped on the reserve, checked the buckles, took a helmet and clamped it on her head.

'Get a proper fix on the drop area,' said the jumpmaster, checking her gear. 'And I don't mean halfway down some tree.'

'Or halfway up a tree,' said a voice she knew so well. 'The fire brigade only rescue stranded cats.'

Lyssa gasped. Jeth was right beside her, all geared up in an overall, kit and helmet in place, his face grim with determination. 'You? Oh, no, are you going to jump?' She had not seen him for months. The joy surging within her was inescapable. She could not take her eyes from his handsome face, acutely aware of him. His face was thinner, drawn, his eyes a smoky pewter.

'Any objection?'

'It's too dangerous.'

'Lyssa, that sounds good coming from you.'

'You have to be properly trained,' she hissed.

'Don't worry, I've done the training, all the procedure and practice landings. I'm a little nervous, of course . . .' Jeth looked down at the ground as if he never wished to leave it. 'This is a far cry from signing cheques and making money.'

Lyssa shuddered. She knew how he must feel, even a big man like Jeth. Perhaps it was even worse for a man: they were not supposed to show fear. His strong dark face was impassive beneath the helmet but it was obvious that he was apprehensive.

'Don't do it, please,' she urged, his long, slow smile turning her heart over. 'Lots of people back out at the last moment. It's nothing to be ashamed of, really. You look too tired anyway. Back out now. I'll see you afterwards . . .'

'I'll back out if you agree to do the same,' he said forcefully, grasping her hand.

'I can't,' she faltered. 'A lot of people have sponsored me. My jump is riding several thousand pounds for RAS.'

'I'll double the sponsorship money if you quit.'

'Oh, you're so bossy, ordering me about, throwing your money in my face,' she said, glaring. 'I won't have it. I'm going to jump whatever you say,' she added. She started walking towards the aircraft waiting at the end of the runway. The engines were warming up, the propellors turning slowly.

'Then we'll jump together,' said Jeth.

Lyssa couldn't believe it. He was walking with her towards the open doorway of the plane. She backed up to the doorway and handed the jumpmaster her static line, shuffling in awkwardly. Jeth greeted the jumpmaster as if he was an old friend.

'This is ridiculous,' she said but the noise inside the aircraft was growing, the fuselage shaking with engine power, and Jeth could not hear her. 'Don't do it. The first time is absolutely terrifying.'

So is the second time, she almost added. She was beyond thinking, beyond caring. She only wanted Jeth to be safely on the ground.

'Don't worry, sweetheart,' he said, taking her hand again as they sat with their backs against the fuselage. 'I served in the Marines. I've done more jumps than you've had hot dinners. We'll do this together.'

Lyssa shrank back with mortification. As usual, he had played a trump card. He had reduced her to nothing with a single sentence. The glittering tarmac was sliding away.

'Then why pretend to be nervous?' she shouted close to his ear. 'I wasted my sympathy.'

'But I am nervous. Nervous of jumping. And

damned nervous of meeting you again. Wondering if you would even speak to me,' said Jeth, his uncomfortably candid eyes full of truth. 'It's been a long time.'

'Not long enough, Jeth Arnold,' she bawled back as the plane rose into the air and soon all she could see was a wing and a wheel. A surge of air filled her lungs. They were airborne, climbing into the delphinium-blue sky. The fuselage shook like an old locomotive.

The jumpmaster signalled to Lyssa. 'I want a good, clean exit, Lyssa. Take your time, then go.'

Jeth was at her side. 'We're going together,' he shouted.

Lyssa looked up at him and knew she still loved him. She was full of an innocent freshness of loving him. He was the one man she trusted. And he loved her. It was in his eyes and the way he took her hand again. A rush of air joined her fear.

'Going together? OK. That's your choice.'

Suddenly they were out, falling through the clean air. They fell together then they were floating, the legs of Lyssa's overalls cracking in the wind. It was like being a bird. Lyssa found herself floating in an ocean of air, moved by the hazy, drowsy scene as she looked sideways at Jeth, then down at the patchwork of land so far beneath them.

Then Jeth nodded and she understood the command. They parted, each skimming sideways, going through the procedure to open their parachutes. 'One thousand . . . two thousand . . . three thousand. Check canopy,' they said together.

The huge orange canopy billowed overhead and Lyssa was filled with amazed delight at the sight. Jeth's canopy opened almost simultaneously and her relief was complete. Now she just had to find the drop zone and make a good landing.

She floated in the silent air, filled with an overwhelming happiness. 'He loves me,' she said aloud. Then she shouted the words. 'He loves me!'

The ground was coming towards her at an alarming speed. She was heading for the drop zone. She hit the ground and rolled over as she had been taught, every bone shaken with the impact. She wondered if she had broken something. She lay, winded. The collapsing canopy dragged itself on the ground.

Jeth landed close by, rolling over quickly, then getting up and coolly collecting his canopy in a way that betrayed his experience. He hurried over to her.

'Are you all right?' He went down on a knee, his expression showing concern. 'Lyssa? Are you all right? Say something, please.'

'Just winded,' she said, struggling to get up. He

took her arm and hauled her against him. She was crumpled, rumpled, very much in a mess. The wall of his chest was familiar, a homecoming. She leaned against him, breathing in the aroma of his skin and sweat. He ran his hands over her arms and legs and that was a new enchantment, confusing her.

'Nothing broken,' he said, and she saw the return of a different concern in his eyes. Here was the special man she had always loved.

He reached out to her but there was no need. She threw off her helmet and was in his arms, their lips meeting in a frenzy of kissing. It was as if their love burst the floodgates and neither could have enough of the other.

'Jeth, I love you,' she murmured, her eyes shining. 'I love you so much. Don't send me away. Don't make me leave you. I only want to be with you.'

'Never, never, my darling. I thought I might never see you again,' said Jeth, wrenching at the straps of his helmet. 'Damn this thing.' At last it was off and he could bury his face in the silkiness of her hair. 'Oh, Lyssa, how I've wanted to hear you say that you love me. And I love you. Adore you, worship you. I was so damned jealous of my son.'

'There was no need. It was all a mistake. But are

you sure, darling?' she asked tremulously. 'After all, Matthew is your son and I was engaged to him.'

Jeth drew back, chilled, uncertain. 'Does that mean you can't you forget Matthew? Is that it? I suppose you still love him and he'll always be first in your heart.'

Lyssa shook her head, cupping the outline of his firm chin with her hand. 'No, no, it's not that,' she said emphatically. 'I don't still love Matthew. Perhaps I never did. I wasn't in love with him. I didn't feel the way I feel about you. It was always a kind of warm affection and I thought it would be enough for marriage. I think Matthew knew it as well and that's why he took any way out. He knew I was short-changing him and it definitely wasn't fair. Everyone deserves a better start to a marriage. I hope he finds a woman who falls head over heels in love with him, and he with her.'

'I think half the female population of New York is chasing him,' Jeth grinned. 'He sounds as if he's having a whale of a time.'

'I'm glad,' said Lyssa.

'But I've been through agonies of guilt,' Jeth went on. 'You were the woman I'd always wanted. To wait years and years to meet someone as daft and spunky and lovely as you and then find you were engaged to my son! I nearly went mad. It was more than any man, any father could bear.'

They began to walk back to the clubhouse, very close, hips brushing, carrying the piles of their rolled-up 'chutes. A glorious spring sun burst through the clouds and new life began to stir in the earth.

'What will Matthew think?'

'I think he'll be pleased we're keeping you in the family,' Jeth chuckled. 'And Sarah will be delighted, of course. She told me I was a fool to let you go but how was I to know . . .? Oh, Lyssa, Hollow House is going to be transformed with you and Bethany around again. I love that kid, too, you know. Do you think Bethany would like a bicycle as a bridesmaid's present?'

'Heavens, no!' said Lyssa emphatically. Jeth's face fell and he caught her arm.

'Am I going to fast for you? I want to marry you so much.' Jeth frowned.

'It's no to the bicycle,' said Lyssa, half laughing. 'Bethany might fall off. You've forgotten about her RAS. A bicycle is a little too dangerous.'

'How about a three-wheeler? And if ridden only on grass?'

'You're going to make a wonderful father,' said Lyssa, stopping outside the clubhouse. She didn't want to go in. The wind blew through her hair, spinning it to a golden haze. 'We're both so lucky to have found you.'

'Let's get married soon, Lyssa. I don't want to wait in case I lose you again.'

Lyssa felt a pang of alarm. 'But no St Margaret's. No Savoy reception. No big ceremony with lots of people. Please, Jeth, can we have a quiet wedding?'

'Of course, sweetheart. Anything you say,' he said kissing her again with a gentleness that made her senses whirl. Their mouths made words unnecessary. They shared those magic moments, knowing this first knowledge of love to be something very special.

They collected Bethany from Maggie's and drove back to Hollow House. Lyssa could not believe her happiness. Aunt Sarah flew to the front door to meet them, hugging Lyssa and kissing Bethany, her face alight with pleasure. The garden was hung with pale sunshine but no one saw it.

'At last,' she said. 'You've both come to yur senses. How I've prayed for this moment. Come in, come in. The champagne is ready.'

'Mummy did a jump again,' said Bethany, torn between pride and rushing off to find Tipsy. 'So did Jeth.'

'Lyssa made me,' said Jeth.

'Oh, yes, I'm sure of that,' said Aunt Sarah. 'And I hope it's the last. There's enough danger in this world without adding any more. Jeth and Lyssa, promise me, no more jumps. My nerves are in pieces.'

'Promise,' said Lyssa, laughing.

'Heavens, you're thinner than ever,' said Aunt Sarah as Lyssa came in took off her jacket. 'Whatever have you been eating, or rather not eating?'

'Mummy hasn't been eating. She hasn't had time. And I've only had baked beans.'

Lyssa groaned. 'Don't you love the honesty of small children? Why don't you go and look for Tipsy? See what mischief she's up to.'

'Well, we're soon going to put an end to all this not eating. You're staying the weekend, aren't you?'

'I'm back to work on Monday. The *Inspector* can't wait. Another series nearly in the bag.'

'And I'm flying to Bangkok on Monday.'

Lyssa hadn't known. But, of course, it would be part of her life from now on. Jeth would always be travelling somewhere. She would have to learn to wait. But there would always be the reunions . . . what glory, a new honeymoon every time. Her body throbbed with desire. Would they be together tonight? She wanted to be with him, but here in Hollow House? Somehow she thought not. Too many relations around . . .

She smiled. This was today and she would enjoy every minute of it. 'Where's that champagne? I promise you that it'll go straight to my head. Breakfast was out of the question before a jump.'

'Are you going to get a little tipsy?' said Jeth, rocking Lyssa in his arms. 'Is that a promise?'

'I've got Tipsy,' said Bethany, interrupting.

'I think I might like to see that. You are always such a cool and calm lady. Sarah, lead the way and we'll open that bottle.'

'Do I get any champing-pain,' said Bethany, her kitten struggling in her grip. Tipsy had grown, become a handful, was trying to climb up her hair. She winced as the needle-sharp claws dug into her scalp.

'There's a special kind for you,' said Aunt Sarah who learned fast. 'It comes in cans.'

Emily had prepared smoked salmon rolls, caviar on tiny biscuits, Greek pastry envelopes filled with goat's cheese and spinach. Lyssa was suddenly hungry. Bethany turned up her nose and went straight for the bowl of crisps.

'Come in, Emily,' said Jeth, giving Emily a glass of champagne. 'Who else is around? Amos? Bring them all in. This is a family celebration. Emily, let's phone Dr Carrington and Miss Reed. I want everyone to meet my future wife.'

Lyssa did not catch Aunt Sarah's quick glance of apprehension; it was over in a moment.

Jeth's happiness produced a kind of ache from the impossibility of understanding this complex man. How could she ever know what went on inside his head? One day perhaps, when they had been married for a long, long time, she would understand him. Or it might be the impossibility which would add the spice to a long marriage.

'Jeth,' she said, drawing him aside with his sleeve. 'Are you sure of that? Do you mean what you are saying? Things haven't been easy between us. You're not just being carried away?'

'I'm definitely being carried away – in your direction. Haven't I waited long enough for you? Much longer than you know. I've lost count of the years I've been on my own. It's been empty time, filled with work and bringing up Matthew. I always kept hope alive by saying that there must be something else to this life, someone to love . . . somewhere. Making money isn't the beginning and end of everything. Now I know . . . there was you. And I was simply waiting for you.'

Lyssa was lost for words. His speech had come straight from his heart. He loved her as much as she loved him. Everything would be perfect from now on.

'I will always love you,' she said. 'Always take care of you, need you, want you. If you have a dream, go for it.'

'You're my dream and I love you, Lyssa. Believe me, whatever happens, that will never change.'

The room was filling up with people. Aunt Sarah had made a few quick phone calls. People arrived from the village, Dr Carrington, Amos and his family. Lyssa recognised the boy who had helped in the flood and smiled at him. He'd grown inches.

'How's school?'

'Leaving soon, miss. Can't come soon enough.'

'Do you know what you want to do?'

'I was hoping Mr Arnold would offer me a job.'

'Ah . . .' said Lyssa. 'You'll have to ask him yourself.'

She had no idea when they all left to go home. Congratulations seemed to have been ringing in her ears for hours. The evening had drawn cool without her noticing, and sable clouds were blowing across the spring star configurations. She stood with Jeth in the porch, saying goodbye and waving. He had wrapped a shawl round her shoulders. It was if they were already married.

He took her arm and strolled her across the lawn. 'I think a little fresh air will straighten you out. How many glasses of champagne did you down?'

'I lost count after fourteen,' she grinned. He wrapped the Paisley shawl more firmly round her. It smelled of Sarah's Blue Grass perfume.

They walked the grounds, her hand tucked into his pocket and held firmly. Bill and Ben scampered ahead in joyous and idiotic freedom. She could not believe her happiness after all the weeks of pain and indecision. And tonight he would hold her close and kiss her, even if they did not make love. She could wait. It wouldn't be long now.

'All this will be your home. Will you like that?' he said as they walked past the stables. He glanced up at the upper windows. Behind them the lights of Hollow House came on and and Lyssa could imagine Aunt Sarah drawing the curtains and helping Emily to clear up.

'You know that I love Hollow House, but your sister . . .? Will she resent another woman coming to live here? After all, it's her home.'

'Do you want Sarah to leave? I could buy her a house in the village near her friends, something really nice. She wouldn't be far away.'

'Oh, no, that's not what I meant. Hollow House will always be her home for as long as she wants to stay. I would never ask her to leave. That would be too cruel. We must reassure her. She's probably wondering . . .'

'I think she'd like it if you told her.'

'She might be nursing a secret longing for a cottage on the green . . . I'll talk to her.'

She thought no more of Aunt Sarah, for Jeth was kissing her with strong and seeking lips, his arms wrapped round her in a hug that promised safety and security and love for a lifetime. His mouth was healing all the terrible times and Lyssa returned his kisses with a blaze of passion that had been dormant since the sun-kissed days of André. But she was not thinking of André now. She leaned against him, memorizing the muskiness of his skin, the shape of his body in all its manly power.

His hands were stroking her spine, running down her back, promising silent delights shead. She wanted to lead him indoors, to take off her clothes, to climb on to him and steal the secrets of his body.

Sunday was their perfect day. Their one day together, making up for lost time, talking all the talk trapped inside them. Jeth tried not to do any work. They walked the Downs with Bill and Ben, took Bethany to the Worthing. The tide was out and they splashed through the puddles and watched the greedy gulls catching crabs in the shallow water.

The time went so fast. Lyssa wanted to lock out

time but it was impossible. The thought of losing him so soon was windowed in her eyes.

That night he did come to her room.

'I can't keep away,' he said, standing in the doorway, his robe losely tied.

'If we lived in a semi-detached house, Bethany and Sarah would be sleeping close by,' said Lyssa, raising her arms to him. 'It's no different . . .'

'We could just sleep,' he said.

'All right,' said Lyssa, drawing him into her arms, smiling. But she knew they would not just sleep.

It was no gentle loving. He loved her first with his eyes, then with his hands. Jeth was fierce and demanding, sliding his arm along the small of her back, enveloping her with a compulsive passion that took Lyssa's breath away. He eased her cotton nightshirt over her shoulders, touched by the pattern of hearts printed on it, stroking her skin, running his mouth over her soft curves, running his fingers through her hair.

Her mouth opened under his and she drew in the moistness from within, glorying in the way he was loving her. His kisses took their pleasure from the softness of her mouth, the roundness of her rising breasts, the moist length of her thighs.

'Jeth . . . Jeth . . .'

She had no fear of him. His long weight was

what she longed to feel on her, the roughness of his chest caressing her skin like a tender brush of fur. She breathed the healthy tang of his skin, her legs eager to wrap themselves round his loins.

It was a blazing communication, filled with exhilaration, joyful, reckless, trailed with burning kisses, scorching surges of delight. She dug her nails into his flesh, her thunderous heartbeats clamouring in her ears. Her breath caught on a sob. They were linked in one mind, one desire, simply wanting to belong.

Her head swam in the darkening landscape. She was lost in his body, no will to stop him, her senses reeling.

It was all over too quickly but they had waited so long, tormented with desire, that the intensity was explosive and shattering. Gasping and shuddering, they fell on each other, moaning each other's names, kissing ears, neck, tips of fingers, longing for more, exhausted but content.

They fell asleep in each other's arms, entwined, buried in the tumble of sheets, rejoicing that the long years of loneliness were over. There were tears on Lyssa's cheeks but they were tears of happiness.

'How long will you be in Bangkok?' she whispered when Jeth rose at dawn. She tried to make it sound as casual as Bristol, Bath, a short trip down the M4.

'A week at the most. It's a quarterly visit to some associate companies in the Far East. I'll phone you as soon as I arrive,' he promised, kissing her warm cheek, aching at the leaving.

But he didn't.

CHAPTER 11

Lyssa waited impatiently for the call from Jeth. Bangkok might be the other side of the world, but modern communications could link them in minutes. She hung around the phone like a teenager waiting for a first date to call back.

She could not believe that he would forget or be so immersed in his negotiations that his promise did not matter. The call would come soon, of that she was sure. Perhaps the line was crowded.

Then the age-old panic lines starting working. He was ill, been in an accident, the plane had crashed. But if the plane had crashed, it would have been on the news. If he was ill, he would get someone else to call.

Day followed day. At first she pretended that it didn't matter; it wasn't happening. Time stretched into nothingness. It was hard to keep going but she had to work, to appear normal, look after Bethany. He was out there, somewhere, not phoning. He must know that he was not phoning and had a reason for it. The agony of waiting was intense, took her breath away, sickened her.

Four days on and the world gloomed into greyness. It was like a bereavement. Jeth had obviously changed his mind and this was his way of telling her. The loss of his freedom was suddenly too much to accept and there was no way of letting her down lightly. Perhaps their lovemaking had been a disappointment. He had rejected her in the only way he knew how: crudely.

But Jeth was in her thoughts every moment of the day. She could not stop thinking about him and reliving their last conversation.

'I'll phone you as soon as I arrive.'

But he hadn't. That one sentence was riveted into her brain. He hadn't. Her work went on to auto-pilot. She was as efficient as ever but she lived on a different plane. Bethany noticed.

'You're not reading this story properly, Mummy,' she said one bedtime. 'You keep saying different words.'

There was a point when she could wait no longer. Her pride went downhill. She phoned Hollow House.

'Sarah?" She held the phone firmly to her ear. 'Have you heard from Jeth? I was sort of expecting to hear from him. He said he would call me when he got to Bangkok . . .' It was like slashing herself with a blade.

'No, I haven't heard, but then I rarely do. He's not one for social calls home. But if Jeth said that he would phone you, then he will. He always does what he says he'll do. Remember there's a time difference, seven hours I believe.'

'Not four days.'

'Perhaps the flight was delayed, diverted, whatever long-haul flights do.' Aunt Sarah had some vague idea of a big jet flight-hopping round the world.

'He could still have phoned.' Lyssa could not stop the hurt showing. Now she was embarrassed at having called Sarah. 'Never mind . . .' she added hurriedly.

'Perhaps you should call British Airways and check with them. That would put your mind at rest. I'll give you his secretary's number. Sybil is a nice young woman and can give you the flight he was booked on. Don't worry, Lyssa. Jeth never calls me when he's away.'

Lyssa remembered Sybil. It was too late to call his office then, and Lyssa spent a restless evening going over their last conversation again. Was it something she had said, something too possessive? Or was it something she hadn't said? The possibilities were endless. She paced her small kitchen till her head ached and she fell into an uneasy sleep in a chair, her dreams all coloured red and black.

She woke up with a start. She was not surprised to find herself shaking. But her back ached and her neck was so stiff that she had to move it carefully with her hands to a more comfortable position.

'Jeth,' she said aloud. 'Where the hell are you?'

At first she couldn't believe it and then she began to believe it. This was the hard, ruthless side to the man which she had chosen to ignore in the bliss of loving him. This was the man who had ignored his schoolboy son for years. OK, he had been rebuilding a home and an empire, but that still didn't excuse his neglect of Matthew.

Then in other moments she remembered his warmth and his passion and knew it had been a real emotion and could not simply disappear on a flight eastwards. Or could it? Her imagination went out of control, saw another woman, dark and mysterious, a secret mistress kept in Bangkok who had a hold over him. Someone he could not give up.

'This is one hundred per cent stupid,' she told herself. 'Go to bed or you won't be fit to locate a bus stop in the morning.'

The next morning Lyssa phoned Sybil. She supplied the flight number and take-off time. Lyssa could not bring herself to ask if they had heard from him. It would be too humiliating to find that he had phoned the office but not her.

'And I made a reservation for him at the Bangkok Hilton, Wireless Street, as usual. He likes the tropical gardens, waterfalls and lily ponds. And I believe he likes the Chuan Chom Pool Pavilion after a game of squash.' Sybil had time to chat now that her demanding boss was halfway across the world.

'Sounds a fascinating place,' said Lyssa.

'I wished he'd take me along sometimes. It would be nice. But I have to keep everything ticking over here.'

'Which I'm sure you do very efficiently. Thank you again.'

Lyssa also checked with BT that her home phone had not been disconnected at any time for any reason but she was assured that the service was in working order. Jeth did not have the number of her mobile phone.

British Airways Customer Information checked the flight number on their computer. It had arrived safely at Bangkok Don Muang International Airport and on time.

'Could you please check the passenger list for a Mr Jethro Arnold?'

'Certainly, madam. Just a moment, please.'

Their computer system threw up the information in seconds. 'Mr J Arnold was booked on this flight but it looks as if he didn't show. Perhaps he missed the flight. The traffic around Heathrow is always horrendous.'

'Didn't show?' The implication didn't sink in.

'No, there's no Mr Arnold, passenger to Bangkok. Sorry, madam.'

'Could he have taken another flight?'

'There are several other carriers. You would have to approach each one directly. I'm sorry I can't give you any more help.'

Lyssa switched off her mobile. She was nearing the location site, the shop which she had found last year. They were using it again as the owner didn't seemed to mind the ensuing chaos. He said it was good for business, being on the telly. And he liked the compensation cheque. The set people were already transforming it into an Asian shop, removing Heinz and Cross & Blackwell bottled sauces from the shelves.

'Glad you managed to make it,' said Greg with heavy sarcasm. 'Hope you haven't had to cancel a more pressing social engagement.'

'I'll just check the catering,' she said.

'It's here,' he said, pointing to a cold coffee. 'But you could get me another while you're about it.'

She floated in a cold shell all day, doing what she was told. Her face was too stiff to smile. She said she had a headache. Heartache sounded hopelessly juvenile and dramatic.

Didn't show. Then where was he? Was he still in this country or had he gone somewhere else? It was puzzling. A small twitch of defiance broke through the gloom. Damn him. She wouldn't be treated like this.

'Mummy, Mummy, wrong feet!' cried Bethany that evening as Lyssa tried to put slippers on wriggling toes that faced a different way. 'This is my left foot and that's my right.'

'Just testing,' said Lyssa, changing the slippers over. 'Time you put your own slippers on.'

'I can, I can,' said Bethany. 'Watch me.'

Checking with the other carriers was a daunting task but Lyssa did it. It took a while. She also made them check other flights on other days. Most of them flew to Bangkok three or four times a week. The clerks were patient, perhaps catching the panic and worry in her voice.

It was a blank everywhere.

'Are you sure you have the right name?' asked one of them.

'Of course,' said Lyssa exasperated. His name was carved on her heart.

Eventually she could stand the inactivity no longer and phoned Sybil again. She could not face trying to get information out of Aunt Sarah.

'It's Lyssa Pasten again. Can you tell me when you expect Mr Arnold back from Bangkok? I don't think he actually told me.' Lyssa injected a degree of casual interest into the words. She said nothing about the no-show and no call.

'Funny you should phone, because Mr Arnold was due back yesterday but he hasn't come into the office this morning. I hate to phone his home in case he's still sleeping off jet-lag. I've got a pile of things waiting for his attention.'

'I'll phone Hollow House,' said Lyssa, glad of something to do. 'It won't matter if I wake him up. I'll ask him to give you a call.'

'Great. Thank you.'

And she was going to give the great Mr Jeth Arnold a piece of her mind. She would tell him exactly the kind of agony she had gone through in the last week, demand an explanation, make him eat humble pie, arrange to see him right away . . . forgive him, hold him, kiss him.

'But he's not here,' said Aunt Sarah vaguely. She was using the kitchen extension and Lyssa could imagine it tucked under her chin. 'Was he supposed to come back yesterday? I didn't know that. But then he never tells me. He could have gone to Timbuktu for all I know.'

'Aren't you worried?'

'No. He always turns up eventually. No point in

worrying. Now when are you and Bethany coming down? Why not this weekend? I'd love to see you.'

Suddenly Lyssa longed for the peace and beauty of Hollow House. She would feel nearer to Jeth there and he might turn up. If he did, then she would be right on the spot. By now she was so worried that she would forgive him anything, just to have him safely home. All she wanted was to hold him in her arms again.

'Wonderful idea,' said Lyssa. 'We'll drive down Friday evening, straight after school. Bethany will be over the moon. She nags me every day about coming to see you and Tipsy.'

'I'll get your rooms ready, dear. We'll have a really good chat about everything,' said Aunt Sarah.

Lyssa knew what she was going to do once she got to Hollow House. She told herself that it was not being nosy, merely making sensible checks.

There might be an appointments book in his study. He might have put a name, an address that he did not want Sybil to know about.

He had been working on something before he came to her bed. Something worrying. For in the night, he had suddenly groaned and said in his sleep, 'Oh no . . . no, no . . .'

Now the time could not go fast enough, and Lyssa threw herself into her work. Greg stopped complaining so often and even told her to hold on and give herself time to breathe. This was a strange remark and took Lyssa by surprise. He had never shown any concern for her before – quite the reverse. He had no patience with human problems or frailties.

'What's all this about?' asked Lyssa. 'Is there a sudden shortage of location managers? Has something happened that you know and I don't?'

'I just think you're being frenetic about things. Take it easy. Be laid back, like me.'

If she had not been so tired, Lyssa would have laughed. But she nodded and longed for the end of the day's filming. Gareth Warwick, scarf flowing, patted her shoulder as he went by.

'Don't worry, Lyssa. We all appreciate you.'

It was the first time he had even noticed her. Lyssa wondered what it was. The look of vulnerability? The look of availability? That shook her. She was not on the market. Not now, not ever.

'I'm glad to hear it,' she murmured.

Then she knew why. Jeth's lovemaking showed. She was a woman who had been loved, fulfilled, and the animal glow was still there, permeating her skin with an essence.

Driving down to Sussex was like coming home. It was an evening of promise, daylight lingering with harmonic clouds and fluttering trees. Spring was clamouring to be recognised. The countryside was bursting with energy and Lyssa felt the same tremor in her veins. If only Jeth were waiting for her at Hollow House. She would fly into his arms, forgive him anything.

Aunt Sarah had heard the ten-year-old BMW coming along the drive and came to the porch to welcome them. She waved cheerfully. Bethany ran into her arms.

'Now you are going to see Hollow House at its best. All the spring flowers and the trees in the grounds coming into leaf. It's a wonderful place for children,' she said later as they were having supper. Bethany had been allowed to stay up and eat with them. It was not the time to mention Jeth's non-appearance at the office.

'I can see that,' said Lyssa. 'Everywhere looks so fresh and green. We'll take Bill and Ben for a long walk tomorrow over the Downs.'

'They'd love that. I can only manage a short walk each day. There's such a lot to do at Hollow House. I don't know where the time goes.'

Sarah had made a salmon quiche to serve with salad and Bethany was eyeing the selection of desserts laid on a side trolley. There was a big trifle and chocolate mousse in little dishes, fruit salad and a jug of cream.

'You've been busy,' Lyssa smiled.

'I know when I've got appreciative guests, though we can't really call you guests now. You're part of the family. Remember that, Lyssa.'

'Where's Jeth?' Bethany asked, picking out the slices of radish which she didn't like. 'I thought he would be here. I want to see him.'

'Not back from Bangkok yet,' said Lyssa lightly.

'Work, work, work,' said Bethany, sounding like a weary adult. They all laughed.

'You'll soon find out what it's all about when you're grown up,' said Aunt Sarah.

'I'm going to work in television when I'm grown up,' said Bethany confidentially. 'So's Pudding, so's Tipsy.'

'The same work as your Mummy?'

'Oh, no, I'm going to be a star and have lots of time off.'

'You've obviously got it all worked out,' said Lyssa, relieved that Bethany was providing light relief for the meal. 'We shall watch your career with interest. Especially all that time off. You'll be able to help at home with the chores.'

Bethany thought that over. 'But Pudding and Tipsy can't do chores. They can't hold things.'

'Tipsy earns her living here,' said Aunt Sarah. 'She keeps the house free of mice. And there are a lot of mice out on those hills looking for a warm home.'

It was not till some time later that Lyssa was able to ask Aunt Sarah about Jeth. But Lyssa learned nothing new. He did not tell his sister much about his business commitments. She had become used to his travelling all over the world.

'He'll turn up. Don't you worry, my dear. Just enjoy your weekend and get some colour back into those pale cheeks.'

'Would you mind if I had a look in his study? There might be an appointments book.' Lyssa asked hesitantly. 'I know he keeps it locked, but . . .'

'I'm sure Jeth wouldn't mind. He has no secrets in there. The key is probably in his bedroom. I'll find it for you when we've finished our coffee.'

Lyssa tried to relax while Sarah chatted on about this and that. She had finished the jersey for Bethany. It was about three sizes too big but that slight drawback simply gave Sarah an excuse to start on another one.

'I've got a pattern with a big panda on the front like the panda Matthew gave her.'

'Do you hear from Matthew?' Lyssa was glad to bring his name up in conversation.

'Not very frequently, but he is having a lovely time and adores New York. I think perhaps you did him a favour when you broke it off.'

'But I didn't –' Lyssa began and then stopped.

What did it matter? She did not want to recall all that bitterness and his accusations.

It seemed odd to be going into Jeth's study, his inner sanctum, his most private refuge. His shadow was there. Sarah did not seem to mind.

'Thank you,' said Lyssa as Sarah unlocked the door. 'I won't touch anything.'

'I doubt if Jeth would ever know,' said Sarah, her glance sweeping over the cluttered desk and files piled on the floor. 'He certainly left in a hurry. He doesn't usually leave it in such a mess.'

Lyssa did not start straight away. Memories were flooding back and the room was so full of his presence. That was his chair, this was his pen; this was where she had sat. He had opened that book, marked that page.

She found an appointments book and opened it to the day he had been flying to Bangkok. The page was empty. She flicked on a week to see if he had made any appointments for his return. But again, there was nothing. Yet the pages before were crammed with times, names and places. He filled every hour of the day with work. On one evening slot he had scrawled 'sleep?' in big letters as if to remind himself, a joke.

The files were unfathomable; only the names of the companies rang bells. Did he own these companies or was he dealing with them? She founded the headed notepaper of Arnold Consolidated Industries and discovered that a Miss Sarah Arnold was on the Board of Directors.

Remembering the *Inspector Dutton* series, she moved books on the shelves to see if anything was hidden behind them. A photograph fell out. It was a small snapshot of Bethany and herself taken in the grounds of Hollow House, Bill and Ben bouncing in the background. Aunt Sarah had taken the photograph the first time Bethany was allowed out after her measles. She was about as good at taking photographs as she was at driving. It was fuzzy and blurred, bits cut off.

Lyssa smiled. Yet Jeth had kept it, tucked between company law books. Not quite framable.

She put the photo back, tired of snooping. She could hardly turn back the carpet and lift floorboards. Her tidy hand went to return the open book on the desk to the shelves but she stopped herself. The page was open at Kuta, some beach resort on the island of Bali. Her heart tripped. Peanuts was underlined. A honeymoon? Had Jeth been planning their honeymoon?

That night, Lyssa found it difficult to sleep. Jeth seemed so close at hand. She would not have been surprised to have him walk into her room, weary and jet-lagged, crawling into her bed and her arms.

At some time in the early hours, she got up and put on her robe, leaning by the window to look on the moonlit garden. A fox ran across the lawn and she was moved by its russet beauty and streaming tail.

Aunt Sarah would not mind if she made some tea. Lyssa hoped that she wouldn't accidentally set off the alarm; she had forgotten the numbers to key in to unset the system. It was even more complicated now that Tipsy lived in the house and some areas had to be cat-free zones.

She crept down the stairs, remembering to avoid the creaky board on the first landing. It always sounded so loud at night.

She switched on the low strip lighting over the working top and filled the kettle jug with water, switched it on. She put her hands round the outside of the jug to warm them. It was a habit from the flat. She not really cold, only sad and lonely.

It only a faint sound but she thought she heard the board creak.

'Sarah?' she said, and went to the door to look. 'Jeth?' The name was hopefully spoken. But no one was there. The house was still.

She took out her favourite flowered mug and an Earl Grey tea-bag, already savouring its fragrant brew. They had been her one luxury during the early days when she had been desperately hard-up. She had rationed herself to one bag a day and made it do for several cups. Sometimes she thought that the anticipation of that cup of tea had been the one thing that kept her sane.

Everything was different now. She earned a good salary and there was talk of a new big classic on television. Jane Austen was enjoying a resurgence of popularity and the company couldn't wait to jump on the band wagon. She was in the running for the job as locations manager, though it might be upgraded to locations director on the credits.

What a joy that would be, and a real challenge . . . to find period villages, big houses, stately homes, hovels, old inns. And with a much bigger budget at her disposal she would not have to bargain or pinch and scrape.

She leaned against the counter, sipping the tea, wondering which way her life would go. For a few heady days she had thought that Jeth was her future, but now . . .

The board creaked again.

It was strange, but Lyssa felt that she was being watched, that some other breathing was pulsing the air. She gave a careful glance over her shoulder but the kitchen was all Rembrandt shadows. The appliances stood in orderly quiet. Nothing stirred.

Fur feathered and twisted round her bare ankles. Lyssa bent down and scooped Tipsy up into her arms, nuzzling the soft tabby head.

'Was it you, you wretch?' she said. But how could this lightweight bundle of fluff make a loose board creak?

Hollow House was an old house, she told herself. Old houses always creaked. The timber expanded and contracted with the heat, cooling at night. It was nothing to worry about. She was quite safe here. Bethany and Sarah were soundly asleep.

She made a second mug of tea and left Tipsy lapping at a bribing saucer of milk. She did not want the cat following her upstairs in case it strayed into a non-cat zone and set the alarm off.

It was nearly dawn before she fell into a fitful sleep but no one came to wake her, and when she eventually staggered out of bed Bethany was already dressed and downstairs having her breakfast.

'I dressed myself,' said Bethany.

'Well done.' Lyssa yawned, making no comment about the jersey on inside out and odd socks.

'Then I fed Tipsy and put her out for a run round. She has to run round the garden, you know.'

'For her health,' said Aunt Sarah who was busy

making French toast. 'Didn't you sleep well?'

'My brain wouldn't stop working and settle down. Did you hear me get up and make some tea?'

'No, but I found the empty saucer. Tipsy may be smart but she's not yet learned how to open the refrigerator door.'

Lyssa followed her daughter out into the garden, the morning freshness waking her up more successfully than two cups of black coffee. Bethany was bounding with energy, rushing about in every direction like a charged rocket. It made Lyssa quite tired watching her. Bill and Ben thought it was a wonderful game and became mildly hysterical, barking at birds, leaves, insects.

She sat on a fallen tree trunk and let her thoughts sort themselves out. On the agenda was another talk with Sarah, a visit to Arnold Place, a telephone call to Matthew. She was not sure what else she could do or if she had any right to probe into Jeth's affairs.

She turned. There was that feeling again. Someone was watching her.

CHAPTER 12

It was a very different Lyssa who went to Arnold Place during a lunch break from filming on Monday. The morning had been spent tying up loose ends of the *Inspector Dutton* series and making sure her records were accurate for future use. Lyssa had made an appointment with Sybil, Jeth's private secretary. Sybil seemed anxious to meet her.

Lyssa had been naïve on that first occasion when she was thrown out; incensed on her second visit, planning to give Jeth a slice of her mind. This time, she was cool, calm, deadpan, hiding her anxiety.

'I'm so pleased you've come in, Miss Pasten,' said Sybil, meeting her at reception. 'I do need to talk to you and I know that Mr Arnold trusts you.'

'Really?' said Lyssa, smiling slightly. 'What did he say?'

'Well, he didn't exactly say anything but I got the impression that you were . . . special.'

'Ah . . .' Lyssa was immensely moved by the thought. 'That's reassuring.'

Sybil Ruston seemed to have realised it was Lyssa's lunch break and had ordered a tray of coffee and a plate of sandwiches from the cafeteria. She showed Lyssa through into Jeth's office. It had a musty look, although the cleaners had been in as usual. The vitality had gone.

'Mr Arnold won't mind if we use his room. It's more private.'

'Thank you, and thank you for the coffee.' Lyssa took a ham sandwich although she was not particularly fond of ham. It was merely to give her body energy, not to enjoy. 'Let's get down to it. Have you heard anything from Mr Arnold and how much do you know?'

Sybil poured out two coffees. 'I'm worried stiff. I haven't heard anything for over a fortnight now and nor has anyone else. It's so unlike him. I've checked with the other members of the board. Nothing like this has ever happened before. Mr Arnold is always reliable, phoning in every day wherever he is. He always wants to know exactly what's happening, to be on top of things even when he's thousands of miles away.'

'But this time, nothing? I haven't had a word from him nor has his sister, Sarah.'

'Do you think we should contact the police?' asked Sybil.

'I'm sure Jeth knows what he's doing and he might think we'd panicked if we reported him as missing. First we must make a lot more enquiries. Can you give me a list of everywhere he's travelled to in the last year with a contact name and number to call? That's just in case he changed his mind about where he was going. And also contacts for this Bangkok subsidiary and anything you can dig up about the firm.'

'They're called Thanit Losmen. It's a building firm. Losmen is the Thai word for bungalow. I'll do a print-out for you. Mr Arnold's itineraries are all on computer.' Sybil looked relieved to have something definite to do. 'And look at all this mail. It's piling up like an ant-hill.'

'This board of directors . . . can't any of them take over the work? Who are they? What do they do?'

'Most of the directors have special responsibilities. Accounts, the legal side, personnel, investments. I'll get you a list. Miss Arnold, of course, has a voting capacity. The directors look after those particular areas and Mr Arnold actually runs the businesses. I've responded to invitations and passed on requests for information, but I don't have the authority or the know-how to deal with the rest.'

'May I have a look at the mail?'

'Please do. There's nothing confidential.'

Lyssa sat behind the desk with her coffee and began reading through the huge stack of opened mail, tidily sorted, some with back-up files attached. It was as if Jeth was sitting beside her, telling her what to do. His voice was inside her head, suggesting what was appropriate action. She was used to organising things and automatically began sorting the mail into three piles, to answer, to delegate, to junk. The piles grew.

She picked up a pencil out of the desk organiser. It was neatly sharpened. It seemed second nature to begin scribbling a few words on the top of the letters and memos to be answered. 'No, sorry, not possible.' 'Go ahead, will confirm later.' 'Two months' sick leave with full pay.' 'Send more information on previous industrial disputes.' 'Delay take-over action.' 'Definitely not, reject offer.'

Her thoughts flew over the pages. They were mostly holding replies. This was the practical side of running a big business, not making visible millions in the bank, not playing with investments, but keeping Arnold Consolidated ticking over till the man himself returned. He would have wanted that.

Past tense. The shock caught her breath. Oh, no, why had she thought of him in the past tense? Was she beginning to think of him as dead? He would want the work moving, she meant. He was not dead.

She looked up with a stricken face. She couldn't wipe away the expression before composing herself. 'We should have a board meeting as soon as possible to give me some authority to act in Jeth's absence. I'm sure Sarah Arnold would propose that. I don't need or want power of attorney; the directors who look after the money side can continue to do that. But I think it would be helpful to keep things going until Mr Arnold returns. Could you please type up these replies using your own form of words? In your own time. Then if I'm given authority they can be posted.'

'I can set up a meeting for the day after tomorrow. Would that suit?'

'Great. Here's my home number and my mobile. We must phone Matthew and get him to come home. Perhaps he could take over. He's the natural –' Lyssa had been going to say 'natural heir' but changed it in time. 'He's a natural stand-in till his father returns.'

Sybil recognized the theatrical term. Jeth must have mentioned her work. 'But what about your own work, Miss Pasten? Mr Arnold told me about the *Inspector Dutton* series. I'm a big fan. You must be terribly busy.'

'We're just coming to the end of a new series. It would be a good time to take a few weeks' leave. And please call me Lyssa. No need for formality.'

'All right, Lyssa, that would be nice. A bit like that film, *Working Girl.*'

'Exactly,' Lyssa smiled. 'And you don't have to get me coffee though I do appreciate this snack lunch. Can you get me Matthew's number in New York? I'm not sure about the time difference.'

'It's five hours, so this would be a good time to phone. Please use Mr Arnold's phone. I'm so relieved that something positive is being done at last,' said Sybil, gathering up the papers.

'The main thing is to find Jeth,' said Lyssa looking out across the London sky-line. Canary Wharf and the Nat-West building towered over the Wren Church spires. 'He must be somewhere.'

Lyssa finished the last sandwich while Sybil used the computer, bringing Matthew's telephone numbers and faxes on to the screen. Lyssa was itching to use the computer. She had to learn. This was part of Jeth's world.

'Did Mr Arnold ever leave messages for you via the computer? It's possible to link up, isn't it?'

'Oh, yes, often. But that's the first thing I check every morning. Not a word.'

Lyssa was not looking forward to talking to

Matthew. They had hardly spoken since Matthew had broken off their engagement. She hoped he had got over the hurt by now and would discuss the situation in a rational manner. He had always been a kind young man at heart; surely that part of his character would not have changed irrevocably? She wanted to be friends with him.

'Mr Arnold is at a meeting,' came the nasal twang of his secretary, crackling over the transatlantic line.

'Would you please get him to call back his father's London office,' she said, giving the direct line number. 'And say it's urgent.'

While she waited, Lyssa phoned the studio and left a message saying she would not be back that afternoon. She began working through the long list of contacts Sybil had provided. Lyssa recognised some of the trips which Jeth had taken during her short but tortured time at Hollow House. Meeting Jeth had been a time-bomb waiting to go off. She had suffered in those weeks but it was nothing to how she felt now, not knowing where he was or what had happened.

She began to draw a line of blanks with her enquiries. A company in Amsterdam said he had missed a meeting fixed with them for the week before. It was most unlike him. Lyssa did not say Jeth was missing; she did not want rumours to start flying around or start a financial panic on the stock market.

The phone rang. It was Matthew. 'Sybil? Miss Ruston?' he asked cautiously.

'Hello, Matthew. It's not Sybil. It's Lyssa. I'm in Jeth's office at Arnold Place.'

There was a horrid pause. For one moment Lyssa thought he was going to slam down the phone.

'What the hell are you doing in my father's office?'

Like a politician being interviewed, Lyssa did not answer the direct question. 'Matthew, we need your help. Can you fly over? I don't want to say too much on the phone but it concerns your father. We're not sure where he is.'

'Why the hell should you know? It's none of your business. I want to speak to Miss Ruston.'

'There's a board meeting in two days' time. Could you make it?'

'A board meeting! I don't like the sound of this. What is this, a take-over?' His voice was caustic.

'Of course not. But it is important. The board will want you there.'

'Too right they will. Whatever you are up to, Lyssa, I'm going to stop you. Don't think you're going to get away with it.'

Lyssa contained her impatience, glad he couldn't see her expression. 'Aunt Sarah wants you to come over. The company needs your help. It's not me. Don't shoot the messenger. Everyone is worried stiff.'

She had no idea if Jeth had told Matthew about their brief day of engagement, the jump, the champagne. It had only lasted a few hours and seemed so long ago that it was like a dream. Lyssa wondered if she had imagined it. She had nothing to show for it although Bethany had the champagne corks which she had gone round collecting like the little hoarder she was.

'I shall make something with them for you, Mummy,' Bethany had said with more enthusiasm than skill. 'A fairy castle, perhaps.'

Hollow House was her castle, thought Lyssa. This was no worse than her knight riding off to the Crusades, away for months, years on end. Those eleventh-century women had survived with no news, no hope, keeping the castle fires burning till their single-minded men returned home. If they survived and came home.

Was this an even darker heaven? It was worse than loving Jeth and being subject, day after day, to his needles of bitterness; Jeth the powerful, critical, caustic, the empire-builder. Now, still loving Jeth and with him not here, no man to see, to be with, to breathe the same air, to feast her eyes upon . . . It was the purest hell.

Lyssa took in a deep, shuddering breath. She had to be strong, find the strength from somewhere, be the kind of person Jeth would love and admire. She had to be him, take on his mantle.

'I will, Jeth,' she said, imagining him right beside her. The image was so strong it was almost as if she could reach out and touch him again. 'I will do everything as you would want.'

Something was nagging her. Some chance remark that had passed by and yet now she realised she should have paid more attention to. But what was it? So much had happened in the last few weeks, her brain was on overload, malfunctioning, only able to cope with the here and now.

Lyssa went to the end-of-series party, although she did not feel she had anything to celebrate. Work well done, maybe. She wore the black skirt and velvet swirled jacket she had bought for her aborted engagement party. A party cancelled more swiftly than it had been arranged.

The party was held in the hospitality suite of the television company's headquarters in London. It was a mixture of class and proletariat; champagne and beer, wine and orange juice, sausages on sticks and smoked salmon sandwiches. Lyssa thought that if indeed there was reincarnation, she would come back to this life as a sandwich.

'Wow, gorgeous girl, where have you been hiding?' Gareth Warwick swung her off her feet in a bear hug. 'Why haven't I noticed you before?'

'Too busy acting the scarf,' said Lyssa, struggling out of his arms. He put her down. He didn't want to crease his Armani jacket.

'I wanted to thank you for all the fabulous locations you discovered,' he said with a smile of insincere sincerity. 'Without you, Lyssa, what would *Inspector Dutton* do?'

'Solve a different crime,' Lyssa suggested lightly. 'So what are you planning to do next, Gareth?'

'A holiday first, somewhere warm. Then a spell on the boards. It's difficult for me to get another part in a TV show because I'm typecast now. I can't suddenly become a vet or a priest.'

'People only see you as Inspector Larry Dutton. That's the price of fame, isn't it?'

'The theatre is the alternative. The punters will show up at a theatre, curious to see Inspector Dutton in the flesh, and hopefully realise that I can do something else, play another part.' He took another glass of champagne from a passing waiter. 'I hear you're going on to great things.'

'Nothing is settled yet,' said Lyssa, feeling a theatrical frisson of bad luck to even talk about it. 'There's a big remake in the pipeline after the success of *Pride and Prejudice*. I'm being considered for part of the production team.'

'Turn up looking like a million-dollar baby and the job will be yours. Who could resist you? I know I can't.'

Lyssa managed to sidetrack the smitten Gareth and joined a larger group. There she could merge into the general talk and stand and listen rather than talk. Her head was spinning from the champagne. She looked around for some orange juice before going home.

It was some time after eight before Lyssa could get away to pick Bethany up from Maggie's flat. Bethany rushed to Lyssa, hugging her legs.

'We've been making biscuits,' said Bethany.

'So I can see,' said Lyssa, brushing flour off her daughter's face.

'I made some for you.'

'Wonderful. I'll eat them tonight when we get home.' Lyssa smiled, knew Bethany's biscuits would need dunking. They had probably been pounded and rolled into near extinction. 'Thank you for looking Bethany, as always. I'm sorry I was late.' She pushed Bethany's arms into her anorak. 'What would I do without you?'

'I'm glad it was a party for once and not your everlasting work search. You should get out more. It would do you good.'

'But I'm always out,' Lyssa laughed.

'You should have more fun. Meet some nice man now that the boy wonder has taken himself off to the States.'

'Are there any nice men?' Lyssa said. 'I think both of them have been snapped up.'

'Tut, tut. That sounds like a bitter woman.'

'Not really. A little disillusioned perhaps but still happy, healthy and getting wiser.'

Lyssa was getting Bethany ready for bed when there was a sharp knock at the front door. She peered through the peephole, trying to make sense of the distorted image. A middle-aged man in a grey suit stood there, rocking on his heels. She half opened the door on the chain. 'Hello?'

'Sorry to disturb you, Mrs Pasten. Couldn't get you all day . . . out a lot, are you?'

She was getting practised at not answering questions. 'What do you want?'

'I'm from the council.' He waved an identity pass at her. 'I take it you've read the notification I put through the door earlier today.'

'I'm sorry but I haven't had time to read anything. I'm busy putting my daughter to bed.'

'Read the notice, madam, and you'll be getting her up again pretty fast. Do you mind if I come in and then I can explain the situation to you.'

Lyssa rifled through the post, found an official-looking brown envelope and tore it open. It was a notice to quit the flat.

'Structural faults,' said the man from the council. 'If you allow me in, I'll show you where.' He sounded as if he enjoyed his job.

He went straight through to Bethany's bedroom. Lyssa had not noticed anything during the redecoration but then she had been pre-occupied, using the painting and papering as therapy. But her eyes cleared now. Two big cracks had appeared along an outside corner of the room, near the ceiling.

'They go right up this side of the block,' said the official cheerfully. 'The whole block may have to be pulled down but of course we'll have to see what we can do in the way of repairs.'

'Pulled down? When?'

'Maybe straight away if the block is deemed dangerous. Before it falls down, and we don't want that, do we? Have you got anywhere you and your daughter can go? Of course, the council will try to rehouse you but you can imagine the problem. It may have to be a bed-and-breakfast.'

Lyssa shuddered. 'When do we have to go?'

'Most of the tenants went today. Didn't you notice how quiet it was? That's why I've come round because you weren't in. If I were you, I'd go tonight. I wouldn't risk a child's life.'

'Thank you for coming. I'm sure you'd like to go home now. I'll take your warning seriously.'

It *was* quiet. She had not noticed it before. No lift doors clanging, other people's television sound, the mega-watts of Walkmans pulverizing the grounds.

Lyssa began to pull down her travel bags from the top of the wardrobe. She piled in clothes for herself and Bethany.

'Are the flats going to fall down?' asked Bethany, who had been all ears.

'No, they're not going to fall down. But the engineers are a bit worried about some cracks so we have to leave the flat while they do some repair work.'

'I'm packing Pudding and all my toys!'

'That's good. Take everything that you might want for a few weeks. Use this bag.'

Lyssa took a last look round the flat. It had been their home for so many anxious years. She would come back later, if it was still standing, to remove some of her furniture and put it in store, although there was little she really cared about. The little flat had been a refuge, a haven, comforted her through a lot of heartache and hassle. But it was time to move on.

She looked at the ugly cracks which had already severed an elephant and a giraffe. The room felt unsafe. Outside, the floor of London stretched into inky blackness, carpeted with residential lights and sulphur road lamps and winking suburban trains. She remembered how the building swayed in the wind and grabbed a few more of Bethany's favourite things. She was growing so fast, it didn't really matter what clothes they left behind.

'It's very late, isn't it, Mummy? Am I staying up late?'

'Very late.'

'What about school tomorrow, Mummy? Aren't I going to school any more?'

'We may have to find you a new school. Don't worry. We'll work something out.'

Lyssa had a lot to work out. She was definitely taking a month's leave. There was holiday time owing, but it wasn't going to be a holiday. She would search the world for Jeth, keeping his empire ticking over, be waiting for his return. Only a few lucky women met a soulmate and he was hers.

'Where are we going?' Bethany asked.

'To Hollow House, of course. Aunt Sarah will have us.'

There was only one place to go. It was the natural decision. It was where they belonged.

CHAPTER 13

Matthew was standing, feet astride, in his father's office like some smouldering Goliath. He was wearing an American suit with heavy shoulder-padding and a tie which made Lyssa wince. She watched his body language. He looked at her as if she were something dragged up from the river bed by the Thames police. She didn't like it.

'Hello, Matthew,' she said pleasantly. 'Thank you for coming over at such short notice.'

'I had to cancel several important meetings. And I wouldn't have come if Sybil hadn't assured me it was necessary.'

'You've spoken to Sybil?'

'Of course. I called her. You don't think I was going to trust anything you might say?'

It was a verbal slap in the face. And it was Jeth's initial distrust and dislike all over again. Surely she wasn't having to go through this again? But there was one major difference. She was not in love with Matthew any more. His remarks would merely irritate and she would put on an antiseptic salve to stop herself scratching.

'I'm glad Sybil has been able to fill you in,' said Lyssa, ignoring his insinuation. 'You can understand that there are decisions to be made so that when Jeth returns, the damage has been limited.'

'Where is he?'

'I don't know. I wish I did.'

'It looks as if you have already made a lot of decisions,' he said stiffly. 'What's this about going through the mail?'

'Would you likc to do it? Another pile has arrived this morning. You are more than welcome to deal with it.'

He began pacing the carpet. 'I don't usually go to board meetings,' he growled. 'So why now?'

He really was thick. Lyssa wondered if he was putting on an act or if he truly did not understand the gravity of the situation.

'These are different circumstances and I think the board should co-opt you as a temporary measure till Jeth returns. I have no ambition to go on the board. I just want the authority to deal with day-to-day work and I believe Aunt Sarah will be proposing that motion.'

Matthew looked somewhat mollified. His body

had slightly thickened around the waist; no doubt the good life in America, hospitality and parties every night.

'Unless you'd like to stay in England and run the business as you are perfectly entitled to do,' Lyssa went on. She strolled over to the window and stared out. This was an afternoon for being very strong.

'No, no,' he said hastily. 'Impossible, out of the question. Oh, no, I've got far too many commitments in NY. It's just beginning to take off. Wrong time to quit.'

'Yes, I do understand,' said Lyssa smoothly, although she was well aware from Jeth's records that the NY office had been in existence several years and run efficiently by a man called Hank Jefferson. He was still Matthew's immediate boss. 'You sound pretty tied up.'

'I think it would be best if you and Sybil acted as caretakers this end with me keeping an overall eye on things.'

'Exactly,' Lyssa agreed placidly.

'But where is my father? Did he leave a note, some explanation? He can't just disappear.'

'He has. Ah, I think the other members of the board have arrived. Perhaps you'd like to go in. I'll stay out here for the decision.'

Aunt Sarah had travelled up from Sludbury

with Lyssa for the meeting. She hated London and the only consolation was a quick invasion of the department stores to buy things for Bethany. Apparently Hollow House was completely unequipped to look after the welfare of one small five-year-old.

'I want to get an ice-cream maker,' Sarah had said in the car. 'And one of those shapes for freezing ice lollies.'

'Bethany can live without ice lollies.'

'I want to make them with real fruit juice, not water and sugar and colouring. And she needs wellington boots for wet days.'

'Shouldn't we buy those with Bethany along with us? She'll need to try them on.'

'Heavens no, I'll guess the size. We can always fill them with socks.'

Lyssa waited in Jeth's office while the board meeting was in progress. It was the headmistress syndrome all over again. Lyssa had once been caught smoking in the school grounds and it had been in the days when that was a cardinal sin. She had never forgotten the lecture she got from the headmistress and she had never smoked again.

She idled through Jeth's appointments diary, taken unawares by the sight of his bold handwriting; Sybil's neater script was quite different. There were comments in the margins. She always thought marginal thoughts revealed a lot about the writer.

Television scripts were full of marginal thoughts.

Jeth's comments were cryptic, wry, funny, resigned. She turned to the day of their jump, their last day together. Jeth had written in the name of the airfield, the time of arrival and in brackets was her name.

(Lyssa), he'd written. And beside her name was the tiniest mark. She could not make out what it was.

Her mind jetted back to that day, jumping from the plane together, held firmly in his arms, the magic of the free fall, the floating down to earth, knowing Jeth was safe and close by. What had he said then? Something about being in the Marines?

She knew she was overtired. Her brain was not working well. She had to pull herself together, be strong, if she was going to work well.

Matthew came out of the meeting, stony-faced. He walked right past Lyssa without a word. But that was what Lyssa expected. Sybil followed with her arms full of files. She winked at Lyssa, which was reassuring.

Aunt Sarah stayed talking to the other members of the board. Lyssa could hear their voices, muted and serious.

'That was a good idea, coming to that meeting,' she said when she joined Lyssa. 'Perhaps I ought to attend more often. Well, you're in, my dear, and welcomed. We need a young and level head like yours. You've permission to do everything necessary to keep Consolidated afloat and the other members of the board have pledged to help you in every way. But the main worry in everyone's minds is, where is Jeth and what has happened to him?'

Aunt Sarah had aged in the last week. Whereas she had always seemed scatty but robust, now her skin was beginning to hang on her and there were shadows under her eyes from poor sleeping. At least the arrival of Bethany was diverting some of the anxiety. But she had begun to dread more news of Jeth, being told he was dead.

'We also decided that it was time that the police were informed. They can make worldwide enquiries, which is something we can't do.'

'I agree,' said Lyssa with relief. 'Would you like me to do it?'

'Oh, yes, you speak to them as his intended wife. Remember the party and all the champagne? That was real. And anyway, I can't talk to the police. I'd get all the facts into a muddle.'

Lyssa left Aunt Sarah shopping at the Army and Navy Store in Victoria Street while she went to the modern Scotland Yard building close by. The police officer she saw was attentive and helpful and took a long statement from her, including details of the enquiries she had made with other overseas contacts.

'I suppose you've searched the house and grounds?' he added. 'Lots of missing people are actually found not far from home.'

Lyssa's colour blanched. She gripped the strap of her bag, nails digging into her skin. She suddenly saw Jeth face-down in the pool, floating . . .

'Sorry, miss. But I had to ask.'

'We'll make a thorough search of the grounds and the house but I'm sure he's not there. If he'd been shut in anywhere, he would have managed to get out somehow. He's that kind of man. Resourceful and very strong. That's why all this is so strange, so unbelievable.'

'We'll get in touch with you as soon as we have any information.'

'Thank you. I hope you soon have some good news.'

Lyssa stood outside on the pavement, letting the noise and clamour of the traffic swirl round her. She wanted more than good news; she wanted Jeth back, beside her, holding her close, kissing her till she couldn't breathe, setting her soul on fire. She was so cold without him, so cold and dreadfully lonely. She could not imagine life without him, not long years. How would she manage?

She shook herself back to earth, back to Bethany, Aunt Sarah, everyone who now depended on her. This was what she had to do, become the mesh of steel on which everyone would cling. She turned wary, afternoon eyes on the world again.

It was still strange waking in Hollow House and knowing this was now her home. Lyssa turned over and stared out of the window at the morning tangle of branches. She had become claustrophobic about drawing curtains and could not bear to have them closed in her bedroom, as if she needed to be instantly in touch with reality when she woke.

Bethany came in, carefully carrying a cup of tea with both hands. She put it down on the bedside table, letting out a long breath. Then she climbed into bed and snuggled up.

'There was a nice lady came and stood by my bed in the night,' said Bethany.

'A nice lady?' said Lyssa, not really listening.

'Yes, she was in a blue-flowered summer dress and she smiled a lot.'

'It must have been a dream,' said Lyssa, stroking the child's soft hair, smelling the cleanness of the bed-time shampoo. 'Or your guardian angel.'

'My garden angel,' said Bethany satisfied. 'That's who she was. Do you think she'll come again?'

'I expect so.'

It was even stranger using Jeth's parking space in the underground car park below Arnold Place. Her battered BMW looked the oldest car there. Perhaps Amos would give it a wash and shine at the weekend; it needed something in this elite company. Sybil had given her keys and tokens for everything: a key to work the car barrier, a key for the lift, a key to the office suite, a key to the private bathroom. Lyssa had refused the key to the safe.

'I don't want that, nor shall I need it,' she said. 'The financial side is not my remit.'

'The board said you were to be paid expenses,' said Sybil, sounding determined. 'They didn't want you running out of petrol or your battery going flat.'

Lyssa slid her a sidelong glance. Did Sybil know about her not being able to start her car after the station halt filming? Surely not? No, she was imagining Jeth talking about her, mentioning the dawn invasion of Hollow House, because she wanted him to have that kind of madness. But that would not have been his way. He would have kept her close to his heart.

Matthew was waiting in reception, looking peeved, face pinched. 'They didn't give *me* a key,' he said.

'You said you were going back to the States,' said Lyssa, walking past him into Jeth's lift. They rode up in silence.

'Well, I'm not going now until next week. I met some people I used to know . . .' He paused, implying that he knew them before he became involved with her. 'They've invited me down to their place in Dorset for the weekend. They've got horses, promised me a ride.'

'I didn't know you could ride.'

'Lots of things you don't know about me.'

Again the cutting hint of a former life which was none of her business. Lyssa shrugged it off. He was being childish but if he was still feeling hurt, this was the armour he was wearing.

'I'd like to use the phone . . . in private,' he added stiffly.

'Of course,' said Lyssa. 'I've got to see Sybil. And there's no need to use that silly tone of voice with me. You could try to talk normally. And sneering does you no favours.'

'My God, woman, you can apologise immediately,' he said, almost choking on his words. 'You may have wormed your way into my father's business and Aunt Sarah's favour but you don't pull the wool over my eyes. I know you for what you are . . . a scheming, loose-living –'

'That's enough!' sid Lyssa sharply. 'When are you going to grow up? I don't have to listen to this childish nonsense. You are either unbelievably naïve or you have a callous disregard for any point of view but your own. Wow, Jeth really knew how to blow your thin veneer of civilized manners.'

'Jeth?'

'When he told you that André and I never actually made it to our wedding day. Another wedding dress I never wore.' She said it without expression but it still hurt. Now it looked as if the same would happen again. Jeth had been taken from her life as surely as André had been wiped out. 'He must have known that you wouldn't be able to take it.'

'Jeth didn't tell me.' Matthew looked at her blankly. 'Whatever made you think that?'

'He knew.' She still believed it must have been him.

'Oh? Did he? He never mentioned it.'

Lyssa absorbed this new information, forward-scrolling a different scenario. She had blamed Jeth without thinking. It had led to another of their furious confrontations, rocking the boat, in this very office. They had wasted so much time fighting when they could have been loving instead.

'So who did tell you? How did you find out?'

'Your boss told me. Greg Wilson. Remember, I made a couple of calls to him the day Hollow House got flooded? He was singing your praises, saying how wonderful you were and how you had coped on your own for so long. It didn't mean anything at first.'

'So, nothing out of the ordinary.'

'But I was curious. I remembered you never wore a wedding ring. How you never talked about your husband. So I phoned him again, and asked him right out when he meant. I was, of course, shocked and horrified. I couldn't believe that you hadn't told me; that I had to learn about it from some weirdo television director of an inferior two-bit detective programme. It made me look such a fool.'

'Only in your own eyes,' said Lyssa simply. She wasn't going to argue with him. He was past listening anyway. It was firmly in his head that she had wronged him in some way and nothing would change that or his opinions. 'Make your calls. I'm busy.'

Sybil greeted Lyssa with a thin laugh and a wave of her hand at another pile of mail. 'Mr Arnold sure creates a lot of work even when he isn't around. Did you go to the police?'

'Yes, I went to Scotland Yard yesterday, right

after the meeting. It's all on their computer network now. At least they have worldwide contacts. Something must come up soon.'

'Perhaps his plane came down in some jungle and he's thrashing his way through the undergrowth to civilization. Sorry, that was supposed to be a joke.'

'He wasn't on any plane.'

'Perhaps that's what he wanted you to think, or wanted someone else to think. Suppose he travelled in another name?'

It clicked.

'The airline clerk said that: was I sure Arnold was the name he travelled under? I thought nothing of it at the time, but supposing, for some reason that we know nothing about, he used a different name? He would have to have another passport.'

'Not too difficult. There must be ways.'

'Needle in a haystack,' said Lyssa, more to herself. 'How am I going to discover if he used a different name? You are sure he was going to see this firm, Thanit Losmen?'

'I was sure. I was a hundred per cent sure. Anything Mr Arnold did was always rock-solid, but now, well, anything goes.'

Lyssa picked up the day's mail. 'Perhaps we'd better start on this. I've arranged to see each of the board members in turn today. I thought perhaps I should get to know them better and see how they can help me.'

The morning went in a flash. Lyssa went to the main office cafeteria for lunch. There was a directors' dining room but it was little used. Lyssa wanted to sit with the staff and talk to them. She stood in line to be served even though Sybil said she could go to the head of the queue.

'And be lynched instead of lunched?' Lyssa smiled. 'No, thank you. I'll take my turn.'

For once she was almost hungry. Since Jeth's disappearance she had hardly eaten and knew she had lost weight from the looseness of her waist-bands. But the lasagne looked and smelt good. The top was oozing cheese, glossily yellow and baked with a swirling pattern of brown lusciousness. She could never resist toasted cheese. She also took a fruit salad and yogurt and was surprised how little she paid. Subsidized, obviously.

Strangely, she was warmed by the thought as well as the food. Jeth had been . . . was a good man. He took care of his employees. She had already discovered that in several ways. She wanted to be the same, to carry on in the same vein . . .

'I'm working here till Mr Arnold comes back,' she heard herself saying to some question. 'It's only temporary.'

People were curious about her and she answered their questions as truthfully as she could.

'Yes, we are going to be married. But no ring yet . . .' she laughed, wavng a ringless hand. 'That's the modern way, isn't it?'

'Yes, I have a daughter, Bethany. She's five, going on fourteen. I'll bring her in one day. She's a poppet. You'll love her.'

'No, come straight to me. I'm here to deal with problems. Don't go through the system. It's quicker if you just knock on the door.'

'You are called an A1 success,' said Sybil a few hours later. 'Lunch in the cafeteria was exactly right.'

'Well, this A1 success wants to go home now,' said Lyssa, stretching an aching back. 'Bethany is probably driving Aunt Sarah up the wall. I have to make arrangements for a new school.'

'The board said you were to have expenses, remember? I've just processed the first cheque.'

Sybil handed over a sealed envelope. Lyssa did not want any money, she wanted to work for love. But love didn't buy petrol. She nodded her thanks and stuffed the envelope into her bag. Later she was to find that it was a cheque for a thousand pounds.

Bethany was standing in the porch, hopping about, waiting for her return. Lyssa put her BMW in the barn, alongside Jeth's Mercedes, and walked back to the house. He had not driven it to Heathrow that morning but had hired a car. That was unusual. Why hadn't it struck her before?

'It's lovely not having to go to school,' said Bethany. 'I've just played all day.'

'Don't you bank on no school forever. That's my first priority tomorrow morning. I hear that there's a good one in the village. Somewhere that will teach you the three R's.'

'I didn't know there were three R's. I thought there was only one, you know, P Q R S T. Do you know that my panda has gone?' said Bethany indignantly, as if she had never ignored him for weeks. 'He's run away.'

'That's a shame. Perhaps he's just gone on walkabout.'

'But he can't walk,' said Bethany, suddenly rational.

The problem of a missing panda went out of her mind. Lyssa had more than enough to cope with. She talked to Sarah, checked that there was nothing from the police, dozed on the sofa half watching the news, then became suddenly tired beyond hope. It was a crushing kind of tiredness. She was burrowing in a dark corridor of trees, searching for Jeth. His name was never more than a second away from her lips.

When she dreamed, Jeth was always very close. It was as if he was talking inside her head. Sometimes she would ride on layers of brilliance, smiling at some secret memory, sailing into ocean sleep with Jeth so close she could almost feel his touch on her skin. She could smell freshly ironed shirt, his washed hair. He was always at her elbow.

When she awoke, there were fresh tears on her cheeks. Yet she never cried now. There was not time.

Lyssa heaved herself off the sofa, drank her cold tea and wandered into the kitchen. Sarah was making supper for Bethany and Lyssa was consumed with guilt.

'I should be doing that.'

'Go and have a swim. It'll wake you up. I'm making a huge pizza. I've no idea how it'll turn out as I've never made one before but your daughter tells me that no one can live without eating a pizza. Pepperoni, onions, tomato puree, cheese – anything else?'

Lyssa glared at Bethany. 'You're bullying Aunt Sarah, you little pest. Back off.'

'Pudding likes pizza.'

'Pudding will end up in the lake.'

Bethany screamed round the kitchen, clutching her bear. 'No, Mummy, don't put him in the lake . . .'

Lyssa clutched her frantic daughter, laughing. 'Only teasing, sweetheart. Only teasing.'

Bethany clung to her legs. 'Jeth isn't in the lake, is he? I heard someone say today that they were going to drag up the lake.'

'That dratted delivery boy,' said Sarah in a low voice. 'He's a mischief-maker.'

Lyssa rocked her daughter closely, stroking her hair and comforting her. 'He's just a silly boy, saying silly things to frighten you. Why would Jeth be in the lake? You know how well he can swim. If he'd fallen in the lake, he'd be able to swim to the bank and climb out, now wouldn't he?'

Bethany nodded, reassured. 'He'd climb out on to the bunk.'

'Bank. Yes, Jeth would climb out. Now tell Aunt Sarah what else has to go on a pizza before she puts it in the oven.'

There were still remnants of light as Lyssa walked over to the stable, swinging her swimsuit. She didn't really feel like a swim, knowing it would only bring back vivid memories of Jeth. But it might do her good, shake off this awful feeling of despair.

She was only half thinking as she went into the entrance of the stables, and instead of taking the first door which led through the fitness room to the pool, she went down the corridor which she thought might take her straight to the pool. The door at the end was locked. It was a perfectly ordinary modern, cream-painted door, in tune with the rest of the complex.

Just as she turned away she spotted a glimpse of brass on the ledge above the door. The number of people who kept their spare keys in a similar place. She would have to tell J– the name caught on her breath.

Shocked, she reached up and took down the key, meaning to return it to Sarah. Instead she found herself putting it in the lock and turning it. The door swung open to a single flight of stairs. Of course this would lead to rooms over the old stable block.

The walls were painted the same cream colour, and on the stairs was a pleasant pale blue carpet. Funny for a stable block. Lyssa went up the stairs. 'Hello,' she called out. 'Anybody there?'

There was no answer.

At the top was a big room with nice teak furniture, a television set, plants and flowers. On the table were spilt painting things and a half-finished picture of a horse. It was a weird-looking horse with lots of spiky green grass and a blazing blue sky splashed on the paper and the table.

Next was a neat, functional bathroom and a neat,

functional kitchen, but, strangely, there were locks on the oven door, the microwave and the refrigerator door. The cutlery drawer also had a lock on it. Lyssa went back to the bathroom, noting now the scattered bath toys and the lock on the bathroom cabinet.

There were two bedrooms. Lyssa paused, hating herself, with her hand on the first door. But it was also locked. Lyssa did not know what she was doing here, but she could not make herself stop.

'Hello?' she said again. 'Anyone at home?'

She was getting a strange feeling, as if she was stepping into another world.

The other bedroom door opened at a touch. At first sight it looked like a very untidy toy shop. There were cuddly toys everywhere and a doll's house with its tiny furniture strewn all over the carpet, and opened Noddy books, pages scribbled on. More crayoned pictures of horses were pinned on the walls. The bed had a pretty cover with sprigs of blue forget-me-knots – and in the middle of the bed, wearing a slightly smug look, sat Bethany's panda.

CHAPTER 14

Lyssa said nothing the next morning. There never seemed to be the right moment. Bethany was a bundle of excitement at the thought of going to a new school.

'We are only going to see if we can enrol you. There may not be room. There may be a waiting list.'

'I'll wait,' said Bethany obligingly.

Miss Reed, the headmistress, a tall, thin woman with frayed hair, whom Lyssa had already spoken to over the telephone, was also obliging. She welcomed Lyssa and Bethany into the school hall. The children had mats out and were doing gymnastic exercises in time to music.

'As you can see, we are a very small school. Sludbury is not exactly in the throes of a population explosion. Bethany can start right away. Today, if you like. If I don't increase my number of pupils, they'll close me down.'

'That's wonderful,' said Lyssa.

'You haven't any more children, have you?' Miss Reed asked hopefully.

'Sorry, not yet. I can't help you out. I'll be able to bring Bethany in the mornings but I'll have to make other arrangements for fetching her as I work in London.'

'No problem. We can deliver Bethany back to Hollow House on the school minibus. I'm afraid there has to be a small charge.'

Lyssa opened her bag. 'I'll pay the cost now, in advance.'

Miss Reed took Bethany's hand and led her towards her new classroom. 'First the other children will want to know all about your other home in London, Bethany. They are always curious. Will you be able to tell them anything interesting?'

'Oh, yes,' said Bethany cheerfully. 'It's falling down. The walls and the bricks might kill people if the flats fall out all over the street.'

'Well, I can see you're going to be very popular,' said Miss Reed. 'A real horror story to start the morning's lessons. Come along in.'

Lyssa waited outside for Miss Reed to reappear in the corridor. This was the part she always hated, having to explain about Bethany's illness.

'I have to tell you something more, about Bethany's health. I mentioned that she has a very rare and unusual condition called Reflex Anoxic Seizure and you said you'd be happy to take her on, but I must be sure you know what you and your school are letting yourselves in for. It's nothing to be frightened of but we do have to make sure Bethany doesn't get bumped or pushed. She won't be able to do gymnastics or play games like rounders in case she gets knocked or falls over. Any bump leaves her looking as if she's clinically dead until she starts to breathe again and comes round. I can bring you some medical notes about it.'

'What does one do if it happens?' Miss Reed had been listening intently.

'Put her in the recovery position, keep her warm, and make sure she doesn't knock herself again. There is sometimes a very short fit before she comes round. Does this make any difference to your having Bethany? Perhaps you won't want her now?'

'No, of course it doesn't.' Miss Reed had absorbed the information with interest. 'How absolutely fascinating. We've never had a pupil with a reflex syndrome before. I'm sure this is the right school for Bethany – we're so small that we can keep an eye on her all the time. And Dr Carrington is her doctor?'

'Yes, but he's never seen her in this condition. It's very frightening when it happens.'

'Half the children here have got asthma. An asthma attack is very frightening too. Don't you worry, we'll cope. Pity about the gymnastics. Mr Arnold bought us all the new equipment for the hall.'

'That sounds like him,' said Lyssa.

'He paid for the minibus too.'

Lyssa smiled at the headmistress, but most of the smile was for Jeth. 'I know that Bethany is going to be very happy here.'

The day went quickly at Arnold Place. As she took his calls, Lyssa was amazed at the variety of industries that Jeth was involved in. She could trace the development, from a very small industrial beginning in importing paper pulp and tar. It had taken years of work to build up Consolidated.

That evening she knew she must find a moment to ask Sarah about the flat over the stables. 'You can tell me to mind my own business,' said Lyssa as they were having their after-supper coffee in the sitting-room. 'But I want to know something else.'

Sarah did not watch so much television now that she had company in the evenings. Bethany was already in bed, exhausted from the first day at her new school. She had enjoyed it and settled in so fast, it might have been her only school.

'What do you want now? The key to the wine

cellar? We could drink the vintage claret Jeth put down for special occasions.'

'So we'll save it for those special occasions. Remember I had a swim last night,' Lyssa began again.

'Something wrong with the pool?'

Lyssa shook her head, taking the pins out of her hair and shaking it loose. 'No, the plant seems to be working fine. There was a door which I had never noticed before, at the far end of the passage. Funny how you can miss something obvious. A cream-painted door.'

Sarah put the cup back on to the saucer with exaggerated carefulness as if not daring to rattle it. She did not look at Lyssa but picked up her knitting, frowned, and started counting stitches. Lyssa knew this was a fake exercise, as Aunt Sarah never counted stitches; she always guessed.

'I opened the door and went upstairs,' Lyssa went on. 'I know I shouldn't have done and it was very wrong of me. Why didn't you tell me that there were tenants over there in the stable flat? And a small child, judging by all the toys and paintings and mess.'

'I don't know why I didn't tell you,' said Sarah casually, giving up her count. 'One forgets all about them living over there. And I rarely see them. Jeth deals with everything.'

Lyssa did not mention Bethany's panda sitting in the middle of the bed. 'He knows that the flat is occupied?'

'Oh, yes, of course, Lyssa. It was his idea in the first place.' Sarah was being deliberately more vague than usual.

'It brings in some sort of income, I suppose,' said Lyssa, hardly seeing Jeth in need of the money. He was not the rural landlord type. 'If they ever move out, perhaps Bethany and I could rent it.'

'What nonsense you talk. Your home is here in Hollow House. Besides, I don't think they'll ever move out.'

'Why haven't I seen anyone coming or going? Does the child go to the village school? I could offer them a lift in the mornings.'

'I've no idea. They keep very much to themselves. Oh, dear, this coffee's gone cold. I think I'll make a fresh pot.'

Sarah escaped any more awkward questions by hurrying into the kitchen with the pot in her hand. Lyssa heard her talking to Emily and then the back door slammed. The draught made the apricot flames in the fireplace flicker and sway like Eastern dancers. Lyssa knew Sarah was keeping something from her. But it didn't matter. She would keep her eyes open and one day she would meet the elusive tenants. A wayward child who had to have everything locked up would not be too hard to spot. Obviously the child did not stray into Hollow House – or did it? Had that been how the panda had changed homes? But perhaps Bethany had left the panda in the garden, since it was always in trouble and being punished by isolation.

Greg Wilson phoned towards the end of the next week.

'I thought you were supposed to be taking holiday time,' he barked. 'This is an Arnold Consolidated Industries number you've given me. Doing a bit of moonlighting?'

'It is a holiday compared to working for your mad outfit,' said Lyssa crisply. She was sitting in Jeth's office, behind his desk, touching the arm of his chair, the edge of the mahogany top. There had been no news from the police. She had phoned every day but they had drawn a blank. Somehow she did not believe them.

'Hundreds of people go missing every day,' the officer said as if that were some sort of consolation. 'They walk out of their lives without a backward glance. No note, no money, not even a change of socks.'

They weren't telling her the truth.

'Jeth wasn't like that. We had just got engaged, the day before. We were going to be married.'

'With all due respect, miss, perhaps that was the reason. Men get cold feet, y'know. Sometimes disappearing is the only way out of a difficult situation.'

'It wasn't a difficult situation,' said Lyssa, getting angry. 'And in no way is Jeth a weak man. If he'd changed his mind, he wouldn't have been afraid to say so, straight to my face.'

'Lyssa, I don't believe you're listening to a word I'm saying,' said Greg, breaking into her thoughts by raising his voice. 'This meeting tomorrow, can you make it? It's damned important.'

'Sorry, Greg, what was that again?'

'Well, your mind is certainly taking a day off,' he growled. 'I hope it sharpens up pretty quick or you won't get the job.'

Lyssa had amost forgotten the *Mansfield Park* project. Arnold Consolidated Industries had filled and taken over her working life and she had barely given the new production a thought. Once it would have been the most important project on her mind. Now she could barely remember who she was supposed to be seeing at this meeting.

'Run through it again, please, Greg.'

'They want to know what ideas you have for Sir Thomas Bertram's mansion. A few place-names, this stately home, that stately home. And Fanny Price's humble beginnings. And the two sisters-in-law, Mrs Norris and Mrs Price, must have quite different homes. Read the book, for God's sake. Lyssa, you know the form. Has falling in love completely wiped out your professional pride?'

'It *has* been a difficult time. The block of flats where I live was suddenly declared unsafe. Structural faults. Great cracks going up one corner of the block. It could fall down any minute. Bethany and I were turned out in the middle of the night at a moment's notice. I think that's enough to raise the stress-levels in any family.'

'Sorry about that, Lyssa. I didn't know. Where are you living now?'

'At Hollow House. I've put Bethany in the village school. We're gradually getting sorted out.'

'And your working at Arnold House is paying the rent.'

'I like the way you put it. So tactful.'

'Well, tell that Mr Arnold you only eat so much toast and you already have a career in television. *Mansfield Park* could lead to big things, Lyssa. It's going to be a classy production. Don't blow this chance.'

'I won't,' Lyssa promised, warmed by the concern in his voice. Greg usually treated his crew in a crude fashion with no sympathy or consideration. If a member of the cast broke a leg, he'd say, 'Get a grip on yourself, mate. We'll do head and shoulder shots.'

She took the book to bed plus a copy of the National Trust Guide to properties and a large-size road atlas of Great Britain. It saved time and money if locations were near each other. Producers liked saving time and money. A stately home in Northumberland, a park in Wales and a village in North Cornwall spelt hours on the road and huge running costs.

The village would be hard to find. One that could easily be taken back in time: street furniture removed, signs taken down, shops converted to a different century. Perhaps Sarah would like to come with her. A day or two touring rural England might take her mind off Jeth's absence. She was looking drawn and felt down.

Lyssa's responsibilities seemed to be growing by the minute. Big house, big business, older sister-in-law, fragile daughter, mysterious tenants and staff at Hollow House and Arnold Place. Somehow she had to fit in the preparations for *Mansfield Park*, *if* she got the job. She had to find the strength for making it all work smoothly. This might be why she had met Jeth, fallen in love with him with such devastating consequences; perhaps it was part of some cosmic plan that she should now shoulder his life's burdens.

'I'll do it, Jeth Arnold, wherever you are, dammit,' she said aloud. She could not believe Jeth was dead. Surely she would know, have some inner feeling? They had been so close. Something would have shrivelled and died inside her, she was certain; instead she had this great conviction that he was alive. He could not have walked out of her life. If he had changed his mind, he would have said so.

She rang her police contact number again the next morning. She tried not to pester the officers, but there were some times when she could not stop herself.

'I'm sorry, Miss Pasten, but we have no further news for you. Has anything occurred at your end?'

'No, I've heard nothing.'

'And you checked Mr Arnold's passport, bank accounts etc?'

'I can't find his passport although it could be in the office safe which only Jeth can open. There have been no withdrawals from his bank account, though I understand he kept currency and traveller's cheques at the ready. Of course, there could be other bank accounts of which I have no knowledge.'

'Our enquiries with the Fraud Squad have –' She heard muffled voices in the background. 'No, sorry, miss. Wrong connection.'

'I didn't know there was any connection.'

There was a slight pause and someone else in the room said something she did not catch. 'Different enquiry altogether, Miss Pasten. Of course Mr Arnold had no connection with the Fraud Squad. Now what about relatives? Have you spoken to them all?'

Lyssa stifled her impatience. 'There are only two, his sister and his son. He lives with his sister and I've seen his son recently.' They were stringing her along. She'd had gone through all this before. If only she had some influential contacts, people in the Foreign Office or Diplomatic Service, people who would pull strings, find out the truth. 'Thank you, anyway.'

'Sarah, I have a wonderful idea,' said Lyssa when she got home that evening. 'Two ideas actually. Will you come with me when I go location-hunting at the weekend? I need to find a village which we can transform and a second opinion will be very helpful.'

'Yes, I'd love that,' said Sarah brightening. 'I'll do a packed lunch for us all.'

'No way! We'll eat out. You spend your life in this kitchen. I've never seen anyone do so much cooking. I'm not sure how you'll take the second suggestion . . . I thought, why don't you have a course of refresher driving lessons? We all forget things over the years. Think what a marvellous surprise it would be for Jeth when he comes home . . .'

Sarah clapped her hands. 'What a surprise that would be! Jeth has always made fun of my driving. I'd like to knock him out with my brilliant parking!'

'There's a woman driving instructor . . .'

'I know. I've seen her around.'

'We'll look in the *Yellow Pages* this evening and phone around. They'll have answering machines.'

Lyssa was pleased that her two ideas had gone down so well. Sarah needed something to take her mind off the aching emptiness in the house.

Sarah went upstairs. Her feet were beginning to drag these days. Her energy was flagging. She came back later with a small black leather box. The leather was scratched and worn, the gold-key-patterned edge almost invisible. 'And I have a surprise for you, Lyssa. I've often thought it was a great shame that Jeth didn't have . . . hasn't had . . . time to get round to buying you an engagement ring before . . .' Her voice faltered, tenses mixed. She was not sure what she believed or thought had happened to her brother. 'I know he was going to, said . . .'

Lyssa put her hand over the older woman's. Her skin was dry and papery, veined with age. 'Don't upset yourself, Sarah. We have to believe that he will come back.'

'That's right,' said Sarah, making a great effort. 'Well, till Jeth can get round to buying you a ring himself, I'd be very happy if you would wear this one, not as an engagement ring of course, but as a sort of betrothal to the family. It's very old, Edwardian I think. It used to be my maternal grandmother's and she left it to me.'

For one dreadful moment Lyssa thought she was going to be presented with the same ring that Matthew had produced. But no, the ring in the box was a dainty circle of garnets in a worn gold setting.

'It's an eternity ring, given to her on an anniversary. I've never been able to wear it, unfortunately; it's much too small for me. My fingers are so broad.'

Lyssa slipped it on. It could have been made for her. 'I love it,' she said simply. 'I'll always wear it. Thank you.' She leaned over and kissed the older woman on the cheek. Even when Jeth returned, she would not want another ring. His grandmother's ring was her link to the family. Jeth could buy the wedding ring to forge the link forever.

Bethany appeared in the doorway, clutching an inky exercise book. 'I've been doing my homework.' She showed off rows of letters and words she had copied out.

'Well done,' Lyssa said. 'But enough work, sweetheart. How about a walk before bed? It's still light. We could take Bill and Ben. I'd like some fresh air after London's pollution.'

'Me, too,' said Bethany. 'I'd like some new air too after plushon.'

The garden at Hollow House was awash with spring. Young leaf and young blossom struggled for life together with glittering energy. The straight blades grew over the damage of the flood. The South Downs in the distance were smudged with new growth as the winter landscape gave up its long rest. The evening sun pink streaked the clouds, sinking with rosy slowness over the horizon.

'It'll have to be a short walk,' said Lyssa. 'We'll go along the bridle path and back to the house the other way.'

The woodland reaching back from either side of the drive was a mass of bluebells and late dwarf daffodils. Under the trees was a thick carpet of blue. Bill and Ben tore in among them, breaking the slender stalks.

'What a shame,' said Lyssa. 'They don't bloom the next year if they are picked or broken.'

'But that lady is picking them. She was picking them when I came home on the school bus.'

Lyssa saw a figure in the distance darting between the trees, bending down now and then. It was a young woman, thin and stick-like, wearing an unsuitable summer dress and no coat. She was barefoot and her hair hung loose and straight over her face. Her arms were full of bluebells, their long white stems already limp and dying.

'I think we should tell that young lady that she has picked enough. There won't be any left to grow for next year.'

'Let's catch her up, Mummy.'

Lyssa hurried after Bethany. Bill and Ben thought it was a game and joined in the chase. The girl was like a will-o'-the-wisp, darting in and out of trees, running up and down banks, exclaiming at the joy of so many bluebells carpeted under her feet. But she could not hold what she had already picked and was dropping them everywhere.

Bethany was quicker. She ran up to the girl and began to gather up the heavy blooms lying on the ground. 'You're dropping all your flowers.'

The girl swung round. It was a shock. The face was lined and middle-aged. The long brown hair was streaked with grey, the eyes pale and empty. She wore a short-sleeved floral print dress with a full skirt and belt. She had stuck flowers in her hair and they hung over her ears in tipsy array.

'These are your flowers,' said Bethany, holding out a bunch.

'Thank you,' said the woman. She held out her hands for them, dropping those which she had been already holding.

Bethany suppressed a sigh and began retrieving them. 'You've picked too many to carry,' she said.

'They're so pretty,' said the woman. 'And they smell like a bottle of scent.'

Lyssa rearranged her thoughts as she collected up the bluebells. She held out her hand. 'Hello, I'm Lyssa Pasten and this is my daughter, Bethany. We're staying at Hollow House at the moment.'

'Hello.' The woman hesitated, then put her hand into Lyssa's. It was icy-cold.

'Heavens, you are cold. You need a coat.'

'I forgot. Sorry.'

This was a forty-five-year-old child, not at ease, expecting to be told off. Lyssa was not quite sure what to do. She could not just leave the woman to wander around, especially as it would soon be dark.

Emily was running along the drive towards them, her wholesome face red with the exertion. She had a cardigan in her hands. She went straight over to the bluebell woman and began putting her arms in the sleeves, flipping out the long hair.

'You'll catch your death, you will,' said Emily, buttoning up the front. 'And look at all these flowers. Dying already. What are we going to do with them all?'

Bethany watched with interest the sight of a grown woman being dressed by Emily.

'Come along now, your tea's ready. We've got sardines on toast. That's your favourite, isn't it?'

Bethany pulled a face. She hated those little fish with their white spines and stringy red bits.

'Emily?' All the questions needing to be asked were in Lyssa's voice.

'It's my sister's day off, so I'm helping out. Nancy's my sister. But this one's a right handful, as you can see. You need eyes in the back of your head.'

Lyssa nodded. 'Good luck with the sardines. Come on, Bethany. Bill and Ben are nearly out of sight. They know the way better than we do.'

The sky was awash with twilight by the time they returned to Hollow House. Bethany was yawning, clinging to her mother's hand, ready for bed after another exciting day. Lyssa took Bethany upstairs and she was soon in bed, washed and pyjama-clad in minutes. Her eyes were closing and her lashes fluttered into sleep.

Sarah was waiting downstairs. Lyssa had a feeling she would be. The older woman was dithering, a glass of pale sherry in her hand. It was not often Sarah resorted to alcohol for support.

'Ah,' said Lyssa. 'I think I'm about to hear something I may not like.'

'Emily tells me that you have met Priscilla in the lane.' She took a quick sip of sherry, tidying away some wisps of hair.

'Priscilla? I presume Priscilla and Nancy are the tenants in the stable flat?'

'Yes, that's right, my dear. And I think I should tell you something else. And you mustn't think hard of him. He only did what he thought would be best.'

'Think hard of him? Who are you talking about?'

'Jeth. Jeth thought Priscilla would be happier in the stable flat, a little home for her, somewhere safe and comfortable, being looked after by Nancy.'

Lyssa stared out of the window as the dark clouds obliterated the last of the day's sun. A silver shiver seemed to wash across the window pane.

'What are you trying to tell me?'

'Oh, Lyssa, I don't know how to say this. It's so difficult. But . . . Priscilla is Jeth's wife. She's Matthew's mother.'

CHAPTER 15

It seemed that everything around Lyssa had changed except the room. How could the well-polished furniture, the beamed walls, the French chiming clock, the flower arrangements by Aunt Sarah, all stay the same while for Lyssa the whole world was changing?

His wife. Strange how she had always felt there was something that no one was telling her. The odd broken sentence, the secretive glances, the unexpected silences. It added up to a conspiracy. They had probably never dreamed that the past would catch up with today and strand *her* on a sandbank of despair. She ceased to know where she ended and the pain began. Perhaps Jeth *had* walked out on her. He had a wife, a wife living only a few hundred yards away from his home, a woman who could not be hidden for ever.

'Tell me about Priscilla,' Lyssa asked in a low

voice, holding on to the table behind her for support. 'I have to know.'

'Of course you'll want to know about her. It was a very brief love affair when Jeth was twenty and Priscilla was twenty-one. She was extremely pretty and delicate and feminine; quite unlike any of the smart young women Jeth had been going around with. She didn't go out to work but stayed at home, helping her mother.'

'Was she already . . . as she is now?'

'I don't know. I'm sure there were indications of instability which only her parents knew about. It was covered up, I'm sure. Then suddenly things happened very quickly. In those days, you didn't live together first, or even sleep together. One minute they were engaged and the next minute they were married. I think her parents pushed it along and Jeth was too much of a gentleman to back out, and too busy working to be actually aware of how he was being manipulated. And he loved her, I'm sure. She was a very pretty and gentle creature.'

'Manipulated? No one could influence Jeth . . .'

'He was twenty. Rather reserved as far as women were concerned. Priscilla made a beautiful bride, pale and fragile, like a doll. If Jeth suspected anything, he never said. He was always loyal; besides, he was working night and day building Arnold Consilidated into the great company it is now. Perhaps if he had been at home more, the actual breakdown might have been averted.'

'So she had a breakdown?' Lyssa felt like a dummy, repeating whatever Sarah said. It was like a dream. Perhaps she would wake up and find it was time to get up and go to work.

'She was very ill during her pregnancy. In fact, she went home to be looked after by her mother. Jeth coped on his own. Then she had Matthew and the trauma of the birth was the last straw. She went into a severe post-natal depression, didn't and couldn't look after the baby, couldn't look after herself. Dear God, the poor soul was a mess.'

'And Jeth?'

'He blamed himself, of course. For getting her pregnant, for working so hard, for leaving her with her parents. He thought he should have recognised that she could never cope with motherhood.'

'That's ridiculous. He was barely old enough to know anything,' Lyssa exclaimed. 'Her parents should have warned him of the risk.'

'They were an elderly couple. I think they were glad to get Priscilla off their hands before they died. To see her settled with a man who would take care of her. And they did die, unfortunately, quite soon after Matthew was born, and Priscilla couldn't cope with that either.'

'And Jeth . . .?' Lyssa sank on to a chair, her legs going weak as if the blood had stopped pumping through her veins. She knew she ought to be pierced with jealousy but she wasn't. A frost was forming on her heart.

'Priscilla was in a psychiatric ward for several years. I had young Matthew to bring up and Jeth employed a nanny to help me. A nice little Swiss girl, I recall. Jeth paid for everything, shouldered the whole burden, paid for the best treatment for Priscilla in a private nursing home. I doubt if Priscilla remembers that Matthew exists, even today. It's very sad. Then, when we moved back to Hollow House, Jeth saw the potential of the stable block and persuaded the authorities to release Priscilla back into his care so that she could have a more normal life, not institutionalised. She's quite harmless, just plays all day. Nancy, that's Emily's sister, lives there and looks after her. Priscilla's mind has retreated back into childhood. Your Bethany is streets ahead of her in development.'

Lyssa absorbed the information, any happiness she'd once had draining out of her.

'And are they still married?'

Lyssa had to ask. The room was suddenly

stifling her; it was as if the ceiling was pressing on her head. She trembled with the possibility of knowing. Had Jeth been deceiving her? His child-wife was being kept by him, housed by him, hidden by him, while he took his pleasures elsewhere it seemed. But would he have asked her marry him if he wasn't free?

'Yes, they're still married. I'm sorry, Lyssa. He never got round to having it dissolved.' Sarah poured herself another sherry. The golden liquid slopped over the rim and ran over her fingers. 'There was never any divorce. "I will get one when I meet someone," he used to say at first. But he never met anyone and so it all got forgotten.'

'He *forgot* to get divorced?' Lyssa could not keep the incredulity bitterness out of her voice.

'But you were that someone, Lyssa, believe me. During the champagne party, when Bethany was collecting all the corks for her castle, he told me. He was full of plans; I'd never seen him so happy.'

'And he said something about a divorce?' Lyssa prompted.

'Oh, yes, quite definitely. "Time for that quick divorce," he said, "one of those instant things." He even asked me to ring his solicitors on the Monday morning.'

'And did you?'

Sarah's face began to fray at the edges. She started to rub at the pleats in her skirt. Her wrists looked brittle enough to break from the friction. She was painting silence, and Lyssa saw all the colours of a rainbow leaking into a grey puddle.

'*You* forgot?'

Sarah was trapped. 'I don't know what made me forget. Perhaps subconsciously I thought Jeth ought to be there to do it and he'd be back soon anyway. I don't like phoning people like solicitors. I wouldn't know what to say, especially about a divorce.'

Lyssa let it wash over her. She was not engaged to Jeth. She couldn't marry him until he got a divorce. If he got a divorce. If he came back. Who was she? Just some woman who happened to be around. Mathew's ex. Bethany's mother. Greg's assistant . . .

She could not survive the rest of the evening even though she knew Sarah was not at fault in any way. She got up from the chair.

'Sarah, I think I'll have a bath and an early night. My head's aching. It's been a heavy day.'

'I'm so sorry, my dear. I'm sorry you had to find out this way.'

'Don't worry, Sarah. I had to know some time. Now I've got Jeth's wife to look after as well.'

'What? I don't understand . . .'

'I'm just talking nonsense. Goodnight, Sarah.'
'Goodnight, my dear.'

Sleep evaded her even though she was bone-weary. How could Jeth have left the matter of a divorce sit on a side burner for years? Yet part of her understood. At the time it had not been important, but rebuilding Arnold Consolidated had been important. He hadn't needed to be free. And probably part of him still felt guilt over Priscilla's fate. If he'd abandoned that tortured soul would he still be the man Lyssa had fallen in love with? She thought not. Priscilla's sad fate must have helped make him the caring man he was today.

And even when *she'd* appeared in his life like a ticking bomb, blowing his carefully structured world to pieces, she had been introduced as Matthew's fiancée. And when that engagement had fallen apart, she and Jeth had gone their separate ways. She had blamed him for telling Matthew about André's death before their wedding.

The day of the jump had been their one perfect day together. The timescale of events had not exactly given Jeth the opportunity to put his life in order.

So Lyssa decided she would do it for him.

Having made that decision, she fell asleep, to dream of the last time he had held her close and she had taken his body into hers. Part of his being still lingered inside her, somehow absorbed into her tissue, and would be with her till the day she died. Wherever she went, to work, to play, here at Hollow House, he was with her, even if only in spirit. They had a bond stronger than friendship or love. And even if they could not be together again, they would never part.

But their love had been such a rare delight, she could not believe it was over forever.

First thing on Monday she phoned his solicitors, Rathbone & Jenkins. Their address and number had been on the list of personal contacts Sybil had given her. She had not needed to approach them before, thinking they would not know anything about Jeth's disappearance. She was put straight through to Mr Rathbone.

'This is Lyssa Pasten, Mr Arnold's assistant. Mr Arnold left an instruction with his sister, Sarah Arnold, just before he left the country. Unfortunately she forgot to contact you.'

'Ah, yes,' said Mr Rathbone. 'Was it about the divorce proceedings?'

Lyssa took the words into her heart and wrapped them round the hurt that existed there. Emotional band-aid for the walking wounded.

'Yes, it was. Had he already mentioned it to you?' Say yes, please say yes, she implored him silently.

'He came to see me about several things before his last trip. I understood he was anxious to regularise his present circumstances and he asked me to find out the legal position when the wife is unfortunately unable to make any decisions for herself. And I have, of course, begun this work. I had expected to hear from Mr Arnold himself by now. Of course, I knew he was going away as he came to collect his passport from his security box.'

'His passport? Isn't that rather odd?' Lyssa heard herself saying, though her mind was singing a different tune. 'I thought his passport was kept with his personal things at home or in the office.'

Mr Rathbone did not respond to this. Suddenly Lyssa knew the answer. It was a different passport. For some reason Jeth had two, keeping one securely locked away. God, what could this mean? Why should he need a second one in safe keeping at his solicitors? She did not let her voice tell Mr Rathbone that she had guessed.

'Please ask Mr Arnold to come in when he returns,' the man said. 'The other document he asked me to prepare is ready for his signature. And, of course, it's not legal until he signs it.'

Lyssa gave up. She did not ask: what document? 'I don't think I need to take up any more of your time, Mr Rathbone. You've been very helpful. I'll pass your messages on to Miss Arnold and Matthew.'

Mr Rathbone cleared his throat. 'Have you spoken to Hank Jefferson?'

'Hank Jefferson?' Where had she heard that name before. Ah yes, he was Matthew's boss in the New York office. 'No, I haven't. Why? Do you think I should?'

The solicitor maintained a discreet silence.

There was just time to call Hank Jefferson before she went to the *Mansfield Park* production meeting. She was wearing her grey pinstriped trouser suit with a scarlet blouse. She'd pinned her hair up the back of her head in a pleat, the way Jeth liked it, and fastened it with a scarlet and gold clip. She felt very much the executive.

Love was geared on memory now. Every morning she stroked his coat which hung in the downstairs cloakroom. When she passed the carver chair in the dining room, she ran her hand along the back as if it still held his imprint. She had no photograph of Jeth but did not need one. She would not fall on her knees before a photograph, but she had taken a black cashmere scarf from the Mercedes and wore it and imagined the fabric was Jeth touching her skin. Sometimes she thought she was losing her grip on her sanity.

Hope only surfaced on some days and now the gaps were getting longer.

She felt a weariness pinning her legs to the polished floor of the office, yet her heart was flying free. Jeth had wanted to marry her, planned to marry her. He had been serious and contacted Mr Rathbone before that eventful parachute jump about the legal situation with Priscilla. He loved her! Was she going to have to live the rest of her life clinging to that knowledge? She knew there could be no other man for her. He was her one special man. The man she would die for.

If life was to be more years of celibacy, what did it matter? Loving him was the source of her joy and her energy. She would run his business, his home, his family, take care of Priscilla as he would want. She would submerge her sexual energy into living a life for both of them.

She had not cried once since Jeth disappeared. But now she sat at his vast desk and let the hot tears run down her cheeks. She drew great gulping gasps of breath, making small primeval, animal sounds of anguish, plucking damply at the papers on the desk, weeping till she thought her heart would break. The windows seemed to shiver with the intensity of her despair; the air misted up, became luminous with washed tears.

She picked at the skin of her hands, wanting to tear her flesh apart, to let blood flow, to die so that she could be with him.

'Jeth . . . Jeth . . .' she started to gasp, shoulders racked. 'Where . . . are you?'

Warm arms went round her and for one startled moment she thought it was Jeth. But the body was feminine, giving and softly rounded, and she knew it was Sybil holding her in a sisterhood of pain.

'I wondered when you would began to cry,' said Sybil softly. 'You're always so strong and so calm. It wasn't natural.'

'I'm sorry . . . sorry,' Lyssa gulped. 'I can't help it. I love him so. I want him back. I can't live without him. It isn't fair.'

'Life isn't fair,' said Sybil, suddenly older, suddenly wiser. 'We have to take whatever it dishes out to us. But you will go on living, because that's what Mr Arnold . . . Jeth would have wanted. You and your little daughter. Did you know that Jeth thought she was wonderful?'

'I think he was just marrying me to gain a daughter,' Lyssa laughed through her tears. She searched for a handkerchief and blew her nose. 'She *is* a nice little girl, very funny, gets her words mixed up.'

'Then you have to live for her . . .'

'I've done all this before,' Lyssa whispered,

thinking of André's death and the lonely years bringing Bethany up on her own.

'Then you can do it again. But this time you have the Arnold money and influence and status to help you. The board are most impressed with your work. You're going to be running Consolidated before you know it.'

'I've got my own career . . .'

'You can do it. Why not do both? Remember that lots of people will help you. Start delegating. Bethany is growing up and before you know it she will be a young lady going to a secondary school in Chichester or Worthing.'

Lyssa could not bear the thought of time passing so quickly. She felt worry lines breaking out on her forehead. Sybil was only trying to help but the air in the office was thickened and dulled with the future she predicted. Sybil did not think that Jeth was coming back.

Lyssa tried to look at her watch but her eyes would not focus. 'I have a production meeting in an hour's time . . .'

'I'll let you tidy up, then.'

'Thank you, Sybil. You've been . . . very kind.'

'Isn't that what friends are for?'

But before she joined the *Mansfield Park* production meeting, Lyssa put through a call to Hank

Jefferson. She was not sure why she was phoning him. Matthew should be back there soon. There was nothing amiss with the New York operation.

'Hank Jefferson? I hope this is a good time. I'm Lyssa Pasten, calling from Consolidated in London.'

'Nice to speak to you, Miss Pasten. Go right ahead. How can I help you?' His voice was the usual transatlantic drawl, friendly.

'I wanted to thank you for letting Matthew come over at such short notice,' said Lyssa, knowing this sounded weak. 'We needed him at a board meeting.'

'Is anything wrong?'

He was quick. How else could he have picked up her distress from her voice and the simple fact of her phoning?

'No . . . yes. Well, nothing's wrong actually. I was told that you've known Jeth Arnold for some years, although I'm not sure if you are going to be able to help me. Do you know him well?'

'We were in the Marines together.' Lyssa again heard Jeth's voice telling her he was in the Marines. 'It was a great time. He was an outstanding officer. And he had a certain quality, the kind of man who inspired loyalty. He was frequently being seconded to special duties. I ribbed him about the SAS, though he never admitted anything. But I think he was sent on missions that were linked with that service.'

'The SAS? Do you think he could still have something to do with them?'

'Yes, he trained for two years when he was eighteen before he went into his father's firm. They never let go of people. Especially those that are good.'

'But it's years since he left the Marines, isn't it? Though he volunteered again during some emergency, didn't he? Was it the Falklands War? I'm a bit hazy about all this.'

'Does it make any difference? A good officer is always a good officer. Jeth has always kept things close to his chest. Is there some problem? Does this help you at all?'

Lyssa cradled the phone, wishing the man were in the room not thousands of miles away. She felt his strength coming over the wire. Someone very much like Jeth. 'Not really but thank you, and I'll send you an invitation to our wedding.' She tried to make her voice light-hearted.

'And I'll accept, Lyssa,' he said, a grin in his answer. 'Don't worry, Miss Pasten. He'll be back. I'd put a bet on it.' He hung up.

How did he know? Perhaps he was just guessing.

She checked her watch. She still had time to make a couple more calls before getting a taxi. It was taxis these days, not the crowded, strap-hanging Underground. The expenses cheque from Consolidated was intended to make life easier and that was how she was spending it. She called several airlines in alphabetical order, asking them to check passenger lists to Bangkok on the Monday that Jeth had left London. She felt sure he had gone abroad, or else why pick up a second passport from his solicitors?

Thai International Airlines was the last on her list. She only just had time to talk to them, knowing that running through an entire passenger list was a lengthy business.

'I'm calling from New Scotland Yard. WPC Dutton.' The lies slid easily off her tongue. 'I'm really sorry to ask you to do this, but it is important. I'm trying to track down the movements of some person who we believe has left the country with Bangkok the destination on a Monday, a month ago.' Lyssa gave the date. 'Could you run through your entire passenger list for that day and read it out to me?'

'Of course, Officer Dutton. One moment please.'

The computer flicked through to the right day, the right destination. The airline clerk began to read the names sing-song: 'Roberts, Deans, Craig, Williams, Chan, Puxley, Smith and Smith, Patpong, Li, Tang, Kai-Yin, Dunn, Miller, Pasten, Davies, Ho, Wan Chai . . .'

'Hold on a moment. What did you say? Did you say Pasten?'

Lyssa thought she had misheard. The air was silent and still, as if a bird had suddenly sung a flat note.

'One moment, please.' The clerk checked again. 'Yes, Pasten. P A S T E N.' She spelt the name.

'Do you have an initial or Christian name for that passenger?'

'Yes. L . . . Larry Pasten.'

It had to be Jeth. No one could exist who had her surname and the Christian name of the fictitious Inspector Dutton. Lyssa's heart volunteered an extra beat. Her breath caught in her throat. It was a message from Jeth. He had known she would start looking for him eventually and he had left a lifeline for her to follow. She grasped it firmly.

'And Mr Pasten flew to Bangkok on the Monday in question?'

'Yes, ma'am. I have the flight number recorded here. It was a perfectly normal flight.'

'And he showed?'

'Oh, yes.'

'And got off the plane, I suppose?' It sounded an idiotic question, stupid.

'No. Mr Pasten was in transit. He was booked

through to Denpasar, Bali. He would have had to wait at Bangkok for the connecting flight to Bali.'

'Could he have made a phone call while waiting for the connecting flight?'

'Unfortunately we had a major communications breakdown during that period. Our public telephones from the airport were out of action for several hours.'

'But he could have phoned from outside?'

'In transit passengers are not advised to leave the building. They could easily be caught in traffic and miss their connecting flight. The traffic in Bangkok is heavy.'

The adrenalin pumped hope into Lyssa's body. Her spirit soared. Jeth, Jeth, so this is where you are . . . Indonesia. 'Thank you, thank you,' she said, trying to sound like a bored WPC on routine enquiries. 'You've been very helpful.'

Lyssa put the phone down and whooped into the air. She didn't care who heard her. Jeth was alive, somewhere. He had flown to Bali, using her name. That must mean something, and God only knew the reason why. But she was going to find out.

A hundred things rushed into her mind. She rang through to Sybil. The secretary came hurrying in, alerted by the excitement in Lyssa's voice.

'I've tracked him down,' Lyssa said triumphantly. 'He flew to Bali under a different name. And I'm going too, now. I'm going to find him. Will you book me a seat on the next possible flight, please? And find out if I'm supposed to get any jabs, although there may not be time for them. My tetanus is up to date.'

'Bali? Why there? Our subsidiary is in Bangkok. We have no contacts with Bali.' Sybil was suddenly suspicious. 'Was he going on holiday? But he never takes holidays. It's not like him at all.'

Lyssa was sure. She didn't have any doubts. 'This wasn't a holiday. There's some other feeling about the arrangements, the secrecy. I've no idea what it is but I'm going to find out. You are going to have to hold the fort while I'm gone.'

'With pleasure,' said Sybil, her plain face alight, suddenly transformed. 'Just find Mr Arnold. Bring him back. In one piece, please.'

A little torch-carrying here, thought Lyssa. It was not unusual among secretaries who liked their boss. And Jeth was the perfect man for distant adoration. But it was no threat to her and Jeth was not the kind to take advantage. He was all hers. She knew that, and hugged the thought close to her body.

CHAPTER 16

Mansfield Park was going to be a classic interpretation with a huge budget and a starry cast that sounded like an Olivier Award nomination list. Lyssa's head was spinning after the production briefing. The whole concept was exciting and Lyssa longed to be part of the team.

Six months ago she would have been over the moon, busting her bra strap to get the job. Now she had more than her name in the credits to think about. She could find sumptuous locations and organize the paperwork; already the ideas were foaming over the edge of her mind. But when? When could she do all this and still carry out her commitments to Hollow House and Consolidated? She felt like Scarlett O'Hara when she found that Tara had been devastated by the Civil War and it was up to her to rebuild the estate. Lyssa would hardly be digging up turnips in the fields with her bare hands but she knew she was going to be close to Scarlett in sheer exhaustion.

And the timing? There was some hope for Lyssa here. The early days of a big production moved slowly. If she kept her nerve and was always one step ahead of the producer she might land the job. They had liked her initial ideas. Haddon Hall, Knole Park, Waddesdon Manor . . . the village of Lempton, near Aylesbury. But Lyssa knew she could do better than that. They had all been used before. She had to get her mind into the right gear and stun her prospective bosses with her originality.

But she was going to find Jeth first. She would catch that plane even if she stayed up all night. She could work on the flight, send back an outline of her plans.

Ideas were spinning through her mind. This was what she really wanted to do; not run a big business that she hardly understood. She was only doing it for Jeth's sake.

But the hope of finding him was surging like a Spring tide. Larry Pasten! Why hadn't she gone down that route before . . . the name had been there to find. Jeth had left it as a clue for her, relying on her to find it some time, knowing she would not allow him to disappear from her life.

Why had she been so slow? But Jeth would not

have visualised all the extra hassle of late . . . moving out of the flat, the discovery of Priscilla, the *Mansfield Park* job. Would he have guessed that she'd step into his shoes at Consolidated? No, he would not have thought it possible or within her capabilities. He imagined she was still trailing the Home Counties looking for lock-up garages and shops and cul-de-sacs.

She hardly knew what to tell Aunt Sarah and Bethany. If she said she was going on a wild-goose chase halfway across the world to a tropical island, it would alarm them more than reassure them.

Sarah could be trusted to look after Bethany. 'Jeth has flown to Bali,' she told Sarah when Bethany had gone to bed. 'I found the name he had used on the flight and it wasn't Jeth Arnold. And he used a different passport, though I've no idea why. But I don't want Bethany to know that I'm going to Bali. We've never been apart before for longer than overnight and she would fret.'

'We could say you are looking for locations in the North of England. She'd understand that. It's sort of true, even you if you actually go later.'

'Would you say that? Would you lie?'

'It's not a proper lie. We used to call it sandpapering when we were children. When are you going?'

'Sybil has got me a flight tomorrow morning, 11

a.m. on Thai Airlines. Thank goodness Bethany loves her new school. She won't be any trouble.'

'Amos will drive her to school. He's very good with my car so that's no worry. Bali . . . oh, dear, it's such a long way away. What on earth is Jeth doing there?'

Sarah's face was a confusion of relief and worry. She liked a plain, simple lifestyle with no complications.

'It's no distance these days, Sarah. And I'll be back in no time. With Jeth in tow.'

'Well, about time too. He's been away long enough. It's time he came home. And I'll have a strong word or two to say to him about not letting us know his whereabouts.'

'You'll be able to rehearse those lines while I'm gone. Get yourself word-perfect. And start those driving lessons right away.'

Suddenly the impossibility of her confidence overwhelmed her. Why was she going? It was a small island about the size of Surrey but where was she going to start looking? It was going to be a nightmare and she had no idea what she was going to do when she got there. She did not know whether to expect a modernised and sanitised island or somewhere still native and rural. Supposing Jeth didn't want to be found?

There was that guidebook in Jeth's study, pages

marked with scraps of paper. Were they pointers she could use? She would take it with her. Quickly she threw some clothes into a travel bag, cotton shirts, jeans and shorts, a swimsuit, just in case, and sun block factor 20. Her passport was up to date and Sybil had efficiently organised her a supply of traveller's cheques and US dollars.

'And you'll need this,' said Sarah, producing an insect repellent spray. 'They breed especially vicious mosquitoes for tourists.'

'How do you know?'

'I saw it on the telly. One of those glossy travel programmes.'

Lyssa managed to contact Matthew before she left. He was offhand and uninterested in her journey. She could hear him tapping on the phone with a ballpoint pen.

'Oh, really? Not another secret? How intriguing. He travelled under a different name, you say . . . you watch too much television. Oh, I forgot, you work in television. Rots the mind, you know.'

'Did you enjoy your horse-riding weekend with your old friends?' she countered, determined not to be riled by his sarcasm.

'Yes, it was very civilized. Delightful people. We went hunting with the the local hunt.'

'Very civilized,' said Lyssa. 'Ripping foxes to pieces.'

There was no point in talking to him. He was polarised in another world. Nothing she might say or do would get through to him. He had built a one-way glass wall around himself that filtered through only what he wanted to see. Lyssa was appalled that she had hurt him so much, but what could she have done to make it easier for him? She was not the type to beg his forgiveness and plead with him to go ahead and marry her. She shuddered at the thought of marrying Matthew now, of the intimate life she would have endured just to please him. It would have been a life sentence.

Lyssa went outside for some fresh air, pulling Aunt Sarah's shawl round her shoulders. She remembered Jeth arranging it around her that evening, making sure she was warm. She remembered how wonderful he had been, so tender and loving.

Priscilla was in the garden playing with Tipsy. She was wearing a short pinafore dress with a floral blouse, sandals, a thin cardigan over her shoulders. Her hair was tied up with straggling ribbons, as if she had done it herself.

'Hello, Priscilla,' said Lyssa, stooping to stroke the cat under the chin. 'Hello, Tipsy.'

'I like cats,' said Priscilla.

'So do I. She's very pretty. Also very lively.'

'She runs away from me sometimes.'

'Are you still painting horses?'

'Oh, no, I'm painting cats now.'

'That's nice. Where's Nancy? She's usually with you, isn't she?' Lyssa stood up and took the older woman's thin, dry hand. 'It's getting cold now, Priscilla. Shall we go back?'

'I came out by myself. I do that sometimes when I find the door open.' Priscilla began to laugh and swirl her skirt about like Bethany did at dancing class. 'It's such fun being in the garden.'

'But it's time you went home.'

'All right. Shall we take the little cat?'

'No, Tipsy belongs to my daughter, Bethany, over at Hollow House. You know, the little girl upstairs in bed. The girl with the panda.'

'Oh, yes. Is it all right about the panda?'

'Yes, you can keep the panda. Bethany has lots of toys. Perhaps you'd like to see them?'

'I'd like that. Tomorrow?'

'No, but soon, I promise. I'll talk to Nancy and Emily. We'll arrange something.'

Chutamat. That was the name painted on the nose of the Boeing 747 that flew Lyssa out to Bangkok. Already the strange-sounding announcements in Indonesian gave her the feeling of having left England a long way behind. The Royal Orchid Lounge had been an oasis of quiet, settling raw nerves with cups of Earl Grey tea and freshly squeezed orange juice floating with fruit flesh.

Lyssa read Jane Austen and waited for time to pass. A tiny-waisted Indonesian stewardess in an ankle-length royal blue, purple and gold striped skirt and tunic top called her personally to board. She wore a flower tucked into her smooth raven hair. It was all very exotic.

Lyssa was flying Royal Executive Class. She had no idea that Sybil had booked her first class until a clerk at Heathrow had directed her to an almost empty checking-in counter. It made her feel even more part of the solidarity of Consolidated.

It was extravagance that Lyssa could easily get used to. Hot towels and mango juice on arrival in the upstairs cabin; pale mauve towels in the toilet; Dior handcream, a goodie bag of toiletries for the flight. Bethany would adore the tiny toothbrush and tube of paste but Lyssa was keeping the miniature Gucci moisturiser for her shoulder-bag.

It was an eight-hour flight to Delhi. Already it was five hours since Lyssa had left Hollow House. She had not intended to wake Bethany before Amos took her to Sludbury to catch the the first train to London. But Bethany heard her leaving and became tearful and upset that Lyssa was going away.

'I'm going to meet Jeth,' Lyssa explained,

sandpapering. 'And remind him to come home. We miss him, don't we?'

'Why can't he remind himself to come home?' said Bethany, going babyish and sucking Pudding's ear. It was a bad sign but Lyssa was relying on the new school and Aunt Sarah's love and spoiling to cheer Bethany up while she was gone.

'Because he's busy,' was Lyssa's bland reply. 'He's a very busy man.'

'Pudding doesn't like you going away,' Bethany complained.

'Then you'll just have to look after him, won't you? And cheer him up.'

Four thousand and seventy miles to Delhi. Lyssa questioned her sanity at 33,000 feet and tried to read Austen. Yet she knew she was right. Jeth hadn't booked a flight in the name of Larry Pasten without good reason. Sybil had combed the records for why Jeth should go to Bali. He had no business contacts there. Bangkok was his Far Eastern contact.

'But he definitely booked through to Bali.'

'I'm sure he hasn't gone just to get a tan,' said Sybil wisely. 'It's only a small island. You'll find him all right. He'll stand out in any crowd.'

Lyssa was even less confident now that she was shut in a vast metal cylinder in a polka-dotted sky and no chance of getting off. She flipped through books on houses, villages, National Trust properties, but Great Britain didn't seem real any more. Her A5 notebook stayed empty. Fax what back? They were waiting for her ideas. Bali had moved on since that *South Pacific* musical and fax machines would be a way of life. Or would they? She knew nothing at all about the island.

If only Jeth were at her side instead of an empty seat. Jantana, the pretty stewardess, had suggested pulling out the centre arm-rest so that Lyssa could lie down. After only five hours of fitful sleep at Hollow House, it seemed a tempting idea.

A straight brandy put her to sleep in moments. When she awoke some time later, the cabin lights were out, blinds drawn and those who were still awake were watching a John Travolta film on a far screen.

She ducked under the screen and washed her face and hands in the barely turn-around loo; helped herself to handcream and Diorissimo eau de cologne, the noise of the engines throbbing in her ears.

It was midnight when they landed at Delhi, though her watch said seven forty-five. She had not enjoyed the computerised information on the screen detailing loss of altitude, wind speed, mph, temperature on the ground. Nor did she like the roar of the reverse thrust as they touched the runway.

The plane filled up with chattering Indians and Indonesians going home. She lost her spare seat on the flight to Bangkok.

Srinapha. That was the name of the A300 aircraft that flew Lyssa the 1858 miles from Bangkok to Denpasar, the capital of Bali. By now Lyssa was uncomfortably hot. She had shed her jacket and jersey, opened the top buttons of her check shirt. It was 86°F outside on the tarmac. The bus that ferried them to the plane was like an oven.

The observation floor at Bangkok airport had filled up in the transit time, busy and bustling as a bazaar, offering high-class duty-free cosmetics and perfume or junk souvenirs. Long-rooted trees were canonised in tubs, their dark glossy leaves casting some shade from the sun that streamed through acres of windows. Passengers without a Royal Orchid lounge to cosset them sprawled in heaps everywhere, trying to get some sleep.

Lyssa was starting to feel homesick. She had not been so far away from Bethany before. She could hardly count the odd location flight to Europe.

The plane took off smoothly. As she cradled a thin flute of champagne in her fingers, she looked down out of the cabin window. The smog over the city of Bangkok was a foul grey blanket.

* * *

Kuta was a shock to the system. It did not help Lyssa to recover from the earlier shock of discovering that her travel bag with all her worldly goods was still in Bangkok Airport. She was forced to fill in forms, standing in the boiling heat in twill trousers, long-sleeved shirt and laced-up boat shoes.

'So what am I supposed to do?' she complained to the airline clerk. 'I've no clothes, nothing.' It wasn't his fault but she wasn't feeling fair. She was being jostled by crowds of people, Chinese, Japanese, Indonesian, Indian. It was some kind of New Year Festival. Western faces were few.

'If you have insurance, you can shop,' he said.

She did not know that Ngurah Rai airport had been built on a seawards headland on the outskirts of the town of Kuta and paid the first price a taxi driver asked. She realised that she had been ripped off when he dropped her in Legian Street in less than five minutes.

'Nice shops,' he said, folding away the ten thousand rupiah note.

Nice shops. Legian Street was a narrow nightmare of blaring cars, bemos, minibuses, jeeps, taxies, motorbikes, bicycles, wandering dogs, street sellers and beggers. In moments she was besieged by the hawkers, spotting a new pale face. The high-rise pavements were twisting ankle-traps of uneven slates with broken slabs of concrete over the open sewer. Cases of rings, watches and jewellery were thrust under her nose. Waiters put menus into her hands; beggers, mostly mothers with small children, clutched at her trousers.

'You buy? You buy? Ten US dollars. Gimme your best price, lady.'

Lyssa tried to shake them off. She was dying of heat, clothes clinging to her skin, sweat dripping between her breasts, feet swelling till her shoes felt as if they weighed a ton.

It was impossible to walk in the road. The traffic was oblivious to pedestrians. Where were they all going? Round and round, it seemed. It was mostly one-way streets. She headed instinctively towards the beach, desperate for a cooling breeze.

But the beach was no better. Sarong-sellers, their goods piled on their heads, massage ladies, manicurists, hair-beaders, men selling lurid carvings, homed in on her like locusts. 'You want good luck today?' they clamoured. Knobbly hands kneaded her shoulders. Another grabbed her hand and exclaimed in horror at her nails. Another tried to start beading her hair.

'No, no, no,' she said, trying to stay polite.

'Yes, you name best price.'

By walking fast, Lyssa managed to escape to a

quieter area of the beach. People were walking on the wet grey sand, flying kites, playing ball games. A burnt-out funeral tower, a twisted and blackened heap of wood, stood on the edge of the beach. The blackened funeral cow effigy, under which the body had lain, had keeled over on to the sand. Lyssa shuddered, hoping the body was now ashes.

'No more funerals,' said a more fluent young hawker selling chopsticks. 'Air purification. One month only.'

Lyssa wished herself back in Hollow House. The cold and rain would be welcome compared to this humid heat. Her waistband was cutting into her flesh. How on earth would she find Jeth in this chaotic mass of people? She had never seen so many people. Somewhere she'd read that the population of Indonesia was the same as the population of the United States.

She bought a bottled Fanta at a beach bar and thought it worth the money to sit on a bamboo stool and watch a glorious sunset. The sky went from apricot to pink; unpolluted splashes of peach and crimson painted the sky in ever changing patterns of colour and size, clouds drifting like silken scarves in the breeze. The luminous beauty soothed her raw nerves.

Somehow she had to find a place to stay the night before it got too dark to find her way around

Kuta. There were hardly any street lights, only lights from the open shops and stalls.

'You got hotel?' asked the bar tender, reading her forlorn look accurately. 'You got room?'

She shook her head. 'Can you recommend a hotel?'

'Air-conditioned? Fan? Or home-stay?'

'Air-conditioned and fan.' She didn't like to think what home-stay meant. 'Somewhere near.'

'I know good place. Pool. Ida Beach Inn. My cousin will take you.'

A slim youth appeared. 'Follow,' he said imperiously.

Lyssa had no option. He led her through a labyrinth of back streets, down a rutted lane, and left her in a yard of banana and coconut trees. She gave him a dollar and he sped off. She peered through the foliage and found herself in a low-lit courtyard and saw that across a pool of water, swimming with fish, was a little wooden bridge leading to a reception desk with a smiling, dark-haired girl. She could have swooned with relief at the near normality.

The thatched-roofed bungalow she secured had woven mat walls, a rickety air-conditioning unit, a swirling ceiling fan and two low single beds each with a single clean white sheet. It looked like paradise.

The bathroom attached to the bungalow was outside. Completely outside. It had no outer walls, only a sloping thatched roof and some plants and palm trees for privacy. Lyssa did not care. She striped off her clothes and stood naked under the lukewarm shower among the quivering plants. The traffic noise was very distant. Only the drip-drip of the air-conditioning unit was going to disturb her sleep tonight.

CHAPTER 17

She awoke to hear little smooth-feathered brown birds singing their own song in the palm trees outside her room. For a moment the cheerful noise heartened her, and then she remembered the traffic and hawker chaos of the Kuta streets and wondered how she could face them again.

The day was already dripping with humidity. The heat hit her as she went outside to see if her washed pants had dried on the towel rail. They were still damp but she put them on just the same. She rolled up the sleeves of her shirt and the legs of her trousers, resisting a scissors job, then went barefoot to the main open-sided breakfast veranda from where she could hear the enticing clatter of plates and smell coffee.

Ida's garden oasis in the heart of Kuta was a surprise. Everywhere the frangipani blossomed and white petals fell to soften her tread on the stones. Coconut trees swayed in the wind. Banyan trees rustled an early morning song. The overflow from the pool ran over the stone wall falling into a pebbled channel. She recognised the helpful cousin as one of the sarong-clad young waiters serving at the bamboo tables. He grinned at her.

A young woman was walking round the grounds with a basket of offerings for the gods, little woven dishes made from banana leaves and filled with flowers, some rice, a biscuit and a stick of incense. She put them on the various shrines in the garden and sprinkled them with holy water.

A boy was decorating the ancient stone statues in the garden with flowers; red hibiscus flowers decorated a hideous frog, one in each ear like earrings; a buffalo and an elephant sported headdresses of flowers and skirts of the powerful black and white check material.

'Fruit, toast and tea,' she ordered, not knowing what to eat, and gave her room number. The fruit came cut into fretted fan shapes on a plate, melon, paw-paw, pineapple, banana. The highest-paid Savoy chef could not have done better.

The toast came served in a basket with packeted butter and jam. No plate. Well, so what? Baskets probably came before plates. She was hungry despite all the food on the plane then she realised that she had not eaten the previous evening. She looked at her watch. It was registering London time and she didn't want to know what time it really was.

She phoned the airport to tell them where she was staying. There was no news of her luggage. It was still in transit somewhere.

She spent the morning touring the concrete beach hotels that fronted the spoilt sea at Kuta. Then she took a bemos to Sanur, jostling on to the bus with a dozen other people, paying over her twenty pence in rupiah like a native born. The cousin had told her which colour bemos to pick up for Sanur. He was turning into her private tour guide.

She tried to explain that she was looking for someone, but that was beyond his grasp of English. He nodded and agreed 'Yes, yes,' but he didn't understand.

Sanur was different, with a long stretch of cleaned-up beach and painted spider boats in neat rows. The big hotels towered white and awesome, over-the-top luxury, ostentatious, breathing money, eating money, Westernised Bali. Not the real Bali. Once she might have enjoyed such a five-star hotel and complex, servants, piped music in the palatial reception area, computerized bills. The tariff said one hundred and fifty US dollars for one night. She was paying thirty.

But Ida's simplicity had converted her in one

night. Lyssa actually pitied the people staying in this sanitized version of Bali. They were missing so much. She liked her outdoor bathroom.

'Excuse me, I am looking for my friend. Male, this tall, very good-looking. Can you check if he is staying here or has stayed here in the last few weeks?'

She asked everywhere, suggesting both names. The desk clerks were polite, smiling in their colourful outfits, consulted their computers, shook their heads, gave her a glossy brochure.

She began to feel sick with disappointment, tired of wandering round in the heat, bought a cup of coffee and discovered that Bali's local ground coffee was the most delicious in the world. By now she was fighting off jet-lag, not knowing what time of day or night it was.

She took a crowded *bemos* back to Kuta, got lost trying to find Ida Beach Inn, but people were helpful with directions. Some even walked part of the way with her. She was discovering how to ignore the hawkers.

'*Tidak*,' she said, shaking her head.

Back at her bungalow, she could no longer ignore the pool but went swimming in her shirt and pants. The cool water was wonderful, rushing out from the monster's mouth and over the wall. Even the monster was decorated with flowers.

Tomorrow she would go shopping, buy, buy, buy like a lottery winner. The shirt clung to her figure but she had to dry it before she could go out.

She needed food now, ordered Indonesian *gado-gado* at Bamboo Corner, a tiny open-fronted café down a narrow side street recommended by the same cousin. This was lightly steamed vegetables with rice, tofu and boiled egg with a spicy peanut sauce. She had watermelon juice to cool down her burning mouth.

Then she began to tour the night-spots, and there were enough of those apparently. 'Cousin' appeared as guide. It was becoming a second career, but after an hour she told him to go.

A flashing neon sign said air-conditioning and videos. Lyssa was hot, so she went in. It was a cavernous disco for Australians and Pommies called Peanuts. It was crowded and low-lit, a cavern of rampant noise. The air was laden with cigarette smoke and pounding with Western dance music. She bought herself a bottled Coke from the long bar and took it to a seat in a far corner, feeling conspicuous on her own. She only planned to stay a short time, to cool off. If she closed her eyes, she would fall asleep. It was way past her London bed time.

A few men glanced at her. Then Lyssa realised why. She was the one burnished blonde among a race of dark-haired beauties. She was a rare sight. She felt that her red-gold hair was the only part of her that was truly awake. Her brain was cyber-spaced, losing its ability to concentrate.

Across the room a group of men were talking round a table littered with beer cans. They were just men, dark-faced, hunched, wearing similar short-sleeved shirts. But the build and bulk of one of the men drew her attention.

She blinked, surfing the hallucination, sipping the cold drink. The man flexed his shoulders and the pain of the so-familiar gesture was like a knife in her ribs.

She slid round in the seat to see the man's profile. The shock was a stunning blow. The same profile, the same strong nose, the firm chin despite the unshaven shadow of stubble. It was Jeth Arnold, holding a can of beer. There was no doubt.

No other man could look like him.

Lyssa watched him for a few minutes, soaking up the nearness of him, letting relief take its measure. He was alive and well. It could be no other than him. There was not one shred of doubt. How well she knew every inch of his skin, every bone in his face. Jeth was here, in Kuta, sitting not more than twenty yards away from her in a disco.

She knew what she had to do. It was like something she'd seen acted on television a dozen times. She stood up, loosened her hair from its butterfly clip and fingered it as it fell around her shoulders. She unfastened the buttons of her damp shirt and tied the ends under her bra so that there was plenty of cleavage and bare waist visible, keeping her eyes on him all the time in case he moved away.

She finished her drink. Her mouth was dry and burning. She began to walk, swaying over to him, hips moving seductively. One of the men looked up and the walk registered. She stood behind Jeth at the beer-laden table. She put her hands squarely on his shoulders and pressed herself against his broad back, feeling the muscles, lowering her face close to his cheek.

'Englishman want good time?' she whispered into his ear.

The shock went through his body like electricity. But he did not move. He was absorbing the impact.

'Lyssa take you to nice beach hotel, have very good time?' she went on in a low voice. The other men could not hear what she was saying but they could read the body language and were laughing. 'Lyssa very good for tired businessman. Plenty dollars? Give me your best price. Special massage.'

He knew who it was. Without moving his gaze from his companions, his hands came up and clamped on to hers. He knew her shape and her feel even if she was hot from the tropical atmosphere. The garnet eternity ring was new to him but he was feeling it, making guesses. Grandmother's?

His hands were every bit as familiar. The longer hair was brushing the curve of her breasts. The skin of his muscled neck smelt of Jeth. She pressed herself still further against him.

'How much?' he asked without looking. His handsome face was rigid. For his companions, this was a straightforward negotiation and they listened with interest. Only Lyssa heard the indecision hidden in his voice.

'Very expensive lady,' she whispered. 'But special price for you. Give you my best price. Promise.'

The other men began making suggestions and for a moment Lyssa panicked, but her trust in Jeth did not waver. He loved her, didn't he? He stood up suddenly, turned and their eyes met. It was an electrifying moment, like their first meeting at Hollow House all over again. She drank in his face, his dearness, his being alive and forgave him.

'Let's dance,' he growled, pulling her roughly onto the dance floor. He wrapped his arms round her, forcing her head against his shoulder, pressing his hand onto her lower spine, brushing the bare skin inside her damp waistband. Then he breathed out against her face.

'What the hell are you doing here?' he said.

He lowered his head so that she could speak against his ear. It was almost impossible for anyone to hear anything over the pounding disco music.

'I came to look for you, you bastard,' she said, looking straight into his glinting grey eyes. 'How could you leave me? Don't you have any idea what I've gone through?'

Touching her was rousing his body's awareness of her. He could hardly think. 'Dear God, I want to kiss you so much.'

'Then kiss me.'

His mouth came down on hers, harsh and demanding and drank in all the lost days. She clung to him, moulding her body like wax against him. The dark disco cavern disappeared and they floated in a space of their own making. He was alive, loved her, wanted her, and even though it was still a total mystery what he was doing in Bali and why he had disappeared, Lyssa didn't care.

'Don't leave me now,' she said, keeping close to him. 'Let me stay with you. I don't care what's happening.'

They danced a few steps, shuffling, weaving in the crowd. The music was half Indonesian-style pop, half Western. In the flashing lights Lyssa saw that Jeth was wearing an open-necked shirt, casual dark cotton trousers, sandals on his bare feet, quite unlike the suited Jeth Arnold. But she recognised the Rolex watch on his brown wrist, brushing the dark hairs.

'Of course you'll stay with me,' he said roughly. 'I'm paying for you, aren't I? Remember what you said? Very expensive lady.'

For a second Lyssa was not sure . . . could she have made a mistake in the dark? 'Tell me my name,' she said.

'Lyssa, mother of Bethany, my beloved wife to be. Marry me soon.'

'And your name?' she trembled.

'Darling will do for now. Don't call me anything else.'

He took her back to the table, gripping her arm, made room for her, ordered a pawpaw juice without asking. 'This is my woman for tonight,' he said in explanation.

The men nodded and grinned, began talking to Jeth as if she did not exist. They had a prosperous look, wore rings and watches. Lyssa wondered if she was dreaming but the closeness of Jeth's arm kept her on this planet. Perhaps when they were alone and soon, he would tell her just what all this was about.

She was so tired, she stopped listening, let her head fall on Jeth's shoulder. Jet-lag, exhaustion, anxiety, worry, was catching up with her. Jeth would have to look after her now. She was in his hands.

Some time later they left the disco after Jeth had obviously made some arrangements with the men. They walked along the dark nightmare of Legian Street, waving on the cruising taxis that stopped to offer a ride, motorbikes accelerating, bicyles, dozy dogs, hens, ducks out for a late stroll, street stalls cooking food, hawkers and beggars still out to make a quick buck.

But Jeth held her firmly, almost lifting her over over the broken slabs of pavement, steering her close to his side. This was a world so far away from the peace of Hollow House, Bethany, Aunt Sarah, that Lyssa began to wonder if she had been taken seriously ill and was in a coma. Only Jeth was real, big and English; she could almost close her eyes and he would take her to safety.

'Where are you staying?'

'Ida Beach Inn. A small place.'

'I'll come with you. Do you know where it is?'

'Not really. Somewhere off Pantai Kuta. I'm not sure where. Sorry.'

'Has it A/C? A bath?'

'Outside bathroom. Very natural. A/C of sorts.'

'Sounds great. Act as if you don't know me.' He seemed to know the way. She recognised the rutted side lane. A skinny kitten slid into the darkness.

'But I do know you.'

'Act, Lyssa. Pretend Greg Wilson is directing you. I don't want anyone connecting you with me. I've bought you for tonight, remember?'

He stopped. Anyone watching could see what he was doing. He was peeling several hundred thousand rupiah notes off a wad from his breast pocket. 'Take these in case you have to get home in a hurry. I presume you have a return ticket.'

'Of course. Consolidated paid. But I'm not going back without you,' she added with spirit. 'So don't even consider it. I'm not leaving you now that I've found you.'

'You'll do as you're told.' He stepped over a pavement offering and Lyssa realised they were nearing the bungalows.

'I could not love thee, dear, loved I not Honour more,' said Jeth enigmatically. It was not till Lyssa got home that she discovered he was quoting Richard Lovelace, a 17th-century poet.

She knew where she was now. She went ahead and collected her carved key, unlocked the padlock on the two entwined rings which fastened the heavy wood doors. The heady secent of frangipani and hibiscus filled the darkness and the lamps in the spirit houses gave off just enough light to see through the shrubbery.

Jeth did not wait for her to even switch on the light. He crushed her in his arms, saying her name over and over again, his mouth devouring her lips, kissing her face, her neck, throat, ears, hair. They fell on to the plain-sheeted bed, their hands discovering the pleasure of each other's bodies. He ripped off what was left of her shirt and buried his head in the softness of her breasts. Lyssa gasped with delight and dug her nails into the muscles of his back, clawing at him.

She was nearly out of her mind with loving him, estatic at finding him safe, glorying that he had missed her as much as she had missed him.

He forced her legs to part and their union was almost terrifying in its intensity. Waves of excitement washed along her limbs, pouring through her pelvis, engulfing the inner core of her woman's body. She drew him in close, willingly accepting his strong manhood, enclosing him with her moist flesh.

She wept at the near pain, taking the passionate intensity into herself, letting it flow through her veins like a long journey of fulfilment, making it grow and last and last until he was groaning aloud in protest, till they came together in a glorious burst of passion.

They lay entwined, panting, slippery, letting the long moment of loving recapture all the depth of their yearnings.

'I love you, I love you,' she whispered against his sweat-covered skin. Her tongue licked at the moisture and took in its saltiness.

'And I love you, darling. One day, we'll make love slowly, I promise you.' He pushed the damp hair off her face. 'Don't ask me anything now. It's too late. You're going to shoot me in the foot.'

'Both feet,' said Lyssa, remembering all the hurt and worry. 'But not yet. Tomorrow will do.' Her voice drifted away into sleep.

Jeth stared at her in the darkness, wondering what he had done. The consequences might grow while his back was turned.

CHAPTER 18

The heat of the morning broke through the thatched roof of the bungalow, following drifts of sunshine tracing the cracks in a moving field of light. The rattle and hum of the air-conditioning unit woke Lyssa from a deep and contented sleep.

She had slept against Jeth's back, unable to believe it was really him until she touched his skin for assurance. It was a moment of the purest happiness yet it was not completely anchored in reality. She put her mouth on his shoulder and bit the soft flesh gently, taking a tuck of skin between her teeth.

'Is this an exquisite form of Balinese torture?' he said without turning.

'Just testing that you're still here and haven't disappeared again. Have you any idea what we've all been through, you monster? Your sister especially, Bethany, me. I've nearly been out of my mind, not knowing if you were alive or dead.'

Jeth rolled over and pulled her into his arms, still on the edge of sleep. 'I know, I know. I couldn't phone. They never let me out of their sight. For the first two weeks they kept me on the Lombok ferry, a rust bucket that plies backwards and forwards between Lembar and Padangbai, east Bali. I nearly went mad. A five-hour crossing each way with no comfort and certainly no telephones.'

'But why? I don't understand.'

'I had arranged to meet someone on the ferry and they didn't show up. Apparently the contact had a heart attack. You can't hurry things out here and too much was at stake. It's all taking far longer than I thought and it's not over yet. But I don't want you here, Lyssa.'

'I'm sure you know what you're talking about but I don't. What's not over? Long enough for what?'

Jeth stroked the sensitive cord down her spine, touching her face with a raw sweetness. 'I can't tell you here. It's a long story.'

'I've plenty of time,' said Lyssa, moving against him and kissing him with her eyes. 'And you've got to tell me. You can't leave me in the dark any more. It's not fair.'

He gave her a long look, seeing the shadows

under her eyes, the haunting agony behind the colour of the irises. He saw the passion and the pain and knew that he was the cause of both.

'Sweetheart, let's have a shower,' he said, leaping out of bed and flinging open the door to the back veranda. A wave of heat rushed in, flooding the room with humidity, saturating it with light.

'There are no walls,' said Lyssa.

'All the better. No walls, no ears.'

She heard him turn on the shower and the water splashing over the tiles. She followed him more modesty, the sheet draped round her, nearly tripping over the long ends. This is very silly, she thought, but then she was not used to nakedness with a man, although she had just slept with Jeth without a shread of cotton between them.

He pulled her into the shower, unfastening the sheet and tossing it aside.

'We've got to get used to this,' he said, reading her mind. 'You and me. It's forever, you know.'

'It's all . . . very new for me.'

'For me, too. My marriage was over very quickly. I can hardly remember it. If it weren't for Matthew, I might think it had never happened.'

And it was not much of a marriage anyway, thought Lyssa, but this was not the time to tell Jeth that she knew about Priscilla.

'So what is all this cloak-and-dagger business?' Lyssa asked, standing close to him so that he could not look at her curving body. The intimate contact of his thighs made it difficult for her to think straight. 'Hank Jefferson said he thought you served in the SAS? Is that true?'

'Hank Jefferson?' He frowned, letting the water wash over his face and hair, rubbing at the skin. 'You've spoken to him?'

'Matthew came over for a board meeting. I phoned Hank Jefferson in case he had any idea where you were. He told me about your time in the Marines.'

'It has some bearing, indirectly,' he said, turning the shower on to full power. The torrent of rushing water nearly drowned his words. 'They approached me because of that expertise despite the passage of time.'

'Who approached you?'

'The Fraud Squad. Lyssa, I'm being followed here. Every move I make is watched.'

'The Fraud Squad in the UK?' Lyssa was astonished, then she remembered the whispered voices in the background of her call to New Scotland Yard. They had known all the time; they had been hiding the truth from her.

'The Indonesian government have a strict regulation about the export of antiquities. There's a vast wealth of Hindu religious and cultural artefacts. They don't want the island ransacked of its treasures. There are ornate beds and chairs, palm-leaf books, fabrics, masks, sculptures and more. So there's a fifty-year rule. Nothing older than fifty years can be taken out of the country. But valuable antiquities have been vanishing, smuggled out of the country and sold to wealthy American collectors.'

Lyssa was horribly confused. 'But what on earth have you got to do with antiques? That's not your business. Consolidated is transport and paper pulp and heavy metals.'

'Right,' he snapped, lathering soap over her smooth shoulders roughly. He was angry with her, angry with her being there, in the way, taking his mind off his purpose. 'But, like this piece of soap, someone is cleverly laundering the pay-off money through one of my companies. And that's very much my business. That's why I'm here, Lyssa, posing as a buyer, trying to find out who is behind it all and how they process the money.'

Lyssa let the information sink in like a thin, driving spike, letting time pass through her mind. 'Those men in the disco? The ones round the table drinking beer and grinning at me. Were they part of the set-up?'

'I'm afraid so. The Kuta connection. I could

only keep you beside me by pretending to buy you. I'm sorry, my darling. They are going to put me in touch with someone who has valuable Dutch artefacts to sell. I'm meeting them tomorrow in Ubud. Bali was once part of the Dutch East Indies but there was fierce fighting and the Royal Family at Klung-Kung defended their Royal Palace to the death. That was in 1908. The Dutch had guns and ammunition. The Balinese King and his court had no more weapons than the famous serpentine *kris* daggers. They knew it was suicide but they fought on just the same. They never gave in.'

'And they were all killed?'

'All but one small boy. A small six-year-old prince. These swords, the genuine ones, fetch an enormous price. The precious gems in the handles are worth a fortune on their own.'

'So New Scotland Yard knew about this but wouldn't tell me. They let me think you were a John Doe floating in the Thames.'

He drew her close under the falling water. 'Oh, my darling Lyssa, I'm so sorry. How else could we have done it? I'd been discussing this with the Fraud Squad for several months. They wanted to send one of their own men, but I wouldn't have it. It is my company that is being used, misused, criminally used. I had to find out how it was being done. Consolidated runs itself. I wouldn't be missed . . . how was I to know that we would fall in love and suddenly find each other again the very weekend before I was due to fly out to Bali? The timing was a nightmare.'

'But you had that passport all ready, using my name?' Lyssa leaned against him, letting the water stream over them. She did not explain how she knew about it.

'The department said choose any name and I chose yours. It leaped to the fore immediately because I was already out of my mind loving you. I never realised it might lead you to following me. That was not my intention.'

The sunlight glinting in Lyssa's hair was like magic. The little elegant brown and olive wren-warblers sang in the palm trees. Jeth took up a handful of her hair and smothered it against his face. His caressing lips slid down the smoothness of her neck, down to the hollow between her breasts. It was a slow and exquisite assault on her body. There were no barriers now. Her hungry body was surrendering to his every move.

'It took me some time . . .' she murmured. 'But I got there in the end. And now, whatever you say Jeth, I refuse to leave you.'

He pushed her away abruptly, severing the mood. 'But you must, Lyssa. You are going straight back to London. You can have a quick swim in that nice pool I spotted in the garden, then you are getting on the five p.m. plane back to London. I'm going to phone for a reservation. I don't want you mixed up in this. You are much too precious to me.'

'I refuse. No, no, I won't go,' said Lyssa defiantly. 'I'm not going back now that I've found you and you can't make me, even if you bodily carry me on to that plane. This set-up is perfect. They think you picked me up in the disco; you told the world you were paying for me, that I was your woman for the night. Why can't I tag along as your girlfriend, your fancy woman? You're supposed to be an unscrupulous dealer with money enough to buy anything you want. Why not buy me, as well?'

'Don't say that, Lyssa,' he said, his control slipping. 'I might give in. You must go home.'

'There's only one problem to staying. My luggage is lost in Bangkok. I haven't any clothes.

'That's exactly the way I like you best,' he said seriously, gathering her back into his arms.

They breakfasted on the front veranda outside Lyssa's bungalow, their eyes feasting on each other. They were hardly aware of the dark beauty in a pink sarong who brought plates of sliced pineapple, pawpaw, and watermelon, banana pancakes topped with honey and coconut and tall glasses of the potent Balinese coffee.

'This is what the Balinese think Westerners eat for breakfast. They eat a bowl of rice or noodle soup.' Jeth sipped the strong black coffee. 'We'd better get you some more suitable clothes or you'll die in this heat. And it isn't even hot yet.'

'Does this mean I can stay?'

'Only for one day, one night, then, true to Western male form, I should tire of you. In the 19th century, the Balinese women were the most expensive slaves in the world.'

'Tire of me? Don't you bet on it.'

He took her down the street market where every cave-like stall sold a variety of colourful clothes. They stepped over little palm dishes on the pavements, the *banten* offerings of flowers and rice made every day to the gods.

The locust swarm of hawkers surrounded round Jeth, sensing a buyer. They thrust shirts, sarongs, sundresses under his nose. Lyssa, alarmed, fingered a pink and apple-green fringed sarong.

'What you buy? What you buy? Twenty-five thousand.' Jeth looked suitably horrified. 'Gimme your best price?'

'Five.' He picked out a white cotton tunic and trouser set. 'Ten for this.'

'Thirty thousand.'

Lyssa shrank with embarrassment. 'Pay them, pay them. I must have some clothes. I'm not used to this haggling.'

'Courage, girl. It's part of life. They won't respect you if you pay their first price. I know roughly what they pay for the stuff from the factories. I'll give them a fair day's profit. Don't you know that? Don't you trust me to be fair? I won't cheat them. What else do you need? Swim-suit and sandals?'

'Bra and pants. Nightshirt.'

'Delete nightshirt. We'll go to the supermarket, Matahari. They sell bras and pants. But be quick. We're leaving for Ubud at midday. And try not to look so intelligent. I don't want you to understand anything.'

'I'll practise a vacant look.'

A wizened brown-skinned woman took Lyssa to the back of her shop and showed her how to tie the sarong round her waist, the Balinese way with gathered folds.

'You give me English clothes?' she asked, eyeing the twill trousers and checked shirt.

Lyssa looked dismayed. 'Lipstick?' the old woman asked hopefully.

Lyssa handed over her Clarins lipstick.

'She wanted my clothes,' she said to Jeth out-side, feeling wonderfully free and cool in the sarong and white tunic. Her legs moved with ease under the loose folds. 'Whatever did she want them for?'

'To sell, of course. Someone would buy them.'

Lyssa was glad to leave Kuta behind, to sit beside Jeth in the rented Suzuki Jimney Jeep, to drive into the countryside with its sculptured rice terraces rising into the breathtaking hills, and through little villages with clusters of family homes within ornate walls and gateways and family temples. Every road was a hazard of wandering dogs, herds of ducks and geese and hens. Now the charm of rural Bali was working on her, and she could see the paradise beyond the chaos of Kuta.

Steep and lush gorges, verdant ricefields, coconut groves, dense bamboo forests, coffee plantations, every inch of land was put to agricultural use. They passed a dozen temples, unspoilt villages, rivers and waterfalls.

They drove through villages that carved wood, and made silver jewellry, and wove baskets and traditional textiles in batik patterns. This was the cultural side of Bali that drew artists from all over the world.

'We shall be in Ubud in an hour.' Jeth put his hand on her knee. 'Then I shall have to leave you, Lyssa. I'll find you a decent place to stay with a bathroom with walls, decent air-conditioning and a pool. Cool off and enjoy yourself. You'll love Ubud, it's the cultural centre of Bali and quite safe to walk around. Travellers come for a day and stay a year. You mustn't worry about me, darling. But you must let me go and get this business finished.'

'I'll let you go,' she said, but it was a journey she did not want him to take without her.

CHAPTER 19

Everyone should have a favourite moment, and this could become one of Lyssa's. Sitting on the long balcony of their first-floor room at Ubud Inn at the lower end of Monkey Forest Road, gazing at the flamboyant gardens and the azure blue swimming pool, a long glass of chilled banana juice at her elbow.

Even the ugly statues in the tropical garden, fat-faced frogs and buffalos and elephants, had gorgeous flowers in their ears. A girl had tucked a flower behind Lyssa's ear when she arrived. The room had two beds, one double and one single and a red hibiscus sat on each pillow.

At the end of the road was a monkey forest with a notice which warned travellers not to take in cameras or handbags. The great trees whispered and swayed with the thieving animals, waiting for the unwary tourists. Lyssa would not be visiting the forest. She didn't like monkeys.

They had arrived earlier in the day but already Jeth had gone out. He had taken the jeep but she had no idea where he had gone.

'I have to go out. See you later,' he'd said, downing a Coke.

Damn the man. How could he make her so happy and then abandon her, putting an unwelcome distance between them? It could be the story of their life together. The breeze-tapped air was loaded with fragrances that she could not identify. But the flowers in the garden were exotic, only bloomed for a day, red-tongued, russet cascades, crimson bells, white and waxy yellow, then they fell to the ground like a carpet before they could decay. The inn's washing lay on the lawns, towels and sheets, drying in no time at all. The air was drier up in the hills.

Lyssa changed into her white trousers and tunic top, put on open sandals, and set out to explore Ubud. She had a map of sorts. It was too hot to eat, though she still had Jeth's money if she wanted a drink. She would walk into the hills. Jeth said it was safe for walking.

The rural villages outside Ubud were unspoilt, with delightful views and people that smiled at her, said hello, waved. Even the ancient villagers, sun-lined and wiry, who had known another, more isolated life, would nod or wave. Puppies gambolled all over the narrow roads; fluffy baby chicks pecked the wayside grass; bamboo baskets held the pride of glossy rainbow-coloured cock birds, flowers bloomed everywhere.

Even the back roads were elaborately walled with individual gateways leading to each family complex, however humble, and the thatched family temples, each *meru* or pagoda decorated with the offerings of the day. A flock of ducklings followed a mother duck to the nearest water in the paddy fields, long necks a sheen of pale feathers.

The villagers smiled at her, offered to sell her a bottled drink, welcomed her to sit in the shade, visit their homes, put flowers behind her ear, marvelled at the fire-touched colour of her hair. They wanted to touch it, exclaimed at it its many shades.

'Hello, lady. Where you from?' The children clustered round her, practising their English.

She followed a steep hill, feeling the midday heat beating down on to her head and wishing she had brought a hat. The only traffic to pass her was a solitary motorbike bumping over the rough surface and a pony and cart making better transit. But the local women planting young shoots in the rice fields showed her how to fold and pin a banana leaf into a hat. They mimed the rain.

'Good for the rain, too? *Bagus. Bagus.*' *Bagus* was the second word that Lyssa had learned. It meant good. And *tidak*, which meant no.

She relaxed into the sun, enjoying the uncomplicated and slow-moving pace of the day. Arnold Place was a million miles away. If only Jeth could be with her. She had to hold on to him for a few days more and then they could start their life together. After all they had been through in the last eventful months, she could not lose him now.

But time caught her unawares and Lyssa panicked. She was sure she knew the way down through the lanes and villages. By now, though, one village was looking very much like another; one small wood-carving workshop like another and the lanes so small they were not even on the map. Had she seen this long flight of steps before or these blackened multi-tiered merus? She prayed for the sight of a bemos to take her back to Ubud.

She quickened her step. White herons hovered over the village from lofty trees.

'Ubud?' she asked, hot and sweating, waving her hat down the paved roadway. People smiled and agreed and pointed ahead. It seemed a long way to walk. She was tiring. Her new sandals hurt. Then she recognised the Ubud crossroads ahead and the Puri Saren Palace. Monkey Forest Road was the long road straight down which passed the football ground. That much she remembered from their earlier arrival.

She practically fell into an open-fronted café and ordered a glass of watermelon juice and a pot of tea. The tea came without milk but with lime slices.

She nearly passed the Ubud Inn where they were staying; it looked different in the dazzling heat. She asked for her key and was also given an envelope marked 'L. Pasten'. She tore it open. Inside was a ticket for that night's Ramayana Ballet.

'Oh, how lovely. A ticket for tonight's dancing.'

'Ramayana Ballet is an old Hindu epic tale of the kidnapping of a beautiful wife in a forest and her rescue by the Monkey God,' said the receptionist. 'Get there on time because the seats are not reserved.'

She clutched the ticket, knowing that Jeth had bought it for her, had wanted her to attend one of these spectacular Balinese dances. She swam in the pool, cooling off, as the sun slowly began to sink behind the hills, painting the clouds with yawning streaks of pink. The day had passed without drama. Now all she hoped was that Jeth would return, safe and sound, before nightfall.

She began to get anxious, went back to the reception desk. 'Are there any messages for me?'

she asked. She tried to sound confident and able to cope with anything.

'Sorry, madam, no message.'

It was dark by the time Lyssa walked up to the dark maze of the Puri Saren Palace where the performance was to be held. No sign of Jeth. People were crowding into the courtyard of the palace, lit by lights strung up in the trees. The musicians' drums and gongs were already laid out and the elaborately carved doorway to the palace was the dramatic backcloth for the ballet.

It was theatre in the round with three rows of stone steps and white plastic chairs. The dance floor was covered in red cloth. It was filling up quickly, late arrivals sitting on the floor for the best view. Lyssa sat on the end seat of the third row so that Jeth could find her easily. The musicians entered wearing richly embroidered red and gold uniforms. It was all very casual. They were chatting and smoking; one had a little girl with him. An older man came round sprinkling the musicians with holy water. Lyssa hoped this helped.

There wasn't a seat left. If Jeth came now, he would have to stand.

The rare instruments of bamboo and gongs made up the glistening tones of the gamelan orchestra. They began to play with vibrant sound and insistent rhythm. The lights dimmed and three courtly dancers came on, the prince, his brother, and his beautiful wife called Sita, according to the cheaply printed programme. They were all played by women. Lyssa was confused.

'The women with arrows in their belts show that they are playing male roles.' It was Jeth. He was standing behind her chair. 'You've got my ticket.'

'It was addressed to me.'

'I'm also L. Pasten, remember? I'm supposed to meet someone here.' He was carrying a shabby backpack. He did not put it down. 'Fortunately reception remembered where you'd gone.'

'Am I supposed to be acting that I don't know you?'

'Yes. Complete strangers.'

'Then I won't share my programme.'

'Suit yourself. I won't share my Coke.'

She smiled into the bright lights of the dancing, not taking her eyes from the glittering scene. Perhaps there was hope that Jeth would return to normality soon. It would be wonderful to go home together.

Lyssa was fascinated by the dancing, the elaborate hand and finger manipulations, the control of every limb and bare foot, expressing the role of a character with eyes, eyebrow and precise head movements. The costumes and head-dresses were exquisite and Sita managed to dance with her long train controlled between her ankles.

A monstrous man in a half-mask and wild wig leaped on stage, flourishing groans and threats.

'The baddie, I bet,' Jeth whispered. But he was looking around, his attention divided.

In the stage forest fauns danced, baby monkeys gambolled, and a bird in spectacular feathers died, trying to save Sita from the warriors. The small, natural setting for the ballet was far better than a theatre. It was then that Lyssa realised that Jeth had gone. She suddenly panicked, empty of feeling. She did not like this being left alone. The gongs echoed in her head.

When he returned, emerging from the darkness of the giant banut trees, Lyssa noticed that he was no longer carrying the backpack. A chill settled on her spine despite the warm evening. This unknown Jeth frightened her.

The Monkey God leaped down stage with athletic bounds, his white outfit sparkling. He was half in love with Sita and determined to rescue her.

As a stylised fight began with characters using flashing daggers and gilt bow and arrows, Jeth leaned forward. 'Make the most of this,' he said. 'It'll be real blood tomorrow.'

* * *

The dark and mottled night filled the room with long shadows. Lyssa's body clock was still out of sync and she was not ready for sleep. She lay thinking of the strange circumstances which had brought her halfway across the world to find the man she loved. And he was fast asleep in a separate bed, exhausted by a day she knew little about. She knelt beside him on the tiled floor, stroking his hair, tracing the set of his jaw, dark against the white pillow. She wanted him back; she wanted him home.

Suddenly something hit the roof of the room sharply. A coconut? But there was no palm tree tall enough near their room for fruit to fall on to it. Lyssa heard a scampering, and then she knew and peered apprehensively into the darkness. Those damned monkeys . . .

They were driving south towards Klungkung, one of the ancient capital towns, not so that Lyssa could see more of the sculptured paddy fields and flower-laden hamlets, but so that Jeth could finish the whole business. That much he had said. He was tired and concerned for Lyssa.

'I won't tell you how many US dollars were in that backpack,' he said, shoulders weary over the wheel. 'And I'm delivering the rest today.'

'Are we ever going to get back to normal, Jeth? I

want you to come home with me. This isn't real. It's not even a holiday.'

'You should know me by now, that nothing about my life is "normal". I travel the world half a dozen times a year. And this is important because it's one of my companies that is being used. I've got to clear my name. But don't worry, my love, I'll be home soon and we'll be together.' He put his hand on her knee, firm and bronzed, and she covered it with her own. 'At least no one is listening when we're in the jeep, but that damned bike has been on my tail for the last five miles.'

Lyssa did not look behind. She didn't want to know. 'Where are we going?'

'We're going to Tenganan, a pre-Hindu village; in fact the only one left in Bali.'

'Why?'

'Because it'll be crowded with tourists and locals and no one will notice me.'

Lyssa did not tell him that his height and powerful build made him noticeable everywhere he went. The Balinese men were mostly slight and slim. And an Aussie could be spotted a mile off.

'You're coming with me because I daren't let you out of my sight. I want to make sure you get on that plane back to London. Bethany will be missing you and Pudding is probably pining, losing his fur.'

'I'm not going home without you,' said Lyssa firmly, not bothering to mention that she had spoken to Sarah by phone every day since her arrival and that Bethany was fine, though, naturally, Lyssa missed her daughter desperately. 'I didn't come all this way to be sent back.'

'Go back to Hollow House and play lady of the manor. Do it for me, Lyssa. I need to know that you're safe.'

He took a left turn and began a slow climb up the worst road in Bali. They were overtaken by swarms of accelerating motorbikes which could swerve round the worst craters.

'I think the road is pre-Hindu as well,' said Lyssa as she was thrown all over the seat by the holes and ruts. She held on to the base of her spine to protect it from the jolts.

'The *geringsing* double woven cloth made here is said to protect people from earthly and supernatural enemies,' said Jeth, finding a parking space among the myriad of strewn bikes.

'I'll buy you some,' Lyssa said, easing herself gingerly out of the jeep. For once, there were no hawkers and the atmosphere of the village was glowing as if even time was reckoned differently, as indeed it was. It was a microcosm of another universe.

Clay-walled houses with thatched roofs had been built along each side of the rough climbing lanes. There were no roads. The lanes rose in terraced fashion, cobbled, sloping steeply at intervals to accommodate the rise. Not a car had ever been in the village. There were walled temples and longhouses and small pavilions with shrines. Chained grey monkeys hung from the trees, bored and bad-tempered.

Most of the longhouses were turned into craft workshops now that tourism had invaded the once isolated community, but no one tried to sell their goods. They worked on, unconcerned, weaving the intricate *ikat* cloth, lidded baskets of natural fibre in every shape and size, carving wood, writing epic tales and holy words with black ink on lengths of dried palm-leaf.

'What's going on ahead?' said Lyssa. Streams of people were converging on the open-sided village hall in the far compound of the village. The noise and activity were humming, voices raised in excitement. But the dozens of free-roaming hens and baby chicks and ducks were as unconcerned as the weavers.

'That's where we're going but you don't have to look. This may be a sacred village but it doesn't seem to stop their favourite sport,' said Jeth. He strode ahead and Lyssa had to hurry to keep up with him, her flimsy sandals not made for climbing the steep cobbles.

The village hall was packed with men, shouting and gesticulating, the air heavy with cigarette smoke. Around the edge of the wall sat food sellers with bananas, peanuts, drinks. There were two rows of descending stone steps. Lyssa suddenly realised that she was the only Western woman there and the only other women were those selling refreshments.

'Jeth?' She was going to ask him if this was taboo for women but he had gone. She stood still as men crowded round, flapped their T-shirts, smoked, waved notes.

On the central floor of the village hall were a group of men. They were each holding aloft a brightly plumaged cock. The colours of their glossy feathers were catching the light, their bright eyes like gems. Bold purples and gold, emerald-green, brown, black, stark white and scarlet. Lyssa was at a cockfight. It was legal in this country and she had seen all the cocks in their baskets on the roadsides, wondering why they were kept separate.

In another corner of the hall, on a flat wooden board, money was rapidly changing hands with the bookmakers. Big money. The floor was littered with plastic bottles, cigarette ends, peanut husks, plastic bags, banana skins.

Lyssa did not want to watch, yet she was

fascinated. This was a million years away from *Inspector Dutton* and *Mansfield Park*. This was raw life.

She did not understand all the arguing going on the floor but she supposed it was to decide which cocks were to fight. The men started binding the cock's legs with red twine, fixing on a spur. Lyssa began to feel hot and sick, looked around for Jeth. He was nowhere to be seen.

Suddenly an uproar went up, but it was not the fighting. It was a pre-fight hype with shouting and waving hands and the brilliant birds held aloft by strutting men and the audience going mad with excitement, waving money. Men surged forward, blocking her view.

She glimpsed nothing but a flurry of feathers and then it was all over in seconds.

'Is it dead?' she asked someone. There was blood on the centre of the floor.

'No,' said Jeth. 'They stopped the fight. The other cock wouldn't fight once its opponent was injured. That often happens. The cocks won't fight to order.'

'Well, thank goodness,' said Lyssa. 'Those birds have more sense than their owners.'

'It's a way of life, Lyssa. No more barbaric than our racing horses over fences that kill them. The world is a cruel place.'

The crowd began to leave the village hall, pouring out into the triumphant air. Dusk was falling. Lyssa clung to Jeth's arm. She would not be parted from him again, even if she had to chain herself to him.

'You're wonderful,' he said. 'Most women, left on their own in such a place, would have panicked.'

'Just keep telling me that and I'll survive,' she said. There was something different about Jeth now. He smiled at her for the first time in days. 'I actually like Bali now,' she added.

'It all depends who you're with,' he said, lifting her fingers to his lips. 'This may be against some local custom but I'll risk it.'

They drove down the terrible road again then stopped in Candi Dasa for a drink. It was a rapidly growing beach resort completely spoilt by ugly concrete walls built to keep the sea from washing away the hotels.

The ginger tea in the half-empty café had never been so welcome. Lyssa sat in the darkness, letting the return of some civilisation wash over her, drinking tea and nibbling nuts. She smiled at Jeth in the gloom and knew that she was happy, simply being with him.

'Would you like to see something incredibly old and really beautiful?' he asked. She nodded.

He began to unwrap a length of cloth. The case was made of tooled leather, fragile with age. Carefully Jeth put his hand on the hilt and drew out the *kris* dagger. The serpentine, scalloped shape of the sword edge was of finely honed silver, elaborately decorated with holy words and symbols. The handle of the dagger was embedded with emeralds, glowing like cat's eyes.

'You're looking at a king's ransom,' he said.

CHAPTER 20

Heathrow at six in the morning was a cold and cheerless place. Passengers were trundling their luggage through customs with white, sleep-starved faces. Jeth had only a small leather hold-all and he looked gaunt despite the taut, tanned skin.

Lyssa spotted him immediately, hurried across the waiting area and knotted her arms around his neck. They clung together, could not speak, savouring the magic of being close, hearts thudding. The seconds ticked by with the sheer relief of seeing each other again.

'Have you anything warm to wear in that bag?' said Lyssa tremulously, pulling back.

'No, not even an emerald-studded *kris* dagger. That's on its way to the safety of a national museum. But I do have a gold hand-made wedding ring from the village of Celuk.' His laughter was rich and deep. 'It's the kind of ring that I hope will ensure you'll keep me warm forever.'

'A ring? That's very formal, Mr Arnold.'

'Everything by the book from now on.'

Lyssa had his winter overcoat over her arm. She had brought it up from Hollow House. 'Good thing one of us has some sense. This month is turning into one of the coldest ever. Talk about global warming. That's a laugh.'

'Wonderful girl. It is damned cold.' He shrugged himself into the coat and pulled her close to his side, his hand on her shoulder. 'I could get used to the Indonesian climate, but not Bangkok's pollution.'

'I've a hired car outside, ready to take us back to Hollow House. I didn't relish a dawn drive along the M25. Everyone's longing to see you.'

'How is everyone? Sarah, Bethany? I suppose they'll never forgive me?'

'They will when they hear your story. They'll want to know everything.' And so do I, thought Lyssa. She had been put on a plane back to London, via Bangkok, leaving Jeth to follow the movement of the marked US dollars. She closed her eyes against the tissue-thin pain of that enforced parting.

'We'll go first to Arnold Place. I'll phone home from there to let them know I've arrived. I want to check on a few things first, find out what's been going on in the office in my absence. Sybil must be grey-haired with the backlog.' Jeth was already shifting gear into his Consolidated mode.

'Sybil's not exactly grey-haired,' Lyssa murmured. 'I'd say everything's pretty well in hand. You'll be surprised.'

'I also have to go to New Scotland Yard right away. The money was being fed through the Bangkok company's books, already converted to *bahts*, and then filtered through to New York, back in laundered dollars. It was damned clever and no one would have noticed if Matthew hadn't gone to the New York office. He sent me a fax, querying where all this money was coming from.'

'Does this mean that someone in New York is involved?'

'I hope not. Hank Jefferson is an old friend. It must be someone else.'

He was mentally ticking off the day's commitments. It was back to normal already. He did not seem fazed by jet-lag but Lyssa knew it would catch up with him later. She had been a zombie for several days. She would wait until he couldn't keep his eyes open.

'Did Matthew know anything about the operation?'

'No, but it was something that he said quite casually that started me wondering if Bangkok was the route. I knew the New York office wasn't making that much profit. The exchange rate isn't good enough.'

'I'll come to Arnold House with you. *Mansfield Park* can stay on hold for a day.'

'Good,' he said but he was not listening. 'Mansfield where? What park? I don't want to let you out of my sight right now, never, ever.'

'That's just what I want to hear.'

They reached Arnold Place long before the early-morning traffic built up and clogged the streets. 'We can let the hired car go,' said Lyssa. 'My BMW is in the car park. It had to be serviced yesterday. So I can drive you home.'

Jeth looked surprised but said nothing. He looked even more surprised when the security guard unlocked the front entrance and said, 'Good morning, Miss Pasten, Mr Arnold. Nice to see you back, sir.'

But his expression when Lyssa produced her piece of plastic which worked his lift was one of amazement. 'Would you like to tell me what is going on?' he said, following her into the lift and pressing the top button. 'How come you have a pass to my private lift? And a place in the company car park?'

'Have you any idea just how long you've been away?' she asked. 'And half the time we didn't even know if you were alive or dead. Did you think

Consolidated was going to tick over with a little genteel help from Aunt Sarah in Sussex now and again?'

'No, but I have a perfectly functional board of directors. They can run the firm.' He did not return her smile.

'That's immensely reassuring,' said Lyssa frankly. 'They look after their special areas adequately but you run the firm.'

She went ahead of him into his office. He recognised, with a jolt, the flowering pot plants brought from Hollow House but said nothing, tossed his leather bag on to a chair. He blinked at his uncluttered desk and the neat line of files on one side awaiting his attention.

'The files are colour-coded for urgency,' said Lyssa, plugging in the coffee machine. 'Red for the most urgent, orange next and so on down the spectrum. Grey you can leave till next week.'

His expression was unreadable.

Lyssa switched on the computer. 'I've put my own password into the WP so that no one else could read this information. There's a complete record of what I've done each day, calls taken, mail answered, decisions made or put on hold till your return.'

Jeth strolled over, taking his time, and leaned across her shoulder, glancing at the screen. He began to scroll down, day after day, without saying a word.

Lyssa grew cold with apprehension, waiting for the explosion. Of course Jeth would not like it. She should have known from the beginning that he would resent any interference. He'd been in charge for so long and no one had ever taken his place before. But it had seemed so right at the time.

'I was only helping out, temporarily . . .' she began, straightening her jacket, unable to stand the silence any longer. 'The mail was mountain-high . . . and Sybil was getting worried . . .'

He reached out to her and pulled her roughly on to his lap, finding her mouth, kissing her thoroughly till she could hardly breathe. His eyes were glinting with amusement and love.

'I think you're wonderful,' he said.

He balanced his chin on her head and began stroking the fiery hair, kissing her spiky, tear-studded eyes. Lyssa felt the old pains fading as she rested against him, the touch of his fingers healing the wounds.

'The sooner you have a baby, the better,' he said at last. 'Or I shall find myself out of a job. Of course, I could take up golf and let you run the company.'

'Miss Reed would be pleased,' she murmured.

'Miss Reed? Who the hell is Miss Reed?'

'The headmistress of the village school. You know Miss Reed. She needs more pupils. Oh, I haven't told you that Bethany goes there now and about the tower block where Bethany and I used to live, cracking up and being demolished. I quite forgot.'

'No, you haven't told me,' he said bluntly. He had been living in a world of black and white, money and international corruption; suddenly it was all colours, vibrant and living. Lyssa was that colour, with her bright hair and laughing face. 'Anything else you've forgotten to tell me? You seemed to have forgotten quite a lot.'

'Well, there is one more thing. I have met someone who used to be special in your life.' It was the last hurdle and Lyssa knew that it was the highest. 'Bethany and I have met Priscilla in the garden and in the woods. I know she lives in the stable block with Nancy. We get on . . . quite well really. She's a sweet . . .'

'Child.' His face clouded. He was holding her tightly as if afraid she might now leave him.

'Yes, Jeth. A sweet child. And we must look after her and make her life as happy and productive as possible. And I don't care if we can't marry legally in a church or whereever. It doesn't matter at all. I just want to be with you all the time.'

'You don't have to worry about that aspect,' said

Jeth leaning back with a huge sigh of relief. 'I have my solicitor sorting it out right now. We shall be married. I knew you would meet Priscilla some time. I was just worried about your reaction. I was afraid that you might hate me for concealing Priscilla's existence. But I had to do something for her, give her some sort of life that wasn't in an institution.'

Lyssa didn't say that she had seen Mr Rathbone. She thought Jeth had had enough shocks for one morning. Instead their bodies touched and melded, the way their hearts and minds always met, and that was how Sybil found them, much later on in the morning, asleep in each other's arms in the chair.

It was not exactly a quiet wedding. Half the village were there and a good many of Lyssa's television friends and crew turned up. Sarah was thrilled to be actually meeting Gareth Warwick, though she kept calling him Inspector Dutton.

'I'm an actor, Miss Arnold,' he said, laying on his usual charm. 'Just call me Gareth. Would you like to come and see some filming some time? We could arrange it.'

'My word, yes. I'd really like that,' she beamed, hanging on to her hat.

The tiny fourteenth-century village church was

crowded. There was Miss Reed and Dr Carrington, Emily and Nancy with their boyfriends, Sybil and Hank Jefferson hitting it off (the police having long ago confirmed Hank's innocence – not that Jeth or Lyssa had ever suspected him), Amos and family in their best clothes, Maggie and her daughter, and the scent of thousands of freesias flown over from Jersey created a mist of delicate perfume in the church. The wine-stained medieval windows cast a warm glow.

Even Matthew turned up, a little late, with a lanky blonde on his arm. One of his Dorset friends, he explained. County horse trials and all that. He looked a shade bashful, but it was obvious that he was smitten.

Lyssa arrived at the church on Greg Wilson's arm. He was very proud to be giving her away, had even shaved properly. It might have seemed a funny choice but she had forgiven him for telling Matthew that she had never been married to André.

André was so long ago now, he existed like a youthful dream, half forgotten in parts. They had both been so young and it had been wonderful. And Bethany had been her legacy of that love. Now life had to move on and Jeth was her future.

But Lyssa could not be angry with Greg for his indiscretion. If Matthew had not been so upset by the news of her single state, she might have been married to him by now and that would have been a real mistake.

'Ouch,' she said aloud, thinking about it, then had to pretend she had stubbed her toe on a paving stone.

Lyssa and Jeth came out of the church into the early summer sunshine, gazing happily at each other, the hand-made gold ring from Bali on her finger. She looked radiant in a shimmering slip of a dress, oyster cream crêpe, authentic Twenties, embroidered with pearls and moonstones, her gloriously bright hair tumbled with flowers.

'Are you going to be able to cope with me for a husband?' Jeth asked, taking her hand, covering it with his own.

'I think I've had very good training,' Lyssa smiled.

'A fully inscribed medal is on the way. You can wear it on your apron when you've finished putting *Mansfield Park* on the map. I'll allow you to make your name on the credits.'

'And no more disappearing, please?'

'Only into your bed.'

'Really, Mr Arnold, more discretion please . . . your new daughter is listening.'

They escaped along the church path and through the lychgate, under a shower of confetti and rice. They began the walk across the green towards the cars that were waiting to take everyone back to Hollow House and the champagne and the wedding cake.

Bethany skipped alongside them through the pale green weeds, stopping to pick daisies and cowslips, the flounces of her pink bridesmaid's dress brushing the new grass. Her exclamations of delight were music to their ears.

'Pudding's coming to the 'ception,' Bethany said cheerfully. 'He's going to drink champing-pain all afternoon.'

'I can see Pudding's going to need watching,' said Lyssa, her heart overflowing with love for the two most special people in her life. The milk-warm air caressed her face with patterns spinning with light. 'We can't have an alcoholic bear in the family.'

THE EXCITING NEW NAME IN WOMEN'S FICTION!

PLEASE HELP ME TO HELP YOU!

Dear ***Scarlet*** Reader,

As Editor of ***Scarlet*** Books I want to make sure that the books I offer you every month are up to the high standards ***Scarlet*** readers expect. And to do that I need to know a little more about you and your reading likes and dislikes. So please spare a few minutes to fill in the short questionnaire on the following pages and send it to me. I'll send *you* a surprise gift as a thank you!

Looking forward to hearing from you,

Sally Cooper

Editor-in-Chief, ***Scarlet***

P.S. Only one offer per household.

QUESTIONNAIRE

Please tick the appropriate boxes to indicate your answers

1 Where did you get this Scarlet title?

Bought in Supermarket ☐
Bought at W H Smith ☐
Bought at book exchange or second-hand shop ☐
Borrowed from a friend ☐
Other ____________________

2 Did you enjoy reading it?

A lot ☐ A little ☐ Not at all ☐

3 What did you particularly like about this book?

Believable characters ☐ Easy to read ☐
Good value for money ☐ Enjoyable locations ☐
Interesting story ☐ Modern setting ☐
Other ____________________

4 What did you particularly dislike about this book?

____

5 Would you buy another Scarlet book?

Yes ☐ No ☐

6 What other kinds of book do you enjoy reading?

Horror ☐ Puzzle books ☐ Historical fiction ☐
General fiction ☐ Crime/Detective ☐ Cookery ☐
Other ____________________

7 Which magazines do you enjoy most?

Bella ☐ Best ☐ Woman's Weekly ☐
Woman and Home ☐ Hello ☐ Cosmopolitan ☐
Good Housekeeping ☐
Other ____________________

cont.

And now a little about you –

8 How old are you?
Under 25 ☐ 25–34 ☐ 35–44 ☐
45–54 ☐ 55–64 ☐ over 65 ☐

9 What is your marital status?
Single ☐ Married/living with partner ☐
Widowed ☐ Separated/divorced ☐

10 What is your current occupation?
Employed full-time ☐ Employed part-time ☐
Student ☐ Housewife full-time ☐
Unemployed ☐ Retired ☐

11 Do you have children? If so, how many and how old are they?
____
____

12 What is your annual household income?
under £10,000 ☐ £10–20,000 ☐ £20–30,000 ☐
£30–40,000 ☐ over £40,000 ☐

Miss/Mrs/Ms ______________________________
Address __________________________________
____
____
____

Thank you for completing this questionnaire. Now tear it out – put it in an envelope and send it before 28 February 1997, to:

Sally Cooper, Editor-in-Chief

SCARLET
FREEPOST LON 3335
LONDON W8 4BR
Please use block capitals for address.
No stamp is required! NODAR/8/96

Scarlet titles coming next month:

CARIBBEAN FLAME Maxine Barry
Revenge is what Ramona King wants and she'll allow nothing to stand in her way – until she experiences true passion for the first time in her life. Damon Alexander can't resist Ramona, even though he already has a mistress and 'Alexandria' is far more demanding than Ramona will ever be . . .

UNDERCOVER LOVER Sally Steward
Allison Prescott knows one thing for sure: the person with the wealth calls the shots. Never again will she allow a man to take over and dictate how she should live. So she needs money – lots and lots of lovely money! What she *doesn't* need is a man like Brad Malone! Brad, too, has other priorities and they sure don't include falling in love with a woman who has dollar signs in her heart.

THE MARRIAGE SOLUTION Julie Garratt
When Amy Weldon discovers that her uncle expects her to marry a man she's never met, she's understandably reluctant. Then she meets Richard Boden and her uncle's plan suddenly seems very, very desirable.

WIVES, FRIENDS AND LOVERS Jean Saunders
Take three friends: Laura had married Nick Dean after a whirlwind romance and was still madly in love with her husband . . . or was she? Gemma wanted stardom at all costs . . . even if it meant denying her love for the one man who was perfect for her; while Penny longed only for success and had no time for romance at all. Friendship, love, marriage or ambition . . . the choice was vital for all three women.